Murmuring Cove

Annie M. Cole

∞ INFINITY
PUBLISHING

Copyright © 2014 by Annie M. Cole

ISBN 978-1-4958-0018-4
ISBN 978-1-4958-0019-1 eBook

Printed in the United States of America

Published April 2014

INFINITY PUBLISHING
1094 New DeHaven Street, Suite 100
West Conshohocken, PA 19428-2713
Toll-free (877) BUY BOOK
Local Phone (610) 941-9999
Fax (610) 941-9959
Info@buybooksontheweb.com
www.buybooksontheweb.com

To my children, their spouses, and my grandchildren...you fill my life with joy. Hannah, Kirk, Zachariah, Brittany, Malachi, Braylon and Amily.

Chapter 1

Somewhere in Louisiana, time flew by at a frantic pace, but not in Sugar Land. It plodded away as if it walked along the low, dirt roads in muddy work boots. But change was coming to the small river town, a simple change, but a change nonetheless. And, as it's often been said, it's simple things that redirect our lives. Those common everyday occurrences that happen at such a creeping pace that we're hardly even aware of them. But in those precise moments, we find our lives and ourselves changed forever.

A strong, swirling wind had tormented Louisiana's lowland around the city of Baton Rouge for most of the day. Erratic gusts of slashing rain pelted the window where McRossen "Mack" Blackwell stood silently, watching a barge as it negotiated the bend in the river. Having swelled her banks with recent rains, the wide, muddy Mississippi River lapped against the levee with swift movements, reminding him that there was always danger beneath the water's surface.

As he stood gazing, a murky shape began forming out of the mist, like that of a woman. *Piper,* he thought, smiling. Then, just as quickly as it formed, it vanished into a wisp of thin air.

Piper Collins-Harding was not the sort of woman a man could easily forget. She was every man's dream of the perfect woman. She was beautiful, charitable, and most importantly, now single. If nothing else good came from the events of this day, Mack could rest assured that life was not always tragic and that sometimes you could get a second chance at love.

Dragging a hand over his roughened jaw, a shallow sense of guilt mixed with relief assaulted him as he turned his thoughts back to the business at hand. He was being relieved of his duties; whether temporarily or permanently, he didn't know. That had yet to be decided. Oh, he had no regrets over the action that had caused his present condition; he'd do it again if he had to. But, he did feel a sense of remorse for all the trouble he'd caused his boss, Rudd England. That was one man he never wanted to disappoint.

Rudd was no ordinary man. In fact, it was Rudd who had first seen Mack's potential as a paramedic. He had given Mack a chance to work his way up to his current position as flight medic, helping him successfully pass the two-and-a-half hour FP-C exam. Not one to ever forget a kindness, Mack always threw his hat in with Rudd. Besides, he loved his job. He was born to it, and everyone around him knew it.

Voices from the hallway drifted through the door and pulled Mack out of his thoughts. He turned from the window and watched as Rudd, along with another man, walked into the room.

"Mack Blackwell." Rudd closed the distance between them with an outstretched hand. "This man is Mr. Jay Anderson, and he's here to gather information and witness the exchange of words by order of the company president. Gentlemen, please take a seat."

Each man casually took his seat around a conference table piled high with maps and loose paper. After clearing a spot for his elbows, Rudd rubbed his hands together nervously and began his inquiry. "So, Mr. Blackwell, please tell us what happened on the afternoon of June fifteenth after you received a call concerning an accident on highway thirty-three. And, for the benefit of Mr. Anderson," he waved his thick hand in the man's direction, "state your position and your duties."

"I'm a flight medic. My *usual* job … is to protect life. But," his voice was low and eerily smooth, "I made an exception in this case."

Rudd choked and cleared his throat, scraping his chair across the floor as he shot to his feet. "What he means, Mr. Anderson, is that he was pushed to the limits of his endurance by this incident! Here is a man who has recorded more flight hours and saved more lives than any two flight medics on our staff put together. And all while performing his duties flawlessly!" Wiping the back of his hand across his forehead, he continued. "Now, what I propose is some type of therapy … some rest, down time, that sort of thing. *I'm* responsible for allowing this man to overwork himself. His record is spotless, with this incident being the only exception, of course. I recommend a three-month leave of absence while all of this gets sorted out."

"Mr. Blackwell," Mr. Anderson inquired after clearing his throat, dismissing Rudd England's ramblings with a wave of his hand. He looked down his hawkish nose as he raised his head from the papers in his hands. "At the accident site, what caused you to react with such hostility toward Mr. Brown, the victim's son? You *were* treating his mother at the time, were you not?"

A muscle in Mack's cheek flexed, the only sign of his apparent agitation. "Yes, I was."

"That being the case, why did you feel it necessary to attack Mr. Brown so fiercely?"

"He was hampering my ability to perform my job."

"In what way? Did he hinder you from administering treatment to his mother?"

"No, he was in the way."

"In the way," Mr. Anderson repeated the words back to Mack, tapping the papers in his hand annoyingly as he appraised him. "So, please tell me, Mr. Blackwell, what was Mr. Brown doing to *so* upset you that you felt it necessary to break his jaw and leave him unattended on the side of the highway?" A smug look crossed the man's face as he waited for a satisfactory answer.

"He was ripping the diamond rings off of his dying mother's fingers while I was trying to administer treatment to save her life!"

Mr. Anderson's eyes widened. Straightening his tie, he looked around the room uncomfortably.

"Oh, I see. So, I suppose you feel that some things are worth the risk."

"And who gets to decide?"

"I suppose the one taking the risk."

"Exactly."

There was nothing arrogant about Mack Blackwell. He simply exuded confidence and leadership, a quiet leadership that others just naturally followed. But at times he could be so private and closed-mouthed, even to the point of letting others think the worst of him with no argument. Mack tilted his head slightly, waiting for a response from the man.

"I can certainly understand Mack's frustration with the situation," Rudd added without reservation. "Sadly, Mrs. Brown could not be resuscitated. All of that, combined with Mr. Brown's actions, proved to be too much. It was a perfect storm of events that sent him over the edge. That's why I'm ordering a three-month leave of absence. What the man needs is rest!" He pounded the table for emphasis. "He's much too valuable to this outfit to allow him to be dismissed. Yes, three months' rest, that's my recommendation. You can pass that up the chain of command for me. My word is final on the matter."

Mr. Anderson rose from the table and raised an eyebrow. "Without pay, of course. And we'll wait for the final word from the president and his council on the matter."

Rudd knew he had pushed the limits. To seek no punishment for Mack's actions would be a sure way to lose both their jobs. "Of course."

The day was unseasonably cool, and a grayish drizzling rain hung over nearly everything in the city of Mobile, Alabama. Bay Rutherford stood at the large window with her face toward Mobile Bay, more intensely awake and aware than she could ever remember being. For the first time in her life, she had perfect clarity of mind. It was as if God had peeled back the curtain of confusion and fear and had given her a brief glimpse of hope mixed with a shot of courage.

"I'm moving to Sugar Land, Louisiana," Bay announced to a chattering room full of management personnel from the St. Bonitus Hotel.

The room grew quiet as all eyes turned toward Bay.

"Oh? And how are you going to manage that, dear?" Rachelle Geroux asked, hiding her distant smile behind her coffee cup. "I'm sure you haven't given this much thought, Bay. There are many things to consider. Think of the boy. Not to mention your … health condition. And, besides that, where else are you going to make this kind of money? Why, didn't we just reach an agreement, giving you the salary you so deserve?" Rachelle calmly placed her cup and saucer on the table and, with a remote manner, picked an imaginary piece of lint from her linen jacket.

Well-connected Rachelle Geroux stood apart with aloof dignity. A former beauty queen, she had managed to marry one of the area's wealthiest businessmen, the owner of the world-renowned St. Bonitus Hotel. Soon after her husband's death, Rachelle had maneuvered and manipulated circumstances so as to arrange a comfy life for herself. Hiring Bay had proven to be a brilliant move. She'd recognized right away that the girl knew how to keep things running smoothly. Bay lacked nothing in the hospitality field, and Rachelle planned to capitalize on it. She was even grooming her son, Sterling, for the role of husband for Bay as assurance to keep Bay securely in the family business.

"I've made up my mind," Bay declared firmly. Looking around the room, she was now more certain than ever that she was making the right decision. The demanding stress of the job was beginning to manifest itself in Bay's health. Headaches were becoming commonplace, and she was losing weight, becoming gaunt and unhealthy looking.

Sterling jumped up, overturning a chair as he stood anxiously to his feet. He crossed the room toward Bay in long, irate strides. He smiled down at her with quivering lips and seemed to regain his composure. "You're exhausted, Bay," he stated softly. His air of cool indifference disturbed her more than his brief outburst of anger. "I'll take you home, and we'll talk about this tomorrow." He turned and addressed his mother. "She's tired and not thinking clearly. All she needs is rest."

Bay spoke up. "Yes, I'm tired. I work hard. It's beautiful here, but I'll not let the geography of this place overwhelm me again. After what I've experienced, I know we're still very much on a fallen planet."

"How dare you." Sterling looked at her with seething eyes. "After all we've done for you! You can't blame us for the actions of one of our guests!"

"One of *your* guests, Sterling, and, yes, I blame you. There are way too many little secrets going on around here for my peace of mind. No amount of money is worth my physical and mental well-being."

Bay's heart gave a fearful leap as Sterling lifted his hand to her. He closed his hand, making a fist, then pointed a long, bony finger in her face. "Mark my words, you'd better take some time to think about this. Think about us! You have *no* idea what you're getting yourself into. You'll regret this, Bay."

She swayed on her feet slightly before lifting her chin and with a confident voice replied, "No more than I already do."

Her tongue involuntarily touched the corner of her mouth. The now-familiar scar seemed to have a way of reminding her of who she was and bolstering her courage. She pressed her lips together tightly and moved to the door, trembling with both apprehension and relief. Nothing mattered now, nothing but her son and the hope of a life lived in peace.

Once outside the hotel, Bay couldn't get away fast enough. After making her way down the brick path toward her car, she stopped by a bench to catch her breath. She looked up at the sky, feeling the cool wetness of drizzle against her heated skin. A sense of freedom came over her, and she smiled, knowing that whatever happened, the peace that now enveloped her was worth the risk.

Chapter 2

The drizzling rain hadn't slacked off since Bay had left the state of Alabama. She'd decided to leave her son, five-year-old Jace, with her mother in nearby Moss Bay, Alabama. She traveled alone to Sugar Land, Louisiana, in hopes of getting a job. A headache, no doubt brought on by the tension of the day and coupled with a lack of sleep, caused her to begin loosening her hair from the confines of the tight French twist. She grew more purposeful, trying to free her hair with one hand and steer the car with the other. She'd thought about maneuvering the car with her knee, but one glance in the rearview mirror changed her mind quickly. Running off the road in the wilds of Louisiana's back country was not an option.

Many miles had passed since Bay turned off the interstate. Now she was making her way into unknown territory. Oh, she'd visited Sugar Land a few times in her childhood, but those times had been so fleeting to her youthful mind that she barely remembered them. This was the land of her mother's people. Most of them were now long-dead or relocated to other more prosperous areas.

She thought back to the morning when she and her mother had shared coffee and a good conversation over a leisurely breakfast. Virginia Rutherford had tossed a newspaper across the kitchen table toward her daughter. "News from my hometown … thought you might find it interesting."

After giving her mother a cautious look, Bay sipped her coffee and scanned the headlines. *Nothing too important here,* she thought. "The local Girl Scout troop is planning a bake sale to help raise money to buy trees for downtown beautification." She cut her eyes to her mother over the top of the paper, then turned the page.

Virginia knew her daughter well. She sat patiently, waiting until Bay's face peered over the top of the paper again. This time a small light shone from her daughter's eyes. And that had been the beginning of this adventure.

The landscape gradually began to change, becoming less populated with houses and more populated with trees and bayou waterways. She came to a bridge and slowed down. Looking out the windshield through swipes of the wipers, she appraised the structure, convinced in her mind that the people of that area hadn't come too far along in bridge building since they'd probably bridged the bayou with a fallen log. Easing her car onto the planks of the old bridge, she heard the loose boards pop and creak as the wheels of the car rolled slowly over the wood.

After crossing the bridge, she noticed for the first time that the road ran parallel with the Mississippi River. You could see the river in brief glimpses over the levee. Through the shrouded mist, she spied a rusted sign hanging precariously on a post. The name Sugar Land was stamped in faded black letters across the front. But, the miles listed to reach the destination had long since vanished away.

Still frustrated with her tangled hair, Bay eased off to the side of the road to deal with the troubling knot, hoping to relieve the pain in her head. Once her fingers worked out the tangle, she looked over her shoulder then pressed the accelerator. The tires began to spin as a sickening feeling came over her. "Oh, no," she whispered under her breath. "I'm stuck."

Closing her eyes, she pressed her fingers against the area of dull ache across her forehead. She could hear the steady, rhythmic beating in her chest as it heaved. Taking a deep breath, she tried to relax. *Well, I can't push this car out of the mud by myself. I'll have to wait until someone comes along, and from the look of it, that could take a while.* Bay turned on the emergency flashers and prayed. *Please, God, send help.*

Rain beat down upon the car as gray misty clouds hung close to the ground. The night was coming on fast. Black and eerily silent, except for the sound of the pelting rain, it seemed as if everyone and everything had already found a warm, dry spot to wait out the storm. Bay turned, and with a last slow look around, rested her head against the headrest and closed her eyes, content to let the rain patter against the windows as she drifted into oblivion.

She hadn't been asleep long when a tapping sound awoke her. Rolling her head to the side, she faced the window. Opening her eyes with a start, she suddenly remembered where she was and what circumstances surrounded her. The rivulets of rain running down the window distorted the image of a man. His head was covered by the hood of a rain jacket. As if sensing her apprehension, he held up for her inspection a card with paramedic credentials.

At her nod, he spoke loudly so as to be heard over the rain. "Stuck?"

She nodded.

"Crank the car and put it in drive. At my signal, slowly give it some gas."

Bay waved her hand, signaling that she understood.

The man walked to the back of the car, positioned himself to push, and raised his hand. The tires began to spin as mud flew out in all directions. Then, with one forceful thrust the vehicle shot forward, grabbing solid pavement under the front tire. Red brake lights flashed brightly in the darkness as the car came to a stop a few feet away.

As the man stepped once more to the window, Bay lowered it a few inches and stuck out a twenty-dollar bill. "Thank you so much," she said, sincerely.

The man waved off the money. "Glad to help." He pushed back the hood from his head, smiling at her in an easy manner.

Something about his deep and smooth voice caused her to look at him more closely. His ice-green eyes seemed at odds with his complexion. Light brown hair and tan skin practically screamed for the warmth of brown eyes. Nevertheless, he had the look of a confident man, and from what she could see in the dark, a very attractive, confident man.

"Are you headed to town?" the man asked, squinting from the sudden onslaught of horizontal rain. He'd noticed her Alabama license plate and was curious to know where she was going or if she happened to be lost.

"Yes, I'm going to Sugar Land."

"Oh? Are you staying with someone?"

"No … I'm staying in a hotel."

He gave a nod of understanding. "Well, there *are* no hotels in Sugar Land, at least not yet. But, don't let me discourage you. You're welcome to stay at our place."

Is he joking? "Well, thanks for the offer, but I believe I'll take my chances in town."

"All the same, here's my card." He slipped a business card through the slit in the window. "Call if you change your mind. Be careful and try to stay on the road. The land of spirits and voodoo can be a bad place to get stranded." The corners of his mouth lifted briefly before he turned and walked back to his truck.

"Spirits and voodoo. Who does he think he's talking to … a tourist?" She mumbled under her breath as she tossed his card on the console.

Traveling toward town, Bay kept glancing up to see the stranger's headlights behind her. Even though she'd never admit it, it brought her a sense of comfort.

The first sign of the approaching town was a gas station with strings of wet plastic pennants flapping furiously in the wind. Checking her rearview mirror again, she noticed the truck had gone. "Well, at least I made it to town," she whispered under her breath, grateful for the escort.

The downtown area was quaint, complete with antiques stores and shops with names like the Lavender Jar, Thibodaux Café, and Just Desserts.

The town was all but deserted. Cutting her eyes to the clock on the dashboard, she noticed it was only half past nine. *Where is everybody?* From the corner of her eye, she spied a flag pole with a light at its base shining upward toward the building. Bold black letters read, "Sugar Land Police Department." *That's a good sign*, she thought as she pulled up to the building.

The door buzzed as Bay stepped inside, pulling the hood of her rain jacket from her head. It was a small office with one desk and an empty rolling chair. An oversized map of the town was fastened to the wall with different colored pins placed in a random pattern. She could hear and feel the footfalls coming from the back of the building.

"Somebody better be dead 'cause I'm missin' the last episode ..." his words dropped off as he entered the room. "Oh, can I help you ma'am?" he questioned, slightly embarrassed as he took in the sight before him. "I'm Chief Mitchell."

She stood as tall and straight as her five-foot-five-inch frame would allow. Nodding, she made an effort to swipe the hair sticking to her forehead. "I'm Bay Rutherford, and I was wondering if you could tell me where I might stay for the night. Is there a hotel or bed and breakfast nearby?"

Bay studied the man. A gold chain was visible through his opened collared shirt, resting on a dark mat of chest hair. The strong scent of Aqua Velva cologne permeated the room as the harsh overhead light reflected on his head displaying a random pattern of baby-doll-like hair plugs.

Inhaling deeply, he paused, filling his cheeks with air as he thought for a minute. "No ma'am. I can't rightly say we've got a place like that for overnight guests just now. We will in about a month, but not just yet."

"Oh, I see."

The look of disappointment on the young lady's face was almost more than the chief could bear, and he grimaced.

"Well, thank you anyway, Chief Mitchell. I'm sorry to have bothered you." She reached inside her purse for the keys and turned to go.

"Well, now, wait a minute, ma'am. I'm sure we can find a bed for you over at Bon Secour. It's a home for unwed mothers. They take in women there all the time. 'Course their circumstances are a little different." He wheezed out a dry laugh. "It's real nice out there. Let me make one quick call." He stepped to the back again, then a moment later emerged with a piece of paper. "This is the address and phone number, and just in case you should get lost, my number is on the bottom. Take this road here and go north until you come to a large pecan grove. You'll drive straight through it. Take the next road to the left and go about a mile. You can't miss it. Mercy Mineree will be waiting for you. Tell her Ludie Earl sent you."

"Thank you so much, Chief Mitchell. I really appreciate all your help."

The butterscotch-colored limestone house glowed under the soft gas lanterns flanking the front entrance. The same wet stone covered the ground directly in front, as if the house had melted and poured down the three shallow steps. Lofty trees stood swaying as they towered over the low and sprawling structure, absorbing the impact of the elements.

As Bay stepped up to the door, it flew open abruptly, startling her.

A small, plump, and wrinkled woman faced Bay wearing a severe scowl. She had the look of a lumpy potato with two sunken eyes.

"Where have you been? This weather is not good for you … breathing in all this dampness! And with no hat to cover your head! Get in here right this minute, young lady, before you catch your death!" the old woman scolded. With that, the woman turned and vanished into the darkened hall, leaving Bay to stare wide-eyed after her.

Bay twisted her lips and mumbled something to herself about it being unhealthier for a person to be frightened half to death than rained on. She looked around the empty foyer and laughed, muttering to herself, "I think I'd be better off sleeping in the car."

There was a sound of soft laughter coming from the dimly lit hallway. "Oh … surely not." A tall and stately woman approached and stuck out her hand, smiling brightly. "I'm Mercy, and you must be Bay. I'm so happy to finally meet you. I recognized your name as soon as Ludie Earl mentioned it during his phone call. Your mother, Virginia, is an old friend of mine. I'm sorry I wasn't here to greet you. I was laying out towels and putting fresh linens on your bed."

Bay half-consciously rubbed her fingers against her forehead. "Thank you, but I don't want to be any trouble. I mistakenly thought there would be a hotel in town. I should have checked. I'll just go back to the interstate and look for something there."

Mercy's eyes were warm and moist as her gaze swept over Bay. "You'll have to forgive Mrs. Antonio for her harshness. You see, she's worked here with the girls for many years. Now she suffers from a mild form of dementia. She's not happy unless she's fussing over one of us. We tell ourselves that that's how she expresses love and concern."

"No explanation is necessary, I assure you," Bay said with a smile.

"I guess we can certainly sympathize with poor Mrs. Antonio. Teenage girls can sometimes present a challenge." Mercy paused and laughed softly. "Come on, I'll show you to your room."

The room was small, but orderly and clean. An iron bed stood against one wall with stark white bed linens and a blue and white quilt folded neatly across the foot of the bed. A bedside table with a single lamp, a wooden chair, and an old kneeler meant for prayers were all the furnishings the room could boast. Mercy walked to the table and turned on the lamp. Then, opening a narrow exterior French door, she explained, "This goes out to the courtyard. Some of us like to sleep with our doors open at night, especially when it's raining. There's just something soothing about the sound of rain. The screen door locks, but I can assure you, you'll be quite safe here. The bathroom is through that door," she stated, pointing to the wall opposite the bed.

"Thank you so much for the use of your room. I'll be gone in the morning, so I'd like to pay you now, if that's okay with you."

Mercy waved her hand in the air, dismissing the question. "We'll have no such talk. God provides for us in every way. We'll send a tray in a moment with a few snacks and one again in the morning with your breakfast."

"Ms. Mercy, I know operating a place like this must be expensive. I only want to make a contribution to help support your work here. I think what you're doing is to be commended."

A slow smile warmed Mercy's eyes, and she responded in a whisper. "We have a benevolent supporter who sees to our financial needs." With that, she closed the door softly behind her.

Bay stared at the door for a few moments blinking. It felt strange being on the receiving end of such gracious hospitality. It was then that she noticed the quiet. Except for the rain hitting the stone patio of the courtyard, she could hear no other sound. Then, a muted chime sounded from somewhere deep within the house, chiming out the hour with ten strokes.

Deciding a shower would help ease the headache, Bay turned and lifted the suitcase onto the bed and popped the lock. She pulled out her robe and pajamas. As she pulled out her slippers, she felt something inside. There, tucked away in the soft satin slipper she found a small Snickers bar, three crayons, and a plastic green army man armed with a bayonet held out ready to defend. Her lips pulled down at the corners, and tears formed in her eyes. "My sweet boy, I miss you so," she whispered, remembering the time her son posted his green guards all around her bedroom because he thought she might be afraid.

After a warm shower, Bay stepped into the bedroom to find a tray laden with an assortment of baked goods, a small teapot, and a bottle of water. There were two cookies, a pecan bar, and a small slice of nut cake—everything needed for a late night snack. Sinking her teeth into the pecan bar, Bay rolled her eyes in pleasure, savoring the chewy goodness.

The clock chimed faintly again, then a muffled thump startled her into full alert. Muted sounds of movement came from within the house, and a girl's voice sounded in the corridor.

Bay finished off the pecan bar and carefully eased open the bedroom door, peering down the hallway. Seeing no one, she slowly closed the door and, with a click, locked it.

Even as Bay sighed with relief against the door, she gave a mental curse at her own stupidity for not checking ahead of time for accommodations.

Stepping to the bed, she noticed a small note. It simply read, "As each one has received a special gift, employ it in serving one another, as good stewards of the manifold grace of God. 1 Peter 4:10."

Chapter 3

*H*enry Clay Blackwell was a tall, barrel-chested man in his early fifties. And, though every man respected him, there was something about the way he handled himself that made most folks keep a comfortable distance. No one ever dared stand one's ground with him, no one, that is, except his nephew, Mack Blackwell.

"Mack! Step in here. I need to tell you something," Henry Clay's voice boomed his words through the empty house.

Mack yanked on the cord to the nail gun, unplugging it. "If you want this house complete in a month, you're gonna have to limit your interruptions to maybe … uh, I don't know, twenty a day?"

"Shut up, and listen to your uncle."

Mack stifled a grin as he walked toward the dining room. He crossed his arms and leaned against the door frame. "What is it now?" he added for emphasis.

"I'm interviewing this morning."

"For my position, I hope."

"No. Blast you," Henry Clay barked. He opened his mouth to speak but immediately began coughing as he choked on his cigar smoke.

"When are you going to quit those things? Can't you see what they're doing to you?"

Mack didn't seem to expect an answer, so Henry Clay didn't offer one.

Mack knew he was pushing it, but teasing his uncle was so enjoyable. He was having difficulty keeping a straight face as he watched Henry Clay's eyes narrow through the smoke. He pushed off the door frame and held out his hands in a truce.

Henry Clay tapped out his cigar in the ashtray and chided, "Don't insult the alligator before you cross the bayou, boy. Now quit your rattlin' and listen. A young lady is about to show up, and I want you to sit in on the interview. We're gonna hire someone to manage the place today—someone with experience. I've included one of the cottages on the property in the deal, plus the salary we discussed. She's already aware of the offer." He rubbed his lips with his fingertip, looking troubled. "I've never been too good with women. Why, my own daughters won't come near me. They're just like their mother, too hard to understand." He stared up at the ceiling, stroking his chin, and continued, "You know, I hear what women say, but that's seldom what they mean." He shook his head as if to clear it. "Anyway, I don't want to do anything to compromise this girl's reputation by having her live out here with a divorced old man and *you*. People talk."

The situation would have amused Mack had he not known how serious his uncle was about the matter. Henry Clay's wife had left him ten years earlier, taking their twelve-year-old twin daughters, Rachael and Rebecca, with her.

Mack shrugged and reasoned, "People live around women all over the world, Uncle Henry. It's perfectly fine. We're all adults here."

Henry Clay lifted an eyebrow. "Yes, and you see the mess it's gotten us into." He eyed his nephew. Women unsettled him. There was something about them that was hard to define. Yet, there had been one woman … He quickly gathered his thoughts before they ran away with him. "But," he added, rolling his chair back from the desk. "You've never impressed me as the kind of man who troubles himself too much over what others think."

A lazy grin twisted Mack's lips. "You're right about that. And, you shouldn't worry about it either. I thought you were the active, not the reflective, type. Why don't you let her decide if it matters? If it does, we can always ask Derlie to move out here as a chaperone."

He thought for a split second, then shook his head, "That will not work, and you know it!" He shuddered at the thought. "Tell you what. Let's meet this woman, ask her direct questions, get a feel for her character, then we'll decide. Pray to God that she's straightforward, so I can understand her."

A morning mist, like gray chiffon being rolled off the bolt, spread over the ground as Bay drove up the long lane to the house known as Briarleigh. The property stretched back from the Mississippi River as far as the eye could see; the land gently sloped and flattened out where large oak and pecan trees dotted the grounds. Between canopies of moss-draped branches, Bay could see the white house which brought back a flood of memories, memories she'd forgotten she even had.

"Briarleigh," she breathed out the name with a soft sigh.

Briarleigh was a large, two-story white house with greenish gray shutters. Pillared porches stretched across the front and rear of the house on both levels. For Bay, it was her mother's home and always would be.

The leaves of the shrubs and trees were glossy green, and, even in the heavy mist, the pale-colored magnolia blossoms could be seen adorning the branches like well-placed decorations. How strange to think that these very same trees were here when her mother was a child. She envisioned Virginia snapping off branches of colorful blooms to decorate the house just as she'd watched her do in their yard at home many times over the years.

Bay rolled to a stop, parked the car, and got out. Thick vines of wisteria covered one end of the porch, and their fragrance wafted up, mingling with her recollection of happier days when her mother and father had taken her to visit Briarleigh years ago. Thinking of her father, Bay's throat tightened with contained grief as she mounted the steps.

A loud Irish woman's voice came from somewhere inside the house, and Bay looked up as the door suddenly flew open. A woman stood there, yelling over her shoulder toward a back room.

"What did your last slave die from?" As the woman glanced around, she saw Bay and jumped, making the sign of the cross on her chest. "Good gracious, girl … you nearly scared the life out of me!"

"I'm sorry. I didn't mean to startle you. I'm here to see Mr. Blackwell."

"Are you now? Which one?" The woman yelled over her shoulder again, only this time, louder, "The big ugly *mean* one or the fine handsome *young* one?"

"Uh … Henry Clay Blackwell. I'm Bay Rutherford, and I have an appointment."

"Oh, they're expecting you. Please come in."

Bay was amazed at how quickly the woman's demeanor changed. She was actually quite pleasant. She kept her eye on the little lady with the Irish brogue. Something about her rosy cheeks and her sparkling black eyes put Bay on guard. It was plain to see the woman was unpredictable and full of mischief.

"I'm Derlie Blevins, the cook around here. And underappreciated I am, too!"

"Nice to meet you, Ms. Blevins."

Polite smiles were exchanged, then Derlie opened the door to the dining room and motioned for her to go inside. As the door was shut behind Bay, she heard the woman say, "And to think, I get in this circus for free."

Mack and Henry Clay looked up from their conversation and noticed Bay standing in the doorway. She was poised in her plain white dress, elegant really, with slight graceful curves and cool features that suddenly turned warm with her smile. She was not glamorous or businesslike with hard edges; she was intriguing, somewhat average in height, and feminine. A small scar turned up from the corner of her mouth giving her the look of holding a secret behind her hazel eyes. Light summer brown hair gathered loosely at her neck and fell down her back to just beneath her shoulders. When her head moved, tiny diamond stud earrings sparkled in the light; they were her only adornment.

Both men stood up and offered their hands.

"Ms. Rutherford?" Henry Clay asked.

"Bay, please." She shook one hand and then the other.

"Have a seat, Miss Bay. I'm Henry Clay Blackwell, and this is my nephew, McRossen Blackwell, but everyone calls him Mack."

Bay took a seat, followed by the men. She looked up at Mack, recognition dawning on her face. "I believe we've met."

Mack had not taken his eyes off the girl since she'd walked into the room. She was not beautiful, yet he found he could not take his eyes off that intense yet serene face. Her storm-colored eyes were set off by dark, thick lashes, and the small scar near her lip inspired in him a desire to know the cause. Surely he would have remembered meeting her. "Oh?"

Bay averted her eyes and blushed. Both men caught her look of embarrassment.

Mack leaned forward, suddenly intrigued. With somewhat of a smile, he waited for her response.

"I was the woman who covered you in mud last night," she stated sheepishly. A smirk touched her lips.

With a nod of recognition, Mack smiled at her and teasingly asked, "How could I forget?"

Henry Clay coughed and reached for his cigar as a distraction. Not at all sure he wanted to know what they were referring to, he cautiously asked, "So, you two are acquainted with each other?"

Turning to his uncle, Mack explained, "Bay's car was stuck in the mud down by Ghost Bridge last night. I pushed her out." He turned back to Bay. "I wondered what happened to you. I expected to get a call."

Did he say, Ghost Bridge? "Oh, I stayed across town at Bon Secour." She tilted her head slightly. "Is that the same bridge I crossed to get here? The one in front of the property?"

Both men nodded, each wondering his own thoughts about the young woman. Bay Rutherford looked and talked and handled herself like a gracious and dignified woman. It was as if she could flip out a fan any second and wave it in front of her face. She was a living, breathing, and slow-moving Southern cliché and seemed to be so unaware of it. But, in spite of that, or maybe because of that, people were drawn to her.

"Well, I'm glad they could accommodate you. Mercy Mineree runs the place. She's a champion of the downtrodden and a fierce defender of those who can't fight for themselves. The world needs more like her."

Getting back on subject, Mack added, "But, I'm glad you made it to us, finally. I followed you into town last night, just to make sure you got there safely." He paused, shifted in his chair, and smiled at her. "There were quite a few people in this town who applied for this position. However, when Uncle Henry found out you were Virginia Rutherford's daughter, he called you first."

Henry Clay's voice seemed to grow thick with emotion. "As you must know, this was your mother's home."

"Yes … and my mother speaks very highly of you. She said that you know each other very well."

"That we do," he replied, with a slow nod and a distant look that made both Bay and Mack take notice. Leaning back in his chair, Henry Clay tapped his fingers lightly on the desk. "So, we've read your résumé, and, I have to say, we're both quite impressed. We have just a few questions for you, if you don't mind?"

"Not at all," she responded, softly.

Mack placed his elbows on his knees, and, with his fist in his hand, he leaned forward and asked, "I'm curious to hear your ideas on how you'd turn this place into a successful inn."

"Of course," she murmured, in a calm and unhurried tone. "I feel that the inn will only be successful when there is a balance between outward beauty and the inner life here. That's what will make it a memorable place where people will want to keep returning year after year. We're asking to become a worthy part of someone's life experience. Our attitude toward and treatment of our guests will make or break this inn. That's why some of the great houses in the South never get visited. They're all outward show, without a soul, so to speak. We'll be the soul of this house, and we never need to lose sight of that. Hospitality is the key."

Mack leaned back against the leather tuft of the chair and slid his fingers over his slightly whiskered chin. Arching his brow wonderingly, he added, "In that case, just for the record ... I don't think Derlie needs to be the door greeter."

Bay broke into a dazzling smile that nearly took his breath. "I'll have to agree with you there."

Henry Clay joined in the humor. "By the way, can you cook? I never know if Derlie is coming back after one of our fights."

"Let's just say I'm a better cook than I am a driver," Bay added playfully.

"Let's hope so," Mack teased in reply, biting back a grin as he watched her head tilt in surprise to his remark.

"Now, I have a question." Henry Clay made a wide, sweeping motion with his arm. "Look around you. This is a blank slate. How would you go about decorating this place?"

Bay glanced around. "My tastes are simple, but, I like to think, refined. I don't like fussy or showy pieces. I don't care for clutter. I like comfortable, elegant pieces and smooth lines. Like oversized couches with ottomans and soft leather chairs arranged for conversation. In this room, I'd have a long mahogany table and sideboard with a simple but stunning chandelier. And, maybe a vase of fresh-cut flowers as the centerpiece or a silver bowl of magnolia blooms." As Bay waved her hand, a delicate fragrance passed and lingered on the air like a whisper. "The guestrooms are where we need to focus most of the attention. You can't skimp on the bed or the bed linens. Whether you settle into bed for warmth to escape howling winter winds or slide your feet into a set of cool, breathable sheets on a humid summer night, you'll want the best to snuggle into."

Henry Clay took a quick glance at Mack before continuing, "How are you at managing people? You'll be over an entire staff if you get the job— Derlie, the cook; a gardener; and a housekeeper."

"I'll make you aware of anything I can't handle. But, I don't see that happening."

She was so confident in her manner that Mack had to cover his amusement by rubbing a hand over his mouth. "Derlie sometimes carries on a dialogue with dead saints, but don't let that bother you. She's mostly harmless."

Henry Clay controlled his grin as he watched the young woman's eyes narrow skeptically. He remembered being young and cocky once himself, having much the same spirit as the girl. He liked what he saw. "By the way, what's that fragrance you're wearing? It's … very nice."

Bay lifted her wrist to Henry Clay. "It's called Sea Briar. A friend of mine back home made it for me as a going away gift. She calls it my signature fragrance and says it's a combination of where I'm from and where I'm going. It's the scent of lavender and wild primroses mixed with a touch of the sea."

Henry Clay took a light sniff. "Very pleasant … I don't think I'll forget it."

Lowering her hand, Bay remarked, "My friend Madeline creates her own fragrances. In fact, I'd like very much to order soaps and lotions from her for the guests of Briarleigh."

Mack raised an eyebrow in response to her sudden change of topic. He rubbed his chin as if unsure how to proceed. "And why's that, Miss Bay?"

"Never underestimate the power of fragrance to evoke wonderful memories and to transport us back to happier times. Fragrances are part of what defines the places and people we love. I want this place to haunt people once they leave so that they'll want to come back often. Most guests take the sample-size soaps and lotions home with them. Whenever they smell our unique fragrance, I want them to think of Briarleigh."

"Then I vote for your fragrance to be the 'house scent.'. It will certainly haunt them when they leave," Mack commented.

"Is that meant as a compliment or a criticism?" Bay questioned.

Mack surprised her with the slightest quirk of a smile, just a twitch of his lips. "A compliment, of course."

Henry Clay leaned forward in his seat. "You've got the job. Now let's look over the schedule for the week. As manager, it will be up to you to fill in when an employee is out, for whatever reason. And I'll expect you to hire a housekeeper and someone to help with serving as soon as possible. Your work day will begin at eight in the morning, and I'll relieve you at four. Derlie *should* be here to start cooking at six every morning, and she will leave after supper. Your days off are Sunday and Monday. The front office is yours, and you'll have an account with a limited amount of funds to work with for decorating the guest cottages." He smiled. "You can begin by decorating your cottage. Any questions?"

"No ... I understand what's expected of me, and I'll be ready to start work in the morning."

Chapter 4

At first glance, the cottage looked as if it had been washed up on shore and caught between two trees. It looked bleached, with the patina of driftwood. The wooden gates in front of the stone path stood open. Bay followed behind Mack as he made his way down the path, carrying her luggage in one hand and the keys to the cottage in the other. A scent of sun-warmed cedar shingles and climbing roses drifted around them as they walked up the few steps to the door.

Pausing at the door, she looked around, trying to analyze her feelings about the place. Running a hand over the weathered wood, Bay remarked, "What a charming place. My son will love it here."

"Oh … I didn't even think to ask if you were married. Will this cottage be big enough for your family? We have several more, seven to be exact." He fumbled with the keys before finding the correct one.

"I've never been married, and this cottage is perfect. My son, Jace, is five years old, and he likes nothing better than to walk around ponds and creeks, scaring frogs and disrupting turtles. Fishing is his sport. He'll love having the creek nearby."

Mack responded with a cautious tone. "Better make sure one of us is with him when he's near the water. There's a big gator down there. We call him Old Joe. He's been known to eat a few dogs. I wouldn't want him to mistake your son for one."

Bay shivered and asked, "Does he ever come up close to the cottage?"

The frightened look in her eyes made him tone down his warning. "No, he stays back toward the swamp mostly, but, occasionally, we'll see him cruise by. That's why we put the picket fence around this particular cottage. Just be careful near the water's edge, and never swim in the bayou." He glanced back at her reassuringly. "You'll be perfectly safe here."

She'd expected a barrage of questions from Mack or at least a reaction from the news about her son. Small towns were notorious for being interested in the little details of the lives of their residents. Taking her mother's advice, she'd prepared herself ... but she was surprised at her disappointment at not having been asked. Now, she simply wanted to get inside and get settled.

A car horn sounded, and they both turned to see a dog scamper across the road and out of the way of the silver Lexus. The car splashed wildly through puddles as it sped toward the large white house.

Mack turned the key, pushed the door open, and flipped the light switch. Glancing at Bay, he replied, "That's Piper, a friend of mine. She'll be staying the weekend."

"Oh ... is she our first guest?" Shading her eyes against the sun, she tried to read his face.

"She's *my* guest … I told her we're not quite ready for visitors. If nothing further develops," a lazy grin twisted his lips, "she'll be staying in the guest cottage near the sugarcane field. It was once a house for chickens a hundred years ago. But that'll be our little secret." He winked as they stepped inside.

The cottage seemed clean, but the air was stale, as if the place had been shut up for months. Dingy dark paneling covered the walls closing in the small space. A glance around the room showed a couch covered in a gold bedspread, positioned in front of the red brick fireplace. A recessed window seat in the same gold, color-washed fabric as the couch was tucked away in an alcove to the left of the fireplace. The window overlooked the bayou.

Bay's legs suddenly began to tremble, and she felt faint. Perspiration started to form on her forehead as the room began to move around her. She held on to the wall and hurriedly rushed through the kitchen to the back door, fumbled with the latch then yanked it open. Stumbling outside onto a narrow porch, she began gulping long, deep breaths. Raising her hand to her forehead, she leaned against a post to steady herself. Two strong hands came down on her shoulders and gently, but firmly, started pulling her backward toward the house. She resisted and wouldn't go until the dizziness stopped.

"I'm fine … I just need air," Bay said, as she tried to steady her trembling voice.

"Let's sit down. I'm just going to grab my paramedic bag. "

A moment later he returned, unfurling the inflatable cuff of a blood pressure meter as he fastened the stethoscope to his ears. He sat next to her on the step, rubbing the end of the disk briefly before applying it below the cuff.

"Are you taking any meds?" Mack asked, never removing his eyes from his purpose of taking her blood pressure. He took her wrist in one hand and pressed his fingers to her pulse.

She shook her head, "No."

His tenderness nearly made her cry. Then she told herself that he was a paramedic and was obligated to treat her this way. A disturbing thought crossed her mind. Had her life so lacked warmth and compassion that she was willing to let this moment stretch out for all eternity?

Reaching into his bag, he took out an otoscope and examined her ears. "Have you been under an unusual amount of stress or anxiety?"

She nodded, gaining more control over her feelings. "Some ... but I can handle it."

"Headaches ... migraines ... unusual or heavy ..."

"Headaches," she supplied, ready for the exam to be over while she still had some dignity. This was getting humiliating.

Mack nodded, placing his instruments back into his bag. He reached over and pulled the skin on the top of her hand and noticed it was tenting. "You seem dehydrated. Let's get some fluids in you." He stood and strode to the kitchen to take out a glass from the cupboard.

"What do you think is wrong with me? And what can I do about it?" Bay questioned eagerly, as Mack handed her the glass of water.

"We need to siphon off a little of that tension."

"Excuse me?" she stated, in growing embarrassment.

Mack responded lightheartedly, "I had in mind a little rest and relaxation. But, I'm open to suggestions." A light of humor shone from his eyes as he reached over and grabbed his bag.

Bay blushed hotly and muttered beneath her breath, "That'll be a cold day in … Biloxi."

"Keep your phone close by, and call me if you feel dizzy again," he said, in a serious but gentle manner. "It'd be a good idea to have a checkup with your doctor, just to be on the safe side. But, you should feel better soon. Now try to relax."

Bay watched him go, and, for a brief moment, she envied the woman in the shiny silver Lexus.

Chapter 5

*G*rayish purple shadows under the trees gradually vanished as morning dawned. Blue morning glories began to awaken in a slow stretch across the fence as Bay stood at the door, dressed and feeling rested. She listened to the sounds of the morning cicadas warming up their instruments for another warm day.

Closing the door behind her, she headed for the main house and toward a cup of steaming-hot coffee, she hoped.

Bay opened the screen door and stepped inside just as Mack was pouring his coffee.

"I'm ready to find something to cook for your guest, unless Derlie has made it back."

"She hasn't. By all means, help yourself." He waved his hand in the direction of the stove. "Yell when breakfast is ready." He grabbed his tool belt from the back of the kitchen chair and, with coffee in hand, climbed the back staircase.

They worked in the quiet of the early morning hours, each busy with separate tasks. Occasionally, the sound of a hammer echoed through the house, mixed with a low, steady whistle. Bay found the noise somewhat comforting. The sound of the wordless tune was both masculine and soothing and seemed to have a calming effect on her first-day jitters.

As Bay pulled a breakfast casserole from the oven, she noticed the hammering and the whistling had stopped. Curious, she glanced around, thinking Mack may have come into the kitchen. To her surprise, Derlie stood in the doorway with arms crossed and a foot tapping as she glared at Bay.

"And just *who* do you think you are? And *what* do you think you're doing in *my* kitchen?" Derlie fumed.

Bay calmly placed the casserole on the counter and slowly pulled off the oven mitts one at a time as she turned to face the woman. "To answer your first question, I'm God's own possession, and to answer your second, I'm doing *your* job, which *you* neglected by *not* showing up for work on time this morning."

Although Bay's words were soft and clear, the look in her eyes told Derlie not to open her mouth, and she didn't.

"I give everything a chance. That's how I am. You should see how I run over a piece of lint a dozen times when I'm vacuuming. Now, if I'll show that much mercy to a vacuum cleaner before I take it to the curb, you know I'll do the same for you. But … hear me well. As your manager, I will not tolerate your disrespect. You will arrive on time and with a pleasant attitude. My patience has a limit. Now, do we understand one another?" Bay paused, noticing the gleam in the old woman's eyes. She felt as if her spirit was communicating with the woman's spirit in some secret way.

"Yes, ma'am," Derlie answered kindly, as she stepped toward the refrigerator. "Would you like me to cut up some fresh fruit to go along with that lovely casserole you've got there?"

Letting out her breath, Bay replied, "That will be just fine, Derlie. As a matter of fact, I'll leave the kitchen to you." Untying her apron, she hung it on the back of the pantry door and grabbed a broom and dustpan. "I'll go make the dining room presentable. Mr. Blackwell has a guest for breakfast."

Bay passed the staircase on her way to the front door to empty out the dustpan, and a movement caught her eye. She looked up. There was Mack, sitting on the landing with his elbows on his knees and his hands clasped together looking down at her. *Why does he always seem to have a grin playing around his lips whenever he sees me?* she wondered. He touched the tip of his fingers to his forehead in a mock salute.

"Looks like we're in for a beautiful day," Bay commented casually. She popped the screen door open with her hip and emptied the dustpan over the side of the porch. Sweeping the cobwebs down from around the door, she tried hard to ignore him and his infuriating grin.

"Looks like it," Mack replied, no longer worrying about the fragile-looking, soft-spoken girl. From the tone of the confrontation he'd just overheard, she had a backbone under those graceful curves.

Later that morning, Piper Collins-Harding nibbled delicately at a slice of orange and sighed as she looked across the table at Mack, who was casually sipping his coffee. Her thoughts ran rampant now that she was finally free from her marriage vows. With the ink barely dry on her divorce papers, Piper began watching the man across from her with growing interest and no small amount of excitement. He seemed far more manly and self-assured than the high-school sweetheart she'd left ten years earlier. She recognized a challenge in his demeanor and was anxious to let the games begin.

"My goodness, Mack, it's been so long since we've seen each other. I'd almost forgotten the power you have over me. You still have a way of making me forget everything but you." The raven-haired beauty flashed him an alluring smile.

Bay was on her way into the dining room with a tray of muffins in her hands when she overheard the woman's comment. Rolling her eyes, she quickly regained her composure, surprised by her action. *I must be tired,* she thought and forced a pleasant smile.

Mack was slow to reply. Usually, he would have jumped on the chance to respond to a beautiful woman, especially *this* woman. But somehow things just didn't feel quite right yet. Maybe too much time had passed. What they needed was a little more time to get reacquainted. And he looked forward to it.

The news of Piper's marriage had come as a shock to Mack, and he could not accept it without a certain amount of pain and regret. But, all of that didn't matter now; she was back. She had left her attorney-husband and was now where she belonged, with him.

He glanced over his shoulder to see Bay busily arranging breakfast dishes on the makeshift sideboard. "Piper, this is the woman responsible for our delicious breakfast this morning. Bay Rutherford. Bay, this is Piper Collins-Harding."

"I'm pleased to meet you, and we're very happy to have you at Briarleigh," Bay replied sweetly.

Piper's eyes shifted from Mack to Bay briefly, then back to Mack without a greeting. "I need a refill of my coffee, if you don't mind." She pushed her cup to the corner of the table where Bay would see it.

The gesture somehow irritated Mack. He cleared his throat and pushed up from the table. Walking toward the sideboard, he met Bay halfway and took the coffee pot from her hand. Turning toward Piper, he threw his thumb over his shoulder and explained as he poured the coffee. "Bay got up at the crack of dawn to see to it that we had breakfast. She runs the place. And, when the cook didn't show up this morning, she stepped in to see that we didn't do without. We don't have servants here, only hardworking employees."

Piper seemed to have the oddest effect on him. Since her return, he tended to blurt things out and regret them as soon as they landed on the intended target. Could it be that he still held resentment toward her? He thought he'd forgiven her. He *had* to forgive her. She was the love of his life.

Piper turned her astonished gaze to him, then to Bay. And, seeing Bay's startled expression, Piper choked out a reply. "Of course … I didn't know. Thank you so much for the delicious breakfast."

"My pleasure," Bay said softly. After picking up the empty tray, she turned to leave the room.

Chapter 6

*B*riarleigh stood erect beneath the humid haze that lay heavy over everything. Beyond the house, a thick growth of lush green sugarcane thrived in the sweltering heat.

Bay let out an exhausted breath as she plopped down on the front steps. Her loose, white shirt molded to her skin, leeched of starch by the humid air. Taking a swig of her iced tea, she paused, noticing a cloud of dust hanging motionless above the road. Following the path of the road with her eyes, she stopped suddenly at the sight of the silver Lexus coming up the drive.

Now restless, Bay felt trapped. If she got up to go inside, they'd see her and know that she was trying to avoid them. Wanting something to do with her hands, she pretended to knead the muscles in her shoulders, straightening her back.

"Daydreaming, Bay?" Piper asked sweetly, as she stepped out of the car swinging her purse over her shoulder. Her words rang out, breaking the serenity of the moment.

As Mack got out of the passenger side, he reached back to collect something from the console.

Seeing the smug look on Piper's face, Bay mentally braced herself for more of the woman's sarcastic tongue. After a week of Piper Collins-Harding, she knew what to expect from the woman, even if her boyfriend seemed clueless.

Piper paused in front of Bay, appraising her. "Mack! You really are working the poor girl too hard. Just look at her, all covered in sweat. Are those chips of paint stuck to your skin?" She spat the words out in distaste, as if she could think of nothing worse.

Mack approached, and Bay lifted her gaze, squinting in the light. A shaft of sunlight hit her hazel eyes, intensifying them, and something flickered there. Beneath his stare, she felt uncomfortable by his concern. She lifted her tea glass and gulped it down until all that was left was the clank of the ice cubes.

"She looks fine to me," Mack said as he brushed off Piper's comment and handed a small wrinkled bag to Bay. "We ate at Mudflats ... they have the best Mississippi Mud Cake you'll ever put in your mouth. We had them wrap up a few pieces for you." He dug around in his jeans pocket, then produced a small gold coin. "My piece had this coin inside. You can redeem it and get a free kid's dessert; thought your son might like to go there."

"Thank you. We'll have to check it out." Bay said warmly, touched by his thoughtfulness.

He turned to his girlfriend. "It was Piper's idea. She has always had a soft spot for kids."

Admiration gleamed in his eyes as he took Piper's delicate hand and rubbed his thumb across it.

Self-consciously, Bay shoved her work-reddened hands between her knees.

"Go on to the cottage and relax, Piper. I'll be there in a minute. I just need to go over a few things with Bay first."

Bay found herself an unwilling witness to Mack's affection. The odd way he'd said Piper's name — it came out softer than the other words. Without protest, Piper smiled tenderly and climbed the steps, disappearing inside the house.

A chasm of quiet came between them as a hum of cicadas rose up in the summer heat.

"What did you do today?" he asked.

"I repurposed a couple of Adirondack chairs, giving them a fresh coat of paint." She extended her arm. "They're now this color," she said, pointing to a gray patch stuck to her forearm. I worked on my cottage, too. It's coming along nicely. I should finish painting tonight, then I'll get started in my search for a few repurposed pieces."

He sat down on the step next to her and took off his med-flight cap and began plucking at the feather of the fly hook stuck into the bill. He pressed his lips together and his face grew serious. "How have you been feeling? Any more dizzy spells?"

"No ... I guess I just needed rest."

He grinned slightly. "If this is what you call rest, I'd hate to know what you consider work."

"This place relaxes me. I know it will be a successful inn. Getaways are about doing things you can't do in your hectic 'other' life, and this place will have plenty of that for me."

"Such as?"

"Well, bike riding for one. I want to keep a few bikes at the ready. Most people over the age of twelve don't get to do that anymore, and most of us love it. A walking trail would be nice, canoes, a pool ... that sort of thing." She tucked her hair behind her ear.

Mack nodded in agreement. "Sounds like a good plan. I'll order pea gravel for the trails in the morning ... I've already marked them out." He gestured toward the river. "It'll circle down by the river."

An awkward silence grew between them, so she quickly added, "Henry Clay told me you bought a house. So, how's the renovation coming?" Her eyes glowed with excitement.

"It's not so much a renovation as a restoration. Except for updating the bath by adding a shower, I haven't modernized it too much."

"Sounds nice ... having a place of solitude in your profession is a necessity, I would say."

He passed his hand reflectively over the porch step, then glanced at her, surprised by her perception. "It's a good antidote to the fast pace and sometimes tragic routine of my work. Hopefully, it'll be ready to move into before I go back to work. I plan on making it home, for the weekends anyway. I'm anxious to show Piper, but I want it finished before she sees it."

Bay nodded, then said, "I really should get back to work." She got up and looked around before climbing the steps. "Everything seems to be coming together."

"Good. Let me know if you need anything. My cell phone number is on the refrigerator. I should be around more after today."

"If it's all right, I'd like to wander around the place later … after work, I mean."

"Help yourself to the place. Just be careful."

Chapter 7

*I*t was a bright Sunday morning. Bay inhaled deeply, smelling the fragrant magnolia blossoms heated by the warm beams of the sun. She closed her eyes, resting her head against the back of the rocking chair as she pushed with her toes to gently set the chair into motion. She wondered how many years her relatives had done the very same thing from the porch of Briarleigh. The warming rays took her weariness and turned it into a relaxed half-stupor.

"You're up early for a day off," Mack stated, as he stepped onto the porch with a mug of coffee in one hand and a plate in the other. He was wearing khaki pants and a comfortable-yet-stylish blue button-down shirt. With his hair slightly damp and lightly brushing the collar of his shirt, he looked as if he'd just come from the shower.

"Derlie sent this to you," he said, holding out a plate of biscuits with a small side dish of molasses and butter. "By the way, the molasses is made from sugarcane from Briarleigh. We have our crop sent to the local syrup mill. It's a century-old maker of one hundred percent pure cane syrup, and there's none better."

Bay widened her eyes, intrigued. "Really? What else is made from the sugarcane?" Already her thoughts were tumbling over each other as she considered ways to use the product for their guests.

"Well, it's a key ingredient in most Southern desserts, like pralines. And then there's always old New Orleans rum, but we don't keep much of that around. Alcohol makes Derlie crazy, and it's hard enough to handle her sober," he said, then winked.

"I see your point."

Mack eased into a chair beside her, holding his cup steady. "What are you reading?"

"Psalms," she answered. "King David … now *that* was a man."

Mack rubbed the cool porcelain of his cup beneath his thumb as his eyes passed over her briefly. "So, you admire the man after God's own heart, huh?"

"That I do." She patted the worn book twice. "He's helped me tremendously over the years."

"Why the Psalms?"

"I guess they make me aware of God's presence everywhere. David prayed to God wherever he was and in whatever situation he found himself."

"Yep … He's everywhere, all right. It always seems a little strange to me that he leaves it to us to notice him, or not … so many never even bother. I'm guilty of that myself."

"Are you a praying man?"

His pale green eyes met hers. "Only recently. The prospect of having a conversation with a holy God who spoke worlds into being has always kind of intimidated me." He laughed slightly. "I guess I never felt good enough—or maybe the word is *clean* enough for it. Then my boss, Rudd England, dropped this on my desk." He reached in his back pocket and produced a thin and worn leather-bound book which he handed to her.

She drew a deep, surprised breath. "The Psalms!"

"Yep … He told me to go home and pray them, which I did. The more I read, the more I realized that I'd been wrong. These aren't the prayers of 'perfect and nice' people. They're rough and raw and honest. I'm beginning to think of prayer as getting everything out in the open before God, nothing hidden."

Bay sensed a passion in him and her curiosity grew. "Why do you think your boss asked you to read the Psalms specifically and not just the Bible as a whole?"

"In our job, we run the scale on emotions. David's prayers are real … not a bunch of rehearsed sentences and Christian lingo. Before reading this book," he slapped it in the palm of his hand. "I sure had the wrong idea about prayer."

"Mack," Piper's voice called from the doorway. "We're going to be late for church." She narrowed her eyes at Bay for a split second before she seemed to catch herself and quickly put on a smile.

The fact that Bay was sitting next to Mack engaged in a conversation seemed to annoy Piper, and if the situation had been reversed, Bay knew she would have felt the very same way.

Feeling suddenly awkward, Bay looked at the open book in her lap, noticing a shaft of light slanting down on the pages from the morning sun. Something thawed in her, and a smile tugged at her lips. "We were just discussing the book of Psalms."

"Oh? Well, then tell me, too." Dropping her dark lashes to gaze at the book in Bay's lap, Piper glanced up at Mack. Bay imagined she warmed with pleasure as Mack looked at her in that ageless way a man looks at a beautiful woman. With a satisfied look, Piper listened as Bay repeated their conversation.

Piper thought a moment. "So, basically, you're saying that God is everywhere. And ... you didn't know that? Bless your heart." She searched Bay's face as if she were looking at a simple-minded child or an idiot, or both!

Bay hesitated a moment, then responded, "Yes, but ..."

"Would you like to come to church, Bay?" Mack asked, intently watching her face for her answer.

"Mack ..." Piper's voice was subdued, but Bay heard the warning in it. "I'm sure Bay has already thought about that and has decided against it. You've just put her on the spot. Besides, she's not even dressed, and we're already late."

Bay's hand was reaching for the arm of the chair when Mack interrupted her. "Next time, then." With that, he reached for Piper's hand and turned to leave, but paused a moment and looked back at Bay. "Rudd always told me that God is not partial to brick and mortar. If anything, he seems to prefer to go along with us through our ordinary day."

After Mack's truck slipped out of sight, his words still hung in the air. Her thoughts seemed to crash over one another like waves hitting the shore. She'd never really thought of that, of God in the everyday, common events of her life. Then a thought came to her. *God is with me, even now.*

It had not been difficult for Bay to avoid Mack's girlfriend for most of the weekend. But, there was no denying that a certain animosity seemed to be developing between them. Try as she might to steer clear of Piper, Bay kept finding herself in the room with the woman.

On Monday morning, the kitchen screen door opened, then slapped shut. Bay wiped her hands down her apron and turned to see who had entered. Her smile of greeting froze on her face as she looked up to see Piper glaring at her from the doorway.

"May I help you?" Bay managed to say without a trace of the apprehension she was now feeling.

Piper laughed mockingly. "Yes, you certainly can." The woman moved near Bay. "I really don't know what you're trying to do with Mack, but I'm here to warn you to keep away from him. He belongs to me, and I have no intention of sharing him with you," Piper stated with blunt frankness. "You see, I intend to marry him as soon as my divorce is final. The last thing we need is for you to try to trap him by getting yourself pregnant again." The shock on Bay's face caused a laugh from Piper. "Oh, yes, Mack told me about your little illegitimate son."

A slow, challenging smile pulled at the corners of Bay's mouth. That was the wrong thing to say to

Bay. The woman had crossed a line, and Bay meant to give her something to think about on her way back to New Orleans.

"So, Mack is your fiancé ... or are you just being hopeful?"

Piper seethed and answered through clenched teeth, "Don't even try to interfere. I've been after him far too long to let some little scar-faced nobody get in my way. I can make your life miserable."

Bay was tired and certainly in no mood to put up with being harassed by a south Louisiana socialite. "I'm sure you can. And, if I have any doubts, all I have to do is ask your husband."

A gasp of shock came from Piper as her words hit their mark. "Why, you little ..."

Just then, the screen door opened, and Bay glanced up to see Mack standing in the doorway. "Everything all right in here?"

Piper turned suddenly at the sound of Mack's voice. "Just having a little girl talk. Are you looking for me?"

"Yeah, I thought we could have breakfast together before you go. What's on the menu this morning, Bay?"

"Beignets, New Orleans-style for our guest, and espresso."

Mack rubbed his hands together, "Great ... no wait. Have you ever made Beignets before?"

"Never in my life ... but ..."

"I know, I know ... you're a better cook than you are a driver."

"No, I was going to say that Derlie made them before she left to pick up a few groceries in town. They're delicious."

His smile started in his lips then spread to his eyes, causing them to glint. Oh, he was a full-blown assault on Bay's senses all right. And that was going to cause some difficulties if she continued to stare at him as if in a trance. Especially when she could feel the heat from his girlfriend's eyes boring a hole through her like the beam from a magnifying glass on a dry leaf.

"Why don't you two go sit in the dining room? I'll bring along some fresh coffee." Bay pushed open the swinging door and waited until they passed through. With a relieved sigh, she leaned against it weakly, casting her eyes heavenward. *Give me strength.*

Chapter 8

*T*he pride Virginia Rutherford had in her home place was almost her backbone. It was the monument that stood as proof that she was no common woman. She, after all, belonged to Briarleigh of Sugar Land, and that made her anything but ordinary.

Briarleigh stood as a rare survivor of the ravages of the Civil War. Legend had it that its survival was due largely to the persuasive reasoning ability of one Miss Julia Breckenridge to the officers of the Union army. Whatever the reason, Julia obtained a letter of protection from an advance officer of the army so that when General William Tecumseh Sherman's troops planned to carry out his orders to burn everything not needed by the troops, Miss Breckenridge's home was spared. Union officers used the home as their winter quarters prior to launching the assault against Vicksburg, Mississippi, in the spring of 1863.

The land was abounding with life, caught in the continual cycle of the seasons and unmindful of the events of man and history that mark the passage of time. It seemed as if the twenty-first century had completely ignored the outskirts of Sugar Land, Louisiana. The landscape hadn't changed much since General Ulysses S. Grant's powerful army marched south through Tensas Parish.

"Virginia …" The name came from Henry Clay's lips like a wind sighing through the trees. His eyes fell to Virginia's lips and throat, and his voice was hoarse when he finally spoke. "You haven't changed at all."

Virginia could almost feel his stare on her skin, and her heartbeat quickened in her throat, until he pulled his eyes away and spoke into the next room where Mack was working.

"Mack, go find Bay and tell her that her mother and son are here."

"Glad to," Mack answered back, tossing his work gloves on the floor. Turning, he gave one last glance at the couple before he strode out.

Mack's first light rap on the door brought no response, so he knocked louder. No sound came from inside the cottage. He stepped back and looked around the yard. There was only one other place where he thought she might be.

Bay dropped to her hands and knees and began scrubbing the bathroom floor of the "chicken coop" cottage Piper had occupied. The floor was a complete mess, and Bay knew the ground-in lipstick and mascara tracks had been deliberately applied to the grout around the ceramic tile.

"Mack must've told his girlfriend that the *unwed mother* of the *illegitimate child* was supposed to clean behind the guests," Bay surmised out loud. "I'm a *good* mother," she told herself as she put her back into the work. "I work hard, and I mind my own business and as far as I know, Lord, You and I are on good terms ... I mean ... I didn't even slap Piper for what she said about my son. That's got to count for something because I wanted to ... You know I sure wanted to."

Twisting around on the bathroom floor, she suddenly found herself staring down at a very large and scuffed pair of work boots. Caught off guard, she raised her head up and knelt frozen by two ice-green eyes staring down at her. Self-consciously, she looked down at the open neckline of her oversized shirt, making certain it hadn't gaped open. When she looked up again, she'd discovered he was doing the same thing. *At least he has the good manners to look guilty before glancing away*, she thought.

"I came to tell you that your son and mother are here," Mack informed her.

Refusing to be embarrassed by her ragged appearance or by the fact that he had obviously caught her venting to God, she stood up and wiped her hands on her jeans and said, "That's the best news I've heard all day."

As they walked back to the house, Mack commented, "I guess your mother must feel like she's come home." He smiled slowly. "She seems to have stirred the blood of the old man. It was quite a sight ... for the first time, I think I actually saw a blush on Uncle Henry's face. But who can blame him? Your mother is quite beautiful. Do you think ...?"

"I have no idea how close my mother and Mr. Blackwell may have been in the past. I know she loved my father, and they had a good marriage.

When he passed away, I was worried my mother would grieve herself to death." She gathered her long shirt tails together and tied them in a knot, letting the ends hang down. "And then Jace came into our lives. He's been the best medicine for all of us."

Stepping up on the back porch, Mack directed Bay through the door and informed her, "They're in the dining room."

Bay went inside and took a minute to comb her fingers through her hair and wash her hands in the sink. She crossed the kitchen and was about to go through the swinging door when she paused and glanced back. Mack was seated at the island in the center of the kitchen, leaning over the countertop with his arms bent and his hands clasped over his head.

"Have you met my family?" Bay asked, waiting expectantly.

He pulled himself up from the counter and startled her with a look of utter defeat as he looked at her. "I … I'm sorry, Bay. What I said to Piper about the situation with your son … I didn't mean it the way she made it sound. I—"

She interrupted him, "Don't worry about it. I'm used to it. Now, would you like to meet my son?"

Stepping into the dining room, they overheard Henry Clay describing his ideas for Briarleigh Inn to Virginia. "The main house has seven guest rooms, six upstairs and one near the kitchen. Mack is staying in that one now. All the outlying buildings are now guest cottages. Three are located near the sugarcane fields. We've just completed the milk house, the smokehouse, the sawmill, and the chicken coop. Bay has the … uh … cottage near the bayou."

A look passed between them that didn't escape notice. Mack cleared his throat.

"Momma!" yelled Jace, as he hurriedly ran toward Bay.

She bent down and scooped him up into her arms. "Oh, I've missed my little man! Have you been a good boy?"

"Uh, huh … but I missed you," Jace admitted sweetly as he pulled his head back and studied his mother's face.

"Not as much as I've missed you," she murmured and nuzzled his neck. "I want you to meet someone. Jace, this is Mr. Mack Blackwell, and I guess you've already met his uncle, Mr. Henry Clay Blackwell."

"Oh, yes, we've met," Henry Clay informed them. "And a fine boy, too … takes good care of his grandmother, I hear."

Mack tilted his head slightly as he looked at Jace, taking in the light green eyes staring back at him with a look of wonder. There was something familiar about the boy. "Well, it sure is nice to have another man around the house. Maybe if your mother lets us, we can go fishing one of these days. There's an old jon boat near the dock. I've wanted to put it in the water to check for leaks."

Jace's eyes lit up, and he turned expectantly to his mother.

"I don't see why not … we have our very own bayou here. I'd imagine you can scare up quite a few turtles and frogs down there," acknowledged

Bay, who couldn't help but smile at the delight she saw in her son's eyes. She turned to her mother. "I'm glad you made it here safely, Mom. This is Mack Blackwell, and I think you already know Henry Clay."

Virginia extended a graceful hand to Mack. "No more talk of the river; it scares me to death. But my, you're as handsome as your uncle. And it's uncanny how much you favor your brother, Shannon."

Virginia's honeyed words sounded fitting in the room, and Mack found her voice something of a pleasure. He raised an eyebrow and questioned, "You know Shannon?"

"Oh, yes, he used to come visit us several years ago. He loved picking on Bay." Virginia smiled at her daughter. "She could always hold her own with him."

Stunned for a moment, Mack could only nod. Why hadn't his brother mentioned the girl? He glanced at Jace again, taking in the features more slowly this time, then turned to Bay. "Holding your own with Shannon is quite an accomplishment. Most people who challenge him sooner or later come out the loser. You should be proud," he said quietly, his eyes measuring her reaction.

They looked at each other for a long moment before she turned away.

The night crept in with its long shadows and the very air seemed to come alive with the sounds of tree frogs and cicadas. Mack sat at the kitchen island and watched through the open window, but even as he strained to see, he couldn't detect any movement in the yard near Bay's cottage. Then, a wobbling, shifting light moved in the night and came ever closer to the house until Mack could hear Henry Clay's boots stomping up the back steps.

"We've got to come up with some kind of outside lighting for the cottages. It's plumb creepy out there once that cove starts murmuring. You should have seen little Jace's eyes when the wind picked up and those sounds started. He held onto my neck so tight I look like somebody snatched me from a hangin'." Henry Clay grimaced and kneaded his neck as he plopped down on a bar stool. "That little fella has a grip that'll choke a mule."

"Want some coffee?" Mack waved him down as Henry Clay shifted in his seat. "Stay put, I'll get it."

"Not much … half a cup will be fine."

Mack glanced over his shoulder and spoke as he poured. "It surprises me to see you and Virginia getting along so well. You must've been close at one time."

"I hate to surprise you, but there's a lot you don't know about me, boy," Henry Clay said impatiently. "And, yes, we used to be close."

"How close?" Mack inquired cautiously, stepping to the counter as he slid the mug in front of his uncle. Straddling the bar stool, he placed his elbows on the counter and took a long pull of his coffee as he waited for the answer to a question that had been nagging him since meeting Jace Rutherford.

Placing his cup down, Henry Clay turned his head and deadeyed his nephew. "There was a time when … when I was forced to do the right thing by your Aunt Hilda. But before that, I was in love with

Virginia Breckenridge. Now, is that clear enough for you, or do I need to paint a picture?"

Mack tilted his head toward his uncle and narrowed his eyes, unable to believe what he was hearing. "You mean Aunt Hilda …?"

Henry Clay was a simple, God-fearing man, but it would have been a mistake for anyone to think of him as unworldly. There was not much he hadn't experienced for himself. Although he'd grown to love his wife, by the grace of God, there had always been a shadow of regret hanging over him.

"Virginia and I were the best of friends. We grew up together," Henry Clay emphasized, as his eyes began to take on a sudden weariness. "Hilda decided that she wanted me … at all cost." He turned a shade darker and cleared his throat. "I was young, weak, stupid, and a little drunk at the time, if I remember correctly. After I found out Hilda was pregnant, I decided we'd go to the courthouse and get married. Word got out, and after the dust settled, I arranged to meet with Virginia. I told her what had happened. Not too long after that, she moved to Moss Bay, Alabama, to live with an aunt." He inhaled deeply and leaned back before continuing. "Oh, I tried to find out about her in a roundabout way, but my life had taken a sudden turn: fatherhood, work, bills … you know … family life."

Mack took in his uncle's features. Noticing the look of regret, he changed the subject. "So, how did the Breckenridge family lose this house?"

Henry Clay ran a thick hand through his hair. "Virginia's brother got sick. In those days, many farmers didn't have insurance, so her father sold the place to pay off the hospital debts. It wasn't long after that that her brother died from complications during surgery. The poor boy never left the hospital. The family was devastated, as you can well imagine. It was then that Virginia convinced her parents to move to Moss Bay and start over."

A hush fell over the room. Henry Clay got up and stepped out onto the porch, retrieving his cigar from the railing. He patted his pocket for a match, struck it, and puffed the cigar to life until it was glowing like the hot end of a poker between his fingers.

Mack walked up behind his uncle and slapped a hand on his shoulder. Having Virginia back on Briarleigh soil seemed to occupy most of Henry Clay's thoughts. It was evident to Mack that Henry needed to be alone.

"You going home tonight Uncle Henry, or are you sleeping here?"

"Here, I'll take the smokehouse."

Mack nodded, "Well, goodnight."

"Goodnight, son," he replied, squinting through the cigar smoke with his attention on the cottage that held Virginia Breckenridge Rutherford.

Chapter 9

Mack Blackwell rose Tuesday morning to what promised to be a calm and serene day. Buttoning his shirt, he stood before the open door of the armoire, relieved that the night was finally over and that he had some manual labor to set his mind to. A phone call from Piper before bed had plagued him for most of the night, running through his head and troubling him out of sleep. She'd made it clear that she wanted more from their relationship and had already set out to prove it on more than one occasion.

Oh, he'd been tempted, but something held him back, something he didn't entirely understand himself. Was he punishing her? He would've liked to think it was because he was becoming a godly man, a man of character and integrity, but deep down he knew that just didn't ring true.

He ran a hand behind his neck, rubbing the tense muscles as he thought about it. The truth was he'd had trouble sleeping since the day he'd been put on unpaid leave, not because of anger or resentment, but because he missed the job and his crew. He couldn't shake the feeling that maybe this was it. Maybe he'd gone too far … to the point of no return. And how he'd cope with that was anyone's guess.

Now he had more pressing matters to attend to. Sterling Geroux, part owner of the St. Bonitus Hotel, had contacted him expressing interest in purchasing their property. After assuring Mr. Geroux that the property was not on the market, Mack couldn't believe that the man refused to take no for an answer, promising that the meeting would not be a waste of his time. Curious, Mack and Henry Clay agreed to meet with Mr. Geroux and hear the man's offer.

The sun was climbing over the river in the east, causing spider webs strung between the fence railings to gleam and shimmer in their dewy symmetry. A deep voice came from the yard, and Bay glanced up from cleaning the chicken coop cottage floor in time to see Mack and another man inspecting the cottages. Through the open door, Bay watched as Mack moved about the grounds, pointing and explaining. After several minutes, the men turned and began making their way toward her. Bay's heart nearly stopped. "Sterling Geroux!" she gasped in horror.

"Am I dreaming?" Sterling put an arm on the door frame and leaned forward into the cottage. From his point of view, the image he projected was nothing short of striking.

Dropping the putty knife to the floor where she'd been scraping tar from the tongue and groove planks, she stiffened her back, stunned by the encounter.

"I see my presence has left you speechless. Is it possible that you still care?"

Looking past him, she saw Mack approaching. "To answer your question, no, it's not possible."

Sterling gave a mock pout. "Now, Bay, that's not very friendly of you."

"I'm not very friendly," she stated, thrusting her chin out defiantly as she looked up at him.

Mack paused just outside the door and watched as the unusual scene played out.

Sterling tossed his head back and laughed, then his gaze warmed with interest as it moved appreciatively over Bay's soft curves. "It's rare to see such a pretty woman scrubbing floors. When I purchase this place, you'll be given a place of honor, and this type of work will be left to the hirelings," he stated with certainty. Her smallness always made him feel powerful and manly.

With the palms of her hands flat on the floor, she stated calmly, "Would it surprise you to know that I find this kind of work infinitely more pleasurable than working for you?"

A feigned weariness came over Sterling, and he let out an exasperated sigh. "Your cruel words pierce my heart. But, you know me … I always get what I want … sooner or later."

Bay's rare show of temper left Mack baffled. It flashed like the blade of a steely knife. She'd never so much as raised her voice to any one of them, handling problems with quiet but unmistakable authority. He raised a brow and asked, "Is there some sort of problem here?"

Surprised, Sterling turned around swiftly and faced a set of hard, cold eyes. It was a full moment before he could speak. "No, no … Bay and I are old friends. We were just catching up. She worked for me before coming to Briarleigh. I have to say, you have quite a jewel on your hands."

Mack glanced down at Bay, seeing a sneer form on her lips. "Well, it seems we agree on one thing, Mr. Geroux. Now, if you don't mind, I'd like to finish our little tour and get back to work."

"Of course," Sterling agreed then turned back to Bay. With a wicked smile, he touched the tips of his fingers to his forehead. "See you soon."

Leaning over so she could get a better view of the two men as they stood next to the fence and talked, she noticed a striking difference in them. Sterling was arrogant with a superior attitude, and Mack was calm and reserved. Mack led by example rather than by orders, and he'd do whatever needed to be done—nothing was beneath him. She liked the way he listened to others and weighed their thoughts before making a final decision. He never questioned loyalty but seemed to know instinctively that others would follow his lead. Even now, with Sterling throwing every ounce of his persuasive abilities toward him, Mack seemed completely unmoved and thoroughly in command of the situation.

Swallowing convulsively, Bay dreaded what may come of the strange turn of events. She couldn't believe that Mack was entertaining the idea of selling Briarleigh! Venting a groan of despair, she got up and gathered her supplies into the cart with a weariness she felt clean to the bone.

She kept her eyes diverted as she tried to hurry past the men.

Sterling commented, "Chasing me, Bay? You know, all you have to do is ask, and I'll take you back."

Abruptly, she turned and faced Sterling.

Moving between the two, Mack pointed to the man and stated, "It seems you've upset one of my employees, Mr. Geroux."

Sterling's eyes suddenly narrowed as he looked at Bay. A stomach-turning smile spread across his face. "I always seem to bring out the passionate side of Bay."

Bay glared at him and, with sheer strength of will, she managed to gather her composure. "This discussion has lost its point. I have nothing to say to you."

"Don't let me keep you from your journey home, Mr. Geroux," Mack remarked, then turned from Sterling, effectively dismissing the man, and said to Bay, "Derlie is looking for you."

Bay clenched her teeth and made her way toward the kitchen.

Sterling turned to Mack and with a raised eyebrow asked, "How many women do you employ here?"

"Enough."

Sterling threw back his head and laughed. "How very enterprising of you … I think we're going to get along better than I expected."

"Don't count on it," Mack stated emphatically, before walking away and leaving the man smiling after him.

A full week after encountering Sterling at Briarleigh, Mack glanced around as the sound of Bay's softly-echoing footsteps stopped in his doorway. Bay was making her daily mid-morning rounds and appeared surprised at his presence. Mack knew she'd probably thought she was alone in the house. She quietly entered the room and placed a stack of towels on the dresser.

"I've ordered a nice mahogany piece to hold your towels," she informed him, neatly straightening the thick towels. "It's taken us a week, but with the help of my mother, Henry Clay and I have finally finished ordering all the furniture we need for the inn."

"Any idea when the shipments will arrive?" Mack grabbed his watch from the nightstand and slid it on his wrist, checking the closeness of his shave as he waited for an answer.

Bay stepped back to the door and paused. "Mother and Henry Clay have gone in the dually truck to pick up a shipment from a supplier in Chattanooga. Jace went with them. They mentioned something about an aquarium across from the hotel where they're staying." She smirked before turning to go. "I think my mother just wanted Jace along as a chaperone. They should be back in a couple of days."

"What? Days?" Mack narrowed his eyes. "When did they leave?"

Bay answered back from the kitchen, "About two hours ago. Your uncle said he didn't want to wake you, so he left you a note by the coffee pot"

Mack looked at his watch. "It's almost … ten! Unbelievable!"

"I'll put on some fresh coffee." She grabbed the pot and took a whiff, crinkling her nose. "This pot has been roasting for hours."

Running a hand through his hair, he replied, "No, I need it strong and effective. I'm getting too soft out here in the country."

"Soft? Hardly." She moved to the sink and began filling up the pot. She called again into the room, "It's because of you we're ahead of schedule. The way you've been working, you *need* a rest. Now, what would you like for breakfast?"

"Nothing … I'll wait for lunch," he said, low and steady from behind her.

His manner held boldness and dominated the scene around him. Bay considered opening her mouth to argue but decided against it and simply nodded.

The aroma of the strong, savory coffee filled the kitchen as she collected Mack's cup. She turned and saw him sitting at the island, his elbows on the counter and his hands clasped together, tapping at his chin with his knuckles. She slipped the cup in front of him, and he never glanced up. He continued to stare unblinkingly at the counter, so preoccupied with his thoughts that Bay had to clear her throat to bring his attention to his coffee.

"Derlie will be back soon to get started on lunch. I sent her to town on an errand."

Mack nodded, then slowly lifted the cup to his lips and took a long pull.

"Well," Bay gently tapped the counter once. "I guess I'll leave you with your thoughts."

Chapter 10

An unpredictable breeze stirred the treetops in the late afternoon as Bay pushed a cartload of supplies down the paths that connected the cottages. She went from cottage to cottage, inspecting each of the rooms, stocking soaps, towels, and linens as needed. As she approached the cottage by the dock, her cottage, suddenly everything became still. There was no wind; nothing stirred the hot summer air. It was so quiet that one listening long might hear a fish jump in the bayou or a turtle slide off a log and plop into the water.

Deciding to explore her surroundings a little more and to find a quiet spot to meditate, Bay parked the cart and snapped on the supply container's lid. She began making her way toward the bayou, carefully watching her step as she walked along the bank to what the locals referred to as the Cove.

It was a beautiful place. The fresh, green expanse of land sloped ever so slightly toward the water; it seemed held in place by the massive oaks and sweet gum trees that anchored the spot.

She spied a fishing boat with a single fisherman casting his line and slowly drifting along. She watched as his boat slipped beneath the great shadow of a live oak near the bank, half-hidden in the tall grass. The boat slowly disappeared from sight as it rounded the bend to join the main river.

Pressing her back to a tree, she took in the tranquil sight, watching as the waters of the cove blended into the Mississippi River. She rested her eyes against the easy flow of the bayou.

In the distance, she heard a faint hum which grew in volume until she strained her eyes to see into the trees on the opposite bank. Thick brush and undergrowth concealed most things, but the feeling of hidden eyes watching her caused the hair on the back of her neck to stand up. She blinked to make sure she was seeing clearly into the trees. The complete stillness of everything frightened her, no sound of insects or animals, no wind ... only murmuring. It was faint and hard to make out, but she listened carefully until the first drops of rain splashed on her arm.

The sky seemed to darken by degrees to an angry shade of gray, when, suddenly, it turned into a downpour, drenching her to the skin. Lightning flashed across the sky as thunder boomed, sending Bay sprinting toward the house. Halfway across the yard, she became aware of a voice calling out to her.

"Looks like you could use a little help ... get in," Mack said, pulling his truck alongside her. He opened the passenger door and extended his hand. She grabbed it like a drowning man grabs a life preserver. As he pulled her into the cab of his truck, he said, "I guess I should have warned you about these summer squalls. They kinda sneak up pretty fast around here."

Trying his best to suppress a grin, he turned his face, not wanting to look at her. Bay always seemed so put together and proper, so cool and confident, that he was finding it hard to reconcile her usual image with the helpless little creature now shivering in his truck. Strangely, as she huddled in the large seat, hugging her arms close to her body with her teeth chattering, she never looked more appealing.

Recognizing embarrassment on her face, he quickly gained control of his amusement. "A hot bath will warm you right up," Mack said and uncharacteristically kept talking, wanting to put her at ease. The poor girl looked like she'd seen a ghost. "Derlie has your dinner in the oven and a chocolate cake on the counter. She'd been watching you from the kitchen window for the last hour. Ever since she heard the weather report her fingers have been worrying the beads of that pearl rosary. When we saw the first flash of lightning, I knew I'd better come get you." He slanted his head as he looked at her. "That woman has always been tenacious when her loyalties take root. It seems she's appointed herself your private guardian. And, where you're concerned, I think you need one."

Bay jerked her head around and glared at him. Straightening in her seat, she held her head high as she tried her best to convey an undaunted sense of pride.

Well, that got a rise out of her, he thought. *At least I know she's not in shock.* "What were you doing down there anyway?"

"If I told you, then you'd know."

"That's the idea," he said.

The windows inside the truck fogged a bit as the coolness of the air conditioner met with the moist heat outside. When she spoke, it was almost in awe. "Why are you concerned about me? I can take care of myself."

Mack shifted in the seat of the truck, his sharp eyes scanning the landscape. "I don't want to pry, but you look like you have serious matters on your mind. Maybe I can help," he offered, trying not to seem overly concerned but wanting to know what was troubling the woman.

"I'm just weighing my options."

"Oh?" He paused, waiting for her to reply. When she didn't respond, he asked, "Mind telling me what's on your mind?"

Crossing her arms over her chest, she peered out the window. "Whether to leave now or wait until I find another job someplace else."

Facing her stiff back, he studied her for a space of time before he spoke. "I see. So you're not happy here?"

An anxious moment passed. "I won't work for Sterling Geroux, *period*. I know I have no say in the matter, but, if you sell this place to him, you'll be making a huge mistake. That's just my opinion." She turned to see his reaction.

"You underestimate your value to us, Bay," Mack assured her. Bay's work ethic impressed him, and he would have sent Sterling Geroux packing with even her slightest disapproval. Now that he knew her feelings, he would have a hard time sitting through the next scheduled meeting with Mr. Geroux objectively. "Right now, we're only listening to his proposal. We have no plans to do anything else."

Slowly, she uncrossed her arms and put her hands down on the seat beside her as thcy rolled to a stop near the house.

Noticing her slight shiver, he said, "Tell you what, you go on to your cottage, and I'll have Derlie bring down your dinner."

"Thank you," she said softly, keeping her eyes away from him. She'd suffered enough humiliation without having to see his subtle grin.

The sun had dipped low in the sky, and the drone of insects grew heavy on the air. A steady rain settled in for most of the evening, but now the storm had moved on, leaving behind a humid heat and a breeze that no one seemed to mind, least of all Bay. She raised the window in the bathroom a crack to catch the fresh air. The scent of rain mingled with bubble bath as she gazed through the cotton curtains, lifted lightly by the gentle wind. As the tub filled, she saw the back screen door of the inn open then slam shut. Derlie, with hands loaded down, made her way toward the cottage.

Relaxing back into the steamy water, she listened to Derlie bustle about the room, humming to herself as she busily arranged dishes on the table. From the sound of it, she had started a load of laundry in the washer.

Bay called over her shoulder, "Derlie, don't bother with picking up after me. I'll take care of that. You just get on home before dark."

Derlie grunted obstinately, "Take your bath and leave me be. I got this."

Bay rested her head back against the edge of the tub and smiled. She was growing fond of the salty old woman. It felt nice having someone fuss over her.

A little while later, she heard the door open and close. Derlie was gone for the night.

Curiosity had always been Bay's downfall; she wanted to see what was around a corner or over a hill. Only this time what she'd discovered down by the cove had robbed her of her peace and, very nearly, her sanity. Already she was growing anxious, fearful of spending the night alone. Something was out there roaming the dark woods. And that sound, that murmur that floated across the cove was beginning to unnerve her.

Wrapping a robe tightly around her, she stepped from the bathroom and looked around the room in amazement. Derlie had arranged dinner on the newly-acquired distressed coffee table. With the warm glow of a candle burning on the mantle, the freshly painted white fireplace looked warm and inviting. The flickering light reflected softly on the off-white paneled walls. The cottage was certainly more appealing after Bay left her personal touches. Settling on the couch, she rubbed her hand appreciatively over the vintage chenille slipcover. She flicked on the radio and began eating her dinner as the voice of the announcer for the Atlanta Braves filled the room, keeping her from feeling so alone.

As the night wore on, one thing was certain … Bay was not going to sleep alone in the cottage *that* night. She began to devise a plan.

Pulling a quilt from the foot of her bed, she brought it, along with a pillow, to the window seat where she waited, staring at Mack's bedroom window. The soft dripping of water from the eaves of the cottage began to lull her senses until she started at his bedroom light going out. She stared at Mack's darkened window indecisively, wondering if he could be asleep. Her feet slid to the floor, and she made her move with the stealth of a panther. Easing out of the cottage, she crossed the soggy, rain-soaked ground to the main house.

She could feel the wetness seep through her slippers, but she would not go back. Creeping up the back porch steps, she carefully unlocked the door and slipped inside. Sliding off her slippers, she tiptoed across the kitchen floor then snuggled carefully and quietly into the corner near the door to Mack's bedroom. At last, she was finally able to relax. Though no light leaked from around the bedroom door, it was comfort enough for her to hear Mack's voice on the other side of the wall as he spoke in low tones to someone on the phone. The sound of his masculine voice assured her of another human being in close proximity. The soothing sound blended with the patter of rainwater dripping down a gutter, and, soon a sense of peace fell over her like a sun-warmed blanket. She felt safe, protected, and secure. Falling fast asleep, she did not wake, not even when the morning sun lit the windows.

The door to Mack's bedroom suddenly pulled open startling Bay from a deep sleep, jerking her awake. Mack turned sharply at the movement then stared down at the crumpled form as if his eyes had played a trick on him.

Seeing the confusion in his eyes, Bay explained groggily, "I … uh, got a little scared last night." She could hear the cringe in her voice and diverted her gaze from his penetrating stare.

The sight of Bay curled on the floor of the kitchen caught Mack completely off guard. Her eyes were sleep–swollen, and a tangle of matted hair stuck up on one side of her head. Still, with the grace of some mythical creature, she emerged from the spot and attempted to stand. But, as she bent down to gather her pillow, her feet tangled in the quilt, causing her to lose her footing. Mack's strong arm came around her waist and pulled her to her feet. The brief contact of their bodies came as something of a shock to both of them and further added to Bay's embarrassment. Modestly hugging her pillow, she didn't wish to contrast herself with Mack's fresh appearance. Grabbing the quilt, too mortified to speak, she slipped by him and eased out of the house without a backward glance.

So concerned was Bay about getting away from the house that she failed to notice the black Mercedes parked in the circular drive under the magnolia tree.

Chapter 11

M ack would have to say that, at first glance, he found the man standing in front of him exactly the kind of man he usually didn't like. He would have guessed him to be thirty, famous and filthy rich, judging by his expensive clothes and the sleek, black Mercedes parked outside. His saving grace, as far as Mack was concerned, were his smiling dark eyes. He didn't spend too much time looking the man over, but he did notice the guy seemed pleasant enough.

"May I help you?" Mack asked.

"I'm Crawford Benton. I was told that I could find Bay Larke Rutherford here?"

Mack looked at the man, his left eyebrow raised, and inquired, "Bay?"

"Yes. Is she here, please?"

"Is she expecting you?"

Crawford shook his head. "No, I'm afraid not. But, if you'll just tell her I'm here, I'm sure she'll see me."

Confident man, Mack thought, as he walked across the foyer and opened the door to Bay's office.

"If you'll wait in her office, I'll let her know that you're here."

Stepping into the kitchen, Mack pulled out his phone and sent a text to Bay. He turned to fill the coffee pot at the sink and glanced out the kitchen window, surprised to see her running across the backyard toward the house.

She flew into the kitchen. Out of breath, she asked, "Where is he?"

"Your office." Mack's curiosity got the better of him, and he walked behind her to the still-swinging kitchen door and pushed it open slightly. Mack watched as she ran into the office and into Crawford's waiting arms. Crawford kissed her and then enveloped her in a tight hug that she seemed to enjoy completely.

Mack let the door close against his fingers, moved toward the counter, and googled the name *Crawford Benton* on his cell phone.

Crawford Benton, New York Times bestselling author.

Pulling out a stool, Mack straddled the seat and slid his cell phone on the counter. With elbows on the marble, he rubbed his hands together and stared ahead as he sat there. Taking a deep breath, he held it for a few seconds before the door suddenly swung open, and Bay came into the kitchen.

"Crawford Benton wants to rent a cottage for the summer and possibly a few months into the fall!" Bay was having a hard time keeping the excitement out of her voice.

"We're a few weeks away from opening. Can he wait?"

"Oh, he won't mind that we're not open yet; in fact, he'd prefer it. He needs solitude, and I'll make sure he gets it. I'll arrange to have all his meals delivered to his cottage. He said he'll pay extra for room service."

The thought that crossed Mack's mind at that very moment was anything but wholesome. It took no small amount of effort to keep his mouth shut as he shifted uncomfortably on the stool.

Seeing his hesitation, she continued, "Don't you think it's a little strange to refuse a guest when we're supposed to be running an inn?"

The tone of her questioning irritated him. When he spoke, his voice was low and firm. "There are matters you're unaware of, Bay. We have an opening day for a reason."

Lowering her eyes before his penetrating green-eyed stare, she could only nod. She was suddenly aware that, in her excitement, she had forgotten just who was in charge here. Mack and Henry Clay were equal partners, and she answered to *them*, not the other way around.

"Which cottage were you thinking of giving him?" Mack rose and leaned forward on his elbows deliberately until his green eyes drew the gaze of the light hazel.

Bay lowered herself onto the stool and, with considerably more respect, spoke carefully and clearly. "I think the old sawmill cottage would be perfect. It's secluded and quiet and very masculine. He'll love the screened-in porch with the woods nearby. It's the perfect cottage for a writer."

"Book him," Mack stated flatly, hoping all the time that the man would change his mind about his visit. Why? He didn't have time to dwell on that question.

Bay's mouth softened into a warm smile when she explained, "Crawford is a well-known author. This is exactly the type of place he seeks out to do his writing." She gently slid off the stool and stood to her feet. "I'll make sure he gets settled in."

After Bay left the room, Mack shook his head. "Author," he spat out the word as if it had been soaked in turpentine.

In the dim, late evening light when the world seemed to let out a deep sigh, Mack walked up the back steps and plopped down in a rocker. After loosening his boot laces, he pulled one muddy boot off then the other, dropping them to the porch floor with a thud. Leaning back, he relaxed his head against the chair and rested his eyes.

The creak of the screen door drew his attention. He rolled his head to the side and saw Bay looking at him, smiling.

"You look worn out. Would you like some sweet tea?" she questioned softly. She held the screen door open and halfway turned, ready to re-enter the kitchen at his request.

"That would be nice, but what I really need is a shower." He rubbed a hand across his bristly chin. "There'll be heck to pay if I track up Derlie's clean floors."

"Well, Derlie is gone for the night, and I promise there won't be a sign of dirt on her floor."

"I'm covered in mud, Bay, almost as much as you plastered on me when we first met," he said mockingly, then flashed a brilliant white smile, even more pronounced against the mud outlining his jaw.

"Oh, I love the smell of wet earth on a man. It makes me think he's been out doing something useful and not simply sitting around whining in a rocking chair all afternoon," Bay explained.

Smiling, Mack pushed up from his seat. As his feet hit the floor, a wind rose up and, with it, came the low murmurings of the cove. Seeing the concerned look on Bay's face as she glanced over her shoulder, he lightly touched her elbow, guiding her toward the door. "I can sleep on the couch, if you'd like to stay in my room tonight."

That was exactly what she wanted. But, how could she ever gain his confidence if he thought she was a baby, afraid of the wind? "No, I'll be all right. I've got to get used to this place sooner or later. But tell me … what is making that sound?"

He shrugged, looking in the direction of the cove. "Some people say it's the way the wind moves over the water. Kind of like the sound you make when you blow over the top of a Coke bottle. Others say it's the ghosts of Civil War soldiers or the spirit of Hezekiah, an old circuit-riding preacher who lived years ago on the other side of the bayou. But, if you're asking me, I say it's just the sound the wind makes in the trees. Or possibly voices from people on the other side … *of the cove*, that is," he added with emphasis.

"It's like something lingers down there ... a certain ... I don't know. All I know is that I don't want to get caught there after the sun goes down."

"We all have to face fear of some kind in this life ... and we all have to fight that battle for ourselves in the end. But tonight, I really insist that you stay up here."

She didn't need another invitation. What Mack was offering her was what she needed most, an understanding friend. "Okay, but I'll take the couch."

"You'll sleep in my bed," he stated firmly, then pulled the screen door open, walked into the kitchen, then disappeared into his room.

Sometime later, Mack emerged from his bedroom through a veil of shower steam. He wore jeans and a white button-down shirt with the sleeves rolled up to his elbows.

"How about dinner out tonight?" he said, in a voice so low Bay thought she was hearing it in her head. "There's a new place near the marina I want to check out. It'll give us a chance to talk over some ideas about the inn. I want your thoughts."

Bay looked at him, seeing not a perfect man, but a man with a sense of morality and a strong work ethic. His casual manner appealed to her on some level. "Okay, that sounds good. First though, we'll need to hide the evidence." She lifted the foil from his supper plate for his inspection.

"I can handle that," he said. Taking the plate from her hand, he walked to the back door and tossed the contents over the porch railing. "There's a family of raccoons that'll eat well tonight." He winked at her conspiratorially, "Our secret or I'm dead meat."

Smiling, she loosened her hair from the elastic band and ran her fingers through it. "I'm really not dressed for dinner out."

"You're fine. This place is nothing fancy," he said, sliding his keys off the counter. He allowed her to lead them out of the house to where his truck was parked.

As the late evening sun heated the remaining moisture from the previous evening's rain, the summer scents of magnolia, jasmine, and honeysuckle permeated the air.

He walked in front of his truck, glanced over at the shiny black Mercedes parked next to him, and opened the passenger door. "My seats aren't leather, but that strip of duct tape down the center does add a certain touch, wouldn't you say?"

"Oh, yes, definitely," she agreed, as she climbed into the seat.

He shrugged as he closed the door, stepped around the truck, and slid in behind the wheel. "I try hard not to show off. Sometimes, you just need to draw a little attention to subtle sophistication."

"I completely agree."

Mack turned the key, and the engine rumbled.

She threw her head back and laughed.

"Oh, Bay. I like you. Since I've stopped hanging out with stoners, I can't make anybody laugh anymore."

"Stoners?" Bay questioned, with a smile still on her lips.

He glanced at her. "We make a lot of calls that involve drugs and alcohol, mostly traffic accidents. I could tell you some stories." Putting the truck in gear, Mack steered down the drive and onto the river road.

Just before the truck reached Ghost Bridge, Bay began looking around the area of the cove. Her eyes scanned the shadowy surroundings, not really sure that she wanted to see what she sought. "Have you lived here long?"

"Not exactly. I live outside Baton Rouge. I've only been here for a few months. But, I did grow up here."

"Oh?"

He nodded, glancing out the window as the truck bumped down the rough road. "This is home … it's a great place to raise a boy, by the way."

She cleared her throat. "That's what I'm counting on."

He glanced at her briefly before turning his attention back to the road. "That boy of yours, Jace, he seems like a good kid."

"Hmm … he is that."

Bay's nature seemed to bring out a protective instinct in Mack. He tried hard to appear as if he didn't hang on her every word, which he did, and often.

"So … does Jace see his father much?"

"No," she said softly, as she looked down at her hands. She had noticed that her son's eyes had taken on depth and a touch of sadness recently. "He's young, I know, but lately it seems he's become aware of loss. Loss for something he's never had, and I'm afraid it's made him feel empty. It's an extraordinary price to pay for someone else's sin."

Mack grew quiet, drawing on his ability to maintain his composure in difficult situations. Being a flight medic requires a steel constitution, but, at that very moment, he felt anything but composed. His brother, Shannon, crossed his mind. The resemblance between Shannon and Jace was uncanny. "So, you know my brother, Shannon?"

"Yes!" Bay answered happily. "I didn't know he had a brother, though."

"I guess you two didn't do a lot of talking." A set of cool, distant green eyes locked obstinately with hers before he looked back at the road.

Before she could respond to his comment, Mack pulled into a parking spot in front of an old dock with a weathered pier stretching out over a marshy lake. About midway, a ramshackle structure seemed to hang precariously to one side of the pier and looked attached there by heavy barge ropes. The sign over the door read *Phatt Bottom Grill*.

"You still game?" Mack asked, noticing her look of apprehension.

"Definitely … we should go for the ambience, if for nothing else."

Now it was Mack's turn to laugh. "That's what I like to hear … lead the way.'

As they approached the restaurant, they could hear music from a live band playing from somewhere inside the structure.

"Is that *Brown-Eyed Girl* they're playing?"

"I think it is. Why? You like it?"

"One of my all-time favorites."

"Good. Let's go in and find a seat."

Chapter 12

Stepping inside the Phatt Bottom Grill, the first impression one got was that of a fisherman's hangout. The walls were covered with an assortment of fish mounted on plaques. Some were suspended in mid-air going after a lure, while others merely hung there, apparently too fat to move. A crowd hovered near the bar, listening to the live band that was set up in a corner.

They were escorted to a booth opposite the bar. The waitress took their drink order, winked at Mack, and said, "This is the best seat in the house … real private."

"Thank you. It's perfect," Mack answered back. "What's the most popular choice on the menu?"

"The shrimp, honey," she answered incredulously.

Mack looked to Bay with a question in his eyes.

"Sounds good to me." Folding the menu, Bay handed it back to the waitress.

"Bring us a little of all the favorites … including dessert," Mack added, then winked at the waitress.

The waitress beamed. "If you trust me that much, sweetie, you're in for a real treat! Old Peggy knows what's good around here."

They watched the waitress shove the menus under her arm and head for the kitchen. As they turned their attention back to each other, a massive muscular arm reached around and hooked Mack by the throat. Bay made a move to get up and confront the man, then pulled her head back sharply when a flash of recognition hit her. "Chief Mitchell?"

As the name rolled off Bay's tongue, Mack reached back and grabbed the man behind the neck and pulled forward.

"Okay, okay, you got me! Now let go!"

Mack released his head and got to his feet, slapping his hand into the chief's ready one. "Ludie Earl, I might have known you'd be prowling around a place like this. Good to see you!" Turning toward Bay, he said, "Ludie, I'd like for you to meet Bay Rutherford. She's our new manager at the inn."

Ludie's smile grew wide. "We've met. But it's good to see you again."

Mack looked sideways at Bay. "Have you been in trouble with the law already?"

Nodding, Bay seized the glass of tea the waitress offered and took a light sip, realizing that Peggy was closely following their conversation and watching them attentively over the eyeglasses perched on the end of her nose. "The chief was kind enough to direct me to the home for unwed mothers."

Gaining instant sympathy from Peggy, Bay suddenly found herself being consoled and pressed against the chest of the pillowy woman. "You poor baby!" She reached into her floral apron pocket for a pen and order pad. Scribbling out her number, she handed it back to Bay. "Listen, darlin', you call me for anything now, you hear? I mean it. I've got five kids of my own." As she straightened to leave, she gave Mack a mean-eyed stare before turning away.

As soon as the waitress was out of earshot, Mack commented, "You'd better sit down and join us, Ludie. Old Peggy may not try to poison me with the police chief sitting here."

Ludie laughed and slid in next to Bay. "If you don't mind, I'll sit with Bay. I don't want people to think I'm friends with a no-count."

"Are we on the Mississippi River?" Bay asked, narrowing her eyes as she looked out from the multi-paned window next to their booth.

"No," Mack explained, "it was once the Mississippi River, but now it's an oxbow lake. The river shifts and curves. Every now and then, it will loop around and almost form a circle. The river cuts through sometimes and cuts off the loop, making a lake, like this one. The river is on the other side of those trees."

Ludie exchanged a glance with Mack. "As a matter of fact, Mack saved my life near here."

Mack raised his hands up from the table as the waitress placed a plate of shrimp in front of him. "Yeah, well, you'd better believe I've lived to regret it."

Bay's curiosity got the best of her. "That sounds like a story I'd like to hear."

Ludie Earl stretched back in the seat, ignoring Mack's headshake, and took a deep breath. "Well, it was like this. It was summer, and, as always, we headed for the river. We had this old, worn-out dugout. I guess you could call it a sorry excuse for a canoe, but it was the best we could do. So we paddled out, going down river just like ol' Huck Finn. As we rounded the bend, a sudden squall came up. It was a violent one, too. We began to take on water from the rough chop of the waves and the sudden downpour. Our boat got swamped and sank. As we swam toward shore, my feet got caught in a tangle of limbs beneath the surface and started dragging me down under the current. I was under water so long that I could hear angels singing. The next thing I know, I was being pulled to the surface by my hair!" He rubbed the top of his sparse head and eyed Mack suspiciously. "He performed CPR on me, and, as they say, the rest is history."

Mack looked at Bay and motioned toward Ludie. "Yeah, and ever since then, he's had a man crush on me," he joked.

"Ten minutes later, the sun was out, and we were fishing from the bank like nothing'd ever happened," Ludie continued. "Those were the good ol' days."

"Well, that experience never made you shy of the river. You spend about as much time on the Old Man as you ever did, from what I'm told," Mack noted, drumming his fingers on the table.

"True … I guess the river gave us both our professions. I'm here most nights when the barge docks. Whenever that rowdy bunch hits town, crime goes up and drunken brawls go down, right here." He tapped his forefinger on the Formica table. "This place can change real fast, but most of the action happens out there on the levee."

Mack smirked and looked at Bay. "Fights always happen on the levee, and Ludie enjoys watching the action unfold. It's kinda like a *sport* to him."

Ludie spread his mouth in a toothy grin.

"But when it's time to round them up, he's got his pistol ready."

Slapping the table, Ludie stood up and said, "I've interrupted your date long enough. I best get back to work and let you guys eat."

Mack opened his mouth to correct him then steeled himself against it. Not wanting to embarrass Bay or his friend, he let the remark pass.

After Ludie had gone, they dug into the shrimp, peeling the shells off the meat as if they were starving. Since it wasn't a date, Bay felt no need to pretend to be anything other than who she was. Mack had already seen her stranded in mud two feet off the road, sick with a mysterious fainting illness, and sleeping sprawled out on his kitchen floor. She couldn't help but wonder why she was reduced to the lowest level of her dignity whenever he was around. She cracked open a shrimp shell and held it up to her mouth. For once, why couldn't he see her the way most people did, as a dignified, competent, and gracious businesswoman? Placing the shrimp back down on her plate, she said, "I know you're not used to having a woman take over your bed."

He looked at her with amusement then raised an eyebrow. "Do you really want me to respond to that?"

Heat began to creep up from her neck, and she felt it fully explode on her face. "I mean, thank you for allowing me to sleep in your room tonight."

"Not a problem." He pretended to think for a minute. "Of course, you'll have to pay me back."

"Oh?" she said in a weak voice, finding it hard to meet his eyes. Her heart began to slam in her chest.

"I've got to go to a funeral tomorrow. Our old gardener, Mr. Willie, passed away. He'd been sick for some time. His cousin Ezra will be taking his place at Briarleigh, and he'll be at the funeral. I'd like for you to meet him. Plus, I hate going to things like this alone."

"Deal," she said, as she scooped up the shrimp and popped it into her mouth.

Chapter 13

*E*arly morning found Bay snuggled under a soft duvet in an oversized mahogany bed. She woke slowly, stretching and breathing in deeply of the unfamiliar scents around her. Sitting up in bed, she looked around for a moment in confusion. Then, remembering her circumstances, she fell back against the pillow and let her mind wander for a while. Her thoughts began drifting down a path she was determined not to follow. She threw back the thick duvet and, after making the bed quickly, headed for the back door and her cottage.

The sun was coming up across the river, spreading its beams through the trees, exposing the secret mist. After bounding down the steps, she felt a feeling of lightness as her foot touched the cool stone.

"Well, look at you!" Bay said to a violet growing out of a crack in the smooth stone. Extending her hand, she gently touched the delicate petals. "Aren't you just the perfect reminder to 'bloom where you're planted'?"

"Do you always talk to rocks?" Mack's deep voice reverberated on the morning air.

Bay jumped before she realized who belonged to the voice. She was surprised to see Mack up and dressed, ready to meet the day. At least, that was her first impression until she noticed the tiredness in his clear green eyes and felt a stab of guilt when she realized she was probably the cause.

"I believe it was an Alabama scientist who said that anything will talk to you if you love it enough. I was just trying to start a conversation."

"George Washington Carver … you see, we learn a little history over here in Louisiana, too." He held up his Styrofoam cup in a mock toast.

Obviously he'd bought his coffee in town, and he seemed in the greatest need of it.

"I'd offer you coffee, but this is just about gone." Mack finished off the last of it. "Doesn't come close to yours, though."

Bay beamed unashamedly. "Glad to hear it. After I get dressed, I'll make a fresh pot."

"Sleep well?"

She nodded. "Too well. I didn't want to get up. Your bed is unbelievably comfortable."

Mack smiled and nodded, then looked at his watch. "The funeral is at ten o'clock."

"I'll be ready."

Midmorning found Bay seated next to Mack on a pew inside a small chapel. There were eight people present, barely, since one man kept going in and out of the room, looking at his watch as if he had someplace else to be.

Beside Bay's diminutive size, Mack seemed massive. Bay slid her small hand over her knee just to size it up against Mack's hand as it rested on the seat beside her. She looked up as the chaplain finished his prayers over the coffin and watched as he turned to console the family.

"Is that Mr. Willie's wife?" Bay whispered, noticing a black-garbed woman passing a loving hand over the casket. Her toffee-colored skin glistened from the paths of tears down her cheeks.

"Yes ... she loved that old man. Nobody could ever understand why."

Furrowing her brow, she turned to him with a question, "What do you mean?"

"Look around ... receiving lines are short at a selfish man's funeral," Mack said under his breath.

Bay gasped, then whispered firmly, "You're not supposed to speak ill of the deceased."

"Why? Just because you're dead doesn't mean you're automatically exempt from the truth of your life. Everyone knows Mr. Willie lived only for himself. Nobody here is shedding a tear, except for his wife."

Given that information, Bay looked around the room with fresh eyes. It was true. No one looked even slightly mournful.

"See that man walking up to the casket? That's Ezra Perkins. He's the polar opposite of his cousin, Mr. Willie."

Ezra was a tall and lean man, slightly bent at the shoulders. His skin was the color and texture of dried tobacco. As he turned, he spied Mack, and a gleam caught in his shining eyes. "Come on," Mack stood and reached down for Bay's arm. "I'd like to introduce you to him."

They walked across the chapel quietly, reverently, paying their respects to Mr. Willie's wife and a few others in the receiving line until they reached Ezra. Extending his hand, Mack made the introductions. "Ezra, this is Bay Rutherford. She's the new manager we've hired from Alabama. Bay, Ezra Perkins."

"We're so sorry for your loss, Mr. Perkins." Bay presented her hand and smiled warmly, looking up into his gentle brown eyes. She smoothed her silky hair behind her ear. "But I'm happy to learn you'll soon be with us at Briarleigh."

"It's Ezra … and I'll be sitting on the doorstep come morning."

Mack held the door open for Bay as she slid into the passenger seat and waited for him to close her door. As he walked around to the driver's side, she thought of something.

"Mack?" She tugged at the corner of her bottom lip with her teeth.

He raised an eyebrow as he sat behind the wheel and faced her, waiting for her to speak.

"I was just thinking. Would you mind driving by Bon Secour … Mercy's place? I need to check about something."

Mack looked at her with a suspicious expression similar to the one she'd seen him give Crawford Benton on occasion. "Is there something you need to tell me?"

A moment passed. She blew a loose strand of hair out of her eyes and said, "There's nothing to tell … yet. I'm going to do my best to convince Mercy to sell their baked goods to us."

They drove toward Bon Secour without exchanging a word. Mack was occupied with a conversation with Piper on his cell phone while Bay was trying hard to ignore the whole thing.

Reaching their destination, Mack ended his conversation and shoved his cell phone back into his pocket. He lowered his hand from the steering wheel. "We never did get around to talking about the inn last night. I'd like to hear your ideas, starting with this one," he said, as he turned off the ignition and gestured toward the house. Facing her, his expression looked intense.

"My first night in Sugar Land I stayed here. They treated me to this amazing assortment of baked goods. All of them contained pecans that I'm assuming came from this grove. I think our guests would enjoy them. Plus, it's a local product, like the sugarcane … visitors love anything local."

"Sounds good. I'll wait here while you go talk to her."

Bay was halfway up the steps when the front door opened and Mercy hurried out, only pausing as she noticed a very startled Bay.

"Well, hello, Bay. It's good to see you. Come in, come in." Mercy stepped back to the door and ushered her inside.

"I don't want to interrupt … you look like you're going somewhere. I can come back at another time." Bay kept her hand on the door.

"Nonsense! I was just going to retrieve the mail. Please, come inside and sit down." She gave a genuine smile that instantly put Bay at ease.

Bay followed Mercy into an open and spacious room with the look and feel of a study. The interior was quiet and smelled of lemon oil and leatherbound books with a faint hint of vanilla.

"Please, have a seat. I'll ask Maundy to make us a tray."

"Oh, no ... that won't be necessary. In fact, that's why I'm here. I'd like to buy baked goods from you for Briarleigh Inn." Sitting down on the couch, Bay watched the facial expression of the woman closely. Mercy's eyes lit up, and Bay could almost see the wheels begin to turn behind their dark depths.

Mercy backed into a seat. "Oh? How marvelous! I've been praying for just such a thing as this. Maundy needs this, in the worst way."

Bay cleared her throat. "I'm assuming Maundy is the baker?"

Mercy fluttered her hands excitedly. "Yes ... and she's been a real challenge for me. I've never been able to reach the girl. I fear she's caught in some sort of cycle, and I can't seem to pull her out of it. She goes days without saying a word to anybody. It's like she thinks she has no purpose in life."

"Does she have family?" Bay asked, scooting to the edge of her seat, intrigued by the girl's story.

Mercy sighed deeply. "Yes, I'm afraid she does. In this case, that hasn't helped matters. Her mother is a well-known New Orleans madame who loves her claim to fame. Not sure about her father, but

Maundy's mother says he's a famous chef from a restaurant on Royal Avenue. As if it's all a big joke, she named her daughter Maundy, after Maundy Thursday, the day she supposedly conceived her daughter in the infamous New Orleans restaurant."

More than a little curious now, Bay asked, "May I speak with her about baking for us?"

"You most certainly can, but, uh … well," she stammered. She brought her hands together in a gentle clap. "We'll see what happens. Wait here, and I'll get her."

A moment later, Bay heard footsteps coming down the hall. Watching the doorway, Bay gasped inwardly as Maundy came into view. She was a girl, no more than eighteen years of age. Clutching a dishtowel close against her like a ragdoll, she seemed terrified. Her large, dark eyes cast a glance at Bay before looking down. She was clean and wore her long hair away from her face, pulled back with a headband. Wearing slim jeans and a gauzy long tunic top gave her an innocent look.

"I'll let you two get on with your business," Mercy said softly, while closing the door behind her.

Realizing the young girl was not going to join her but stay hovering against the wall, Bay stated her business. "My name is Bay Rutherford, and I'd like to know if you'd be interested in supplying Briarleigh Inn with your baked goods. Of course, you'd have to bake in our commercial kitchen, but we'll supply everything you need and pay you a fair wage."

Bay watched as Maundy blinked her large eyes and looked inquiringly at her.

"I'll pay you each Friday. And, if you're interested, we have a position available for some light housekeeping and meal deliveries to our guests."

Maundy contemplated the woman who had spoken to her with such authority. She was intrigued but watched Bay cautiously.

"Tell you what," Bay said as she gathered her purse. "You think about it, and if this is something you'd be interested in, come out to the inn." She stood, smiled at the girl, then made her way out the door.

Once outside, she let out a breath.

"Well?" Mack asked as Bay got in the truck and fastened her seat belt.

"It's up to her now so ... we'll see."

Chapter 14

*B*right and early Monday morning, Bay's heels
tapped rhythmically across the polished floors
of Briarleigh. Her hair had been pulled back into a
loose "messy" bun, allowing the soft mass to gently
sway with her steps. Wearing a white button-down
blouse tucked into a khaki pencil skirt, a single
silver bracelet, and tiny diamond earrings, Bay had
nothing detracting from her simple elegance.

It encouraged Bay to see Ezra seated in the
foyer, his countenance warming as he watched her
approach. "It's good to see you, Ezra. Have you had
breakfast?"

"Oh, yes, ma'am," he said and stood up,
smiling down at her. "I'm ready to start this day."

Bay instructed him about his duties, and he
listened attentively, seeming to hang on to her
every word of instruction. He probably knew better
than anyone else what was to be done around the
place as well as where everything was kept. He'd
helped his cousin, Mr. Willie, for years and was no
stranger to Briarleigh.

After Ezra left to start his duties, Bay sat down at her softly curved mahogany desk and began checking e-mail, replying when necessary about inquiries, updating their new website and working on menu items. It was midday when she finally managed to get up and appease her curiosity as to where her mother and son could be. They had arrived in the night, tired and travel-weary but smiling. Henry Clay had taken a cottage for the night after seeing to it that Virginia and Jace had settled in, but, so far, no one stirred.

Stepping to the tall front window of her office, she parted the sheer curtains and paused to watch Ezra's progress in the front flowerbeds. He seemed to be wrestling with an overly eager morning glory vine. She rapped lightly on the window, drawing his attention. Straightening up slowly, he placed a hand on his lower back and peered through the window. Bay indicated the rocking chair on the porch and called to Derlie to send out a drink.

"It's time for a break, Ezra," Bay pronounced in the soft cadence of a South Alabama drawl as she stepped onto the porch. She held out a glass with two fingers.

The silky smoothness of her voice caused him to smile. "The sound of your voice reminds me of my momma's. She was from Alabama, too." Trudging up the steps, he wiped his forehead with the back of his arm. "I'm sure glad you called for time-out. That vine was whoopin' me." He half-sat, half-reclined against the rocker and leaned his head back. Without glancing around, he indicated the chair beside the table where Bay placed a tall, cool glass of lemonade.

She took a seat beside him and asked, "Where is Mack? I haven't seen him all morning."

He lifted his shoulders in a brief shrug. "I haven't seen him either." Looking up at the sky, Ezra mused thoughtfully, "But on a fine day like this you could always find that boy on the river."

She looked over at him. "You knew Mack as a boy?"

"I've known the Blackwells all my life. Mack's granddaddy was a good friend of mine. When we were boys, we'd sell fruits and vegetables from a wheelbarrow we'd push to town." He gave a half-laugh, "Course, most of those vegetables and fruits came from *somebody else's* garden. We robbed poor Mr. Kennedy blind. He had the best garden around … the man could grow anything. His muscadines and grapes were always a big hit. We got so brazen that when the old man fixed the fence where we'd been climbing through, we built steps to go over it." Ezra shook his head in shame. "He got us, though. That old man caught us one afternoon and handed us each a galvanized bucket and said, 'Load up, boys. Take all you want.' We looked down at that old farmer's hands all worn out from work … and that did it … shamed us to the core. We both started crying, and, after that, we never stole anything from that old man again."

Bay smiled, then turned serious. "Derlie says you're gifted. That people tell you things they'd never tell another soul. Is that true?"

He shrugged dismissing the comment. "There's no magic to it. All I know about people I learned from Jesus. He dwelled on one person at a time, giving them his full attention. That's all I do. I try to forget myself and focus on them. When I do that, I really see them, and that's when they usually start talkin'. That's when I see things about them, too."

There were so many things she wanted to know from him. Under the guise of small talk, she asked, "So what kind of children were the Blackwell boys?"

"Those boys may look similar, but they're way different. For one thing, Mack is far less tame than Shannon. He's calm and collected most of the time and likes to cut up with you, but there is a thread of something you can't define running straight through him. Smart people don't cross him. But you can trust Mack with anything. Shannon, on the other hand, is easygoing. He likes to joke around and have fun, too. Not sure I'd ever trust him completely, though. It's hard to know what that boy is thinking."

Bay tilted her head slightly as she heard a stirring. "I think I hear my lazy bunch now." Before she stood, she asked one more question. "Ezra, what do you think of the murmuring sounds coming up from the cove?"

Lifting the slick glass of lemonade from the table, he took a swig and propped it on his knee. "The murmurs need to be heeded."

The front door opened suddenly, startling Bay. "Jace! Come here, little man! I want you to meet Ezra."

While Ezra engaged Jace in a conversation about fishing and catching lightning bugs, the old man's words nagged at Bay. It was the cadence of his voice, the way he had said "The murmurs need to be heeded" that troubled her. She shivered, but, as the shivering slowly abated, her curiosity grew. She thought better of asking another question for fear the answer might frighten her son, then the noise of a truck engine pulled her attention to the road where she saw a UPS truck turning into the drive.

Bay got up and walked to the edge of the porch. "Well, now, looks like our first shipment has arrived."

Following closely behind the delivery truck was a small car carrying two women. As the truck pulled up to the house, the car veered off to the side and parked under the magnolia tree. After receiving the package from the delivery man, Bay glanced over to see Mercy step out of the car and wave toward the cottage, then she looked up at Bay.

"I brought Maundy. I'm going over to visit with your mother while you two talk."

With that said, Mercy headed toward the cottage leaving a lost-looking girl standing in the drive.

Ezra stood and extended his hands, "Here, let me take that. Where do you want it?"

"On the bar in the kitchen … and, thank you. Jace, wait here while I see about Miss Maundy."

Bay called to Maundy as she came down the porch steps. "Is it my understanding that you're here to work?"

The young girl's manner bore the submissive posture one might expect from a beaten-down slave. Her voice was weak and cracked softly, but, for the first time, she spoke. "I'm here to do whatever you need me to do. All I need is a ride back to the home after work," she said, her lines sounding rehearsed.

If the girl had raised her eyes from the ground, she'd have seen the briefest smile touch Bay's lips. Then Bay grew serious, careful how she handled the girl. She'd learned from single motherhood that pity was not helpful or constructive, and she refused to give in to it. "Good. Then you can follow me into the kitchen."

Moments later, the three walked into the kitchen, making Derlie lookup from her mixing bowl. Jace climbed up on a bar stool as Bay approached with a young girl in tow. Derlie hit the switch to turn off the noise of the mixer, almost afraid to ask the question, but she couldn't resist. "Is this the new housekeeper?"

Bay smiled, knowing that Derlie felt territorial about her kitchen domain. "Yes, and she'll help you with baking in the mornings before she goes on her rounds. This is Maundy. And Maundy, this is Derlie, the head chef around here. This is her kitchen."

Derlie broke into a wide grin and appeared suddenly straighter. "I'm always right here, Maundy girl, if you're ever in need of anything. Just ask me. I know the place backward and forward."

Bay opened a utility drawer and took out a case cutter. Slicing open the box Ezra had left on the counter, she reached in and pulled out a stack of purple and gold aprons. "Perfect!" she exclaimed. "Girls, you'll wear one of these each day and alternate colors by the week. So, this week you'll wear purple." She rummaged through the stack then held up a crimson apron and a blue apron, one in each hand. "Except for two days out of the year."

"I know, I know … except for Christmas and the Fourth of July," Derlie interjected, pleased with herself.

"No … except when LSU plays Alabama and Auburn. I'm no traitor to my state!"

Maundy wrestled with her smile and struggled to keep a straight face as Derlie's eyebrows shot upward.

"Now, Derlie, I'll leave it to you to show Maundy how to bake … uh, I don't know … let's start with pecan bars. I think Mr. Benton would just love something with a little local flavor."

"Well, pecans *are* local; there're tons of them around. I'll see that little Miss Maundy here learns a thing or two about baking today … I can promise you that."

Before Bay turned to go, she opened the fridge and grabbed a Coke bottle and a juice box. Popping the cap off her Coke, she winked discreetly to Maundy, causing the girl to display a small grin. "Then I'll leave you to it. Maundy, help yourself to anything in the kitchen. Something tells me you're going to be a fast learner." After handing Jace the juice box, Bay took hold of his hand and walked through the swinging door.

"Bay Larke!" Crawford Benton crossed the polished wood floors outside Bay's office and stopped in front of her. "I need to have a word with you, if I may."

"Of course." Bay turned in surprise as Jace let go of her hand. Looking up, she saw Derlie motioning for the boy from the kitchen door.

Once Jace was out of sight, Crawford reached down and lifted Bay's hand to his lips, turned it over, and placed a light kiss on her palm. "I'd like for you to join me for dinner … in my cabin. I've been alone too long now, and I'm in need of company. You can be my muse … to inspire me." His lips peeled back displaying a white-toothed, devilish grin. "So what do you say? Will you honor an old recluse with your bright and cheerful presence?"

"Well …" She found it hard to admit that she was concerned about what the others might think if she were to spend time in a guest's cabin. And, not just any guest, but a famous and attractive bachelor with a reputation for having many such casual relationships scattered all over the world. She worried her bottom lip with her teeth as she thought about how she should respond. "My son just got home, and I really need to spend time with him … but, maybe another time."

Crawford nodded understandingly. "Well, if you should change your mind, you know the way to my cabin. My door will always be open to you."

Bay watched him go. The thought of having dinner with Crawford Benton was almost overwhelming. She shuddered at the thought. Lifting her drink to her lips, she took a cooling sip. "Some other time, Mr. Benton, some other time," she said to an empty room.

Casually, she wandered out on the front porch, swinging the bottle lightly between her fingers as she watched Crawford make his way down the path to his cabin. *He strolls*, she thought, noticing his wandering movements as he stopped to admire a low-lying oak limb laced with moss. Sighing wistfully, she slowly turned around and plowed right into a granite-hard chest. She braced a hand against it and looked up into Mack's smiling eyes. His hand on her arm was firm and warm against her skin. She had the undeniable feeling of suddenly being caught.

"The girls put Jace to work cracking pecans … he should be occupied for the next hour or so if you need to be somewhere," Mack informed her with a raised eyebrow.

Irritably, Bay jerked her arm free and folded it tightly across her chest. "*This* is where I need to be, Mr. Blackwell," she emphasized clearly.

Mack shrugged, "Suit yourself." He gestured casually over her shoulder. "You looked like you wanted to take Mr. Benton up on his offer. Just thought I could help out."

"I have my weak moments … just like everybody else," she said, annoyed at the smug look on his face. "But, I don't need your help in my personal affairs."

Mack chuckled, "You do surprise me, Bay."

Shading her eyes against the sun slanting across the porch, she tried to read his expression. Once again, she'd overstepped her bounds with him. "Mr. Benton is an old friend, nothing more. He was a regular guest at my former place of employment."

"He's not the one for you," Mack explained, like it was really just that simple, and he was saving her the trouble of having to find out.

He took a long swig of her drink, his lips covering the opening of the bottle as he emptied the contents. There was a shallow cleft in his shadowy chin that moved when he swallowed. Her eyes were fixed on his relaxed lips pressing against the lip of the bottle. The excitement she felt frightened her a little, especially when her eyes traveled up his face and found those ice-green eyes locked on hers so intently. She took a firm hold of her courage and would not look away even though her heart nearly jumped out of her chest.

Mack lowered the bottle and handed it to her. That simple gesture seemed to somehow seal the matter, and he turned from her and walked away.

With Mack now out of sight, she relaxed a little, too shaken by the encounter to even be upset at the audacity of the man. Turning her attention toward the slow, meandering river just over the levee, she tried to forget him, but, in her mind, she saw only those penetrating green eyes.

Chapter 15

Walking around the side of the cottage, Bay turned a piece of contorted driftwood in her hand as if it were a famous sculpture, fascinated by all the intricate curves. Near the gate, she found Jace on Henry Clay's shoulders and her mother's hand linked through the older man's bent arm. Since their return from Chattanooga, she'd seen a change in all of them. They seemed bonded together in a familiar sort of way, like a family somehow. A brief picture of her father passed through her mind as she watched her mother smile with complete and utter joy as she looked up at Henry Clay. With her father now gone, Bay felt a stab of loss sweep through her. The life she'd once known seemed even more distant … now, gone forever.

Virginia smiled as she saw her daughter. "We want to take Jace for ice cream. Do you mind, dear? You don't have any plans do you?"

Bay chafed at the reminder. "No … I'm just going to work on a little project."

Virginia furrowed her brow. "Project?"

Henry Clay cleared his throat. "Yes, Bay was telling us that she wanted to create a few gathering places around the property. She's convinced us that, with the wide lawn and plenty of shady trees, this will be the perfect place to hold family reunions."

"Oh, I completely agree. This place is perfect for reunions!" She exchanged a flirtatious glance with Henry Clay.

Bay stepped back and pointed toward her son, anxious to get away from her mother. There was a serious "ick" factor involved in witnessing Virginia flirt openly with a man other than Bay's father. "You be good, and don't eat too much ice cream."

"I won't, Momma, and I'm gonna bring some back for you … ain't we, Nanny?"

"*Aren't* we? And not this time … I'm afraid it will melt before we get back. You see, we plan on taking you to see a movie, too!"

Bay glanced around her, not sure about her feeling at the moment. "I'd better get started before it gets dark. Have fun, and I'll see you all later."

Henry Clay cautiously warned Bay as he lifted Jace from his shoulders. "Mack is going out tonight, so you'll be here by yourself, except for Mr. Benton, of course. But he'll do you no good if you should need help because I doubt he'll hear you. Keep your phone on you, and stay near the house."

Bay nodded, "I will."

Dressed only in jeans, Mack watched Bay warily from his bedroom window while he toweled his hair dry. He turned and hurled the towel into the corner, snatched his shirt from the bed, and grabbed his boots off the floor as he headed toward the back door.

"Bay!" His tone was low but challenging.

She turned, her glance sweeping him briefly, and then continued to drag a large piece of driftwood across the lawn.

"Never drag anything up from the bayou, especially driftwood. You never know what may live in, around, or under what you find there," Mack warned.

Mocking light hazel eyes peered up at him as her full lips formed a thin line.

He grinned confidently. It was as if he'd touched a dry match to smoldering wood and it burst into flame. He nodded toward the wood. "See what I mean."

She clamped down tightly on her arms, digging in with her fingernails, as his words registered. Following the path of his eyes, she saw a short grayish-black snake slithering away through the grass.

"They say you can cross the bayou on the backs of alligators and water moccasins and never get wet. Course, I think that's just an exaggeration," he mocked. "But if you don't mind telling me, what do you want with an old piece of driftwood?"

"I want to use it for seating around a bonfire." She pointed to a clearing near the edge of the woods.

He kicked the wood with his heavy boot then reached down and grabbed it by a weathered limb. "Point the way." A shadow of a smile played across his lips. "If you see anything crawl toward me, be sure to inform me, would you?"

"I'll consider it," she responded, with a hint of a grin.

As they passed the smokehouse cabin, Bay commented on it. "That cabin has wasted space. It's dark and closed in. I don't care for it. We've got to come up with better names for the cabins, too. I mean, who wants to sleep in a smokehouse?"

Mack's eyes fastened on hers. There was an unspoken intention in it. "Oh? What do you suggest, then?"

"Break through to the attic and open it up. You'll have natural light from the attic windows and a higher ceiling. It'll seem much larger. Build some bunk beds under the old stairwell, and you can sleep six instead of four." She brushed her hair behind her ears and looked down, seeming to realize her outspokenness. "I guess I kinda sound bossy sometimes."

"Yes ... you do. But I think you have a good idea. I'll see what I can do." He dropped the wood next to the fire pit and pushed it securely into the soft dirt. "Now, if this is all you need from me, I'll be going."

"Thanks for your help. I'm finished here, so I'll be going, too."

Mack raised his brow. "Are you going out?"

What, like I don't have a life? She'd planned on heading straight for the bathtub then reheating the plate Derlie had made for her dinner, but seeing the surprise in Mack's eyes, she quickly changed her mind. "Mother and Henry Clay have taken Jace to the movies, so I'm free tonight and thought I'd go out."

Though Bay was bound and determined that he would never again treat her casually or offhandedly, she realized he was no dawdling schoolboy, and she would have to carry out what she had stated or lose credibility with him for good.

"Oh, well, maybe I'll see you in town."

"Maybe."

Chapter 16

*L*ater that evening, Mack halted abruptly as a familiar scent wafted past him. His eyes traveled across the hazy smoke-filled room and stopped at the sight of Bay standing in the doorway. A light breeze from the open door blew around her, tousling her hair as if releasing her scent to a room full of hungry predators.

The Bloody Bucket had certainly never carried that type of fragrance in the air before. He leaned over the pool table and casually took his shot, pretending to keep his attention on the game while watching her with sideways glances. Her head was down as she flipped through papers clasped tightly in her hand. Straightening, he'd already noticed a slow move of men circling while her attention was on the papers.

A large shadow blocked the already dim light in the pool hall. Bay looked up to see the cause of it. A bulky, sweaty man wearing a cocky grin and a dingy T-shirt slammed a booted foot on the chair in front of her.

"Whatever you're selling ... I'm buying," he said, forcefully.

Bay moved over to carefully put the table between them. "I'm just passing out these flyers to let everyone know about Briarleigh Inn. We'll be opening soon, so tell your friends," she said, trying hard to keep her voice from shaking.

The man's eyes narrowed and a sickening smile twisted his lips to display a partial set of stained teeth. "What extras come with a room at that inn of yours? You, maybe?" He reached out and grabbed her arm, forcefully yanking her to his chest.

In the fraction of a second it took for the aggression to register with Bay, two strong hands grabbed the man and jerked him around. She heard a loud smack, then watched as the stranger crashed into the table before sprawling out onto the floor. The next second, Mack was lifting a glass of beer from a nearby table and pouring it on the man's face. The guy sputtered and spit, wiping his hand down his face as he slowly regained consciousness.

"Sorry, Mack, I didn't know she was your girl … you should've said somethin'."

Mack reached down and pulled the man up. "I'm not the one you should apologize to."

The man cut his eyes toward Bay. "Real sorry about that … I didn't know you was Mack's." With that said, he turned and grabbed his beer off the table and stumbled out the door.

Ezra waited outside the Bloody Bucket for Bay to come out. They'd spent the past hour passing out flyers all around town to let the people of Sugar Land know about opening day at Briarleigh Inn. He was beginning to have second thoughts about allowing her to go in by herself, even if it was only briefly. He started for the door and was about to go inside when he spotted Mack's truck parked next to the building. Smiling to himself, he walked over to the truck and leaned against it, blowing out a tuneless whistle as he waited. A surprisingly brief amount of time passed before the door flew open and a rather large man staggered out, wiping at his bloodied lip with the back of his hand. He appeared eager to put some distance between himself and the place as he crossed the parking lot, hopped into his car, and sped away.

Ezra turned an apprehensive eye to the northwest. A dark and angry squall line approached. Pushing off the truck, Ezra decided that this time he was intent on retrieving Bay. But, before he could take a step, Mack came through the door and stopped as he waited for Bay to follow him out. Once outside, he lightly touched the small of her back and led her toward his truck.

Upon seeing Ezra, Mack asked, "Where did you park?" He opened the passenger side door of his truck and motioned for Bay to get in.

"I'm just around the corner," Ezra informed Mack with a knowing smile. "Looks like you got this, so I'll be going on home."

Mack nodded, "I'm headed to the inn, so I'll take Bay back for you. Keep a weather eye out," he said, glancing up as a distant flash of jagged light streaked across the sky. "Looks like a strong one."

"Will do … see you tomorrow."

Mack got into the driver's seat and cranked the engine. "If you don't mind, I need to see about something before we head back." He checked the side mirror and backed out slowly, then glanced at her. "You need anything else from town?"

Bay shook her head. "No, I'm good."

"You want coffee? I'm gonna run into Perks for a coffee to go. How do you take yours?"

"Uh … black with a dose of half-and-half," she answered, noticing how his eyes were shadowed under the brim of his cap.

After the strange rush of excitement back at the Bloody Bucket, her heart began to thump wildly in her chest. She looked away, keeping her eyes fixed ahead, hoping he wouldn't notice the sudden way her breathing increased, moving the collar of her shirt up and down. She held her breath for a moment, hoping to slow the rhythm of her heart. Once they pulled into the café parking lot, he left the truck running and hopped out, glancing at the sky before yanking the door open to the coffee shop.

Once her heart slowed its rapid beating, she looked around the truck, becoming aware of the manly scent of leather and oil. A half-eaten roll of butter rum Life Savers was tossed in with change in the cup holder and a spool of Weed eater twine sat next to her feet in the floor board. She liked the way his truck made her feel. The dirt, oil, and hard surfaces made her feel feminine and soft by comparison. The corner of a photo stuck out from the visor on the driver's side, catching her attention. Her eyes darted to the coffee shop, then back to the picture. Slowly, she eased the visor down just enough to see Piper's dark eyes staring back at her.

Hearing voices, Bay snapped the visor back in place just as Mack got to the truck. She smoothed her white tunic over her jeans and reached for her seat belt.

"Best coffee in town … doesn't even begin to compare to yours, though," he added with a lazy smile.

"Good to know," she said, reaching for the Styrofoam cup.

The road stretched before them, shrouded in an eerie yellow haze against a backdrop of black. White, lacy clusters of Queen Anne's lace lined the road, giving Bay an idea. "Would you mind stopping so I can cut some of that Queen Anne's lace? I think a few pastel-colored flowers arranged on the dining room table will be simply beautiful … not to mention inexpensive."

He glanced at her with a look that said he thought she'd lost her mind.

Clearing her throat, she began offering an explanation as if she were speaking to a child. "You see, when you take the freshly cut flowers, you can stick them in colored water, and the head of the flower will change colors."

"We've always called those *chigger weeds*."

"Oh? Well, how dreamy. And I suppose you call Spanish moss *strangling fungus*, too."

He started to grin then quickly covered it. "It's an air plant, not a fungus. It only hangs from the branches to take in sunlight and rain."

Redness slowly rose to her throat. He grinned, knowing he was irritating her, but he just couldn't stop. "That little plant is a concentrated form of natural estrogen. Healers around these parts brew it as tea to help mood swings, irritability, and … other female discomforts. So feel free …"

She shot him a scathing look that silenced him, but it didn't wipe off his grin.

She noticed the storm when they drove straight into the rain. It pelted its fury on the truck unmercifully. The wind tugged and pulled at the vehicle as if trying to yank it off the road. With the windshield wipers frantically slapping, Mack turned off the highway and onto a gravel road. They drove for a while, then turned onto another, more narrow and unkempt road, with shattered limbs and low-hanging branches thrashing about in the wind. Entwined overhead were vines so tangled with tree limbs that one could only glimpse the sky in brief snatches, though it did provide a canopy of sorts to shelter them from the brunt of the storm.

The truck bumped over a fallen log, and he glanced at her. "You'd better hold on. I wouldn't want you to bump your head."

Just when Bay was about to question him, they came upon a clearing. The heavy woods ended, and an arrangement of shrubs indicated a yard near a small house. Overgrown blue and purple hydrangeas spilled away from the corners of the house unchecked, now bowing low under the heavy beating of rain. The steeply-pitched roof was mottled and shimmered as streams of water washed down her surface before gushing over the gutters in a wild torrent.

Bay took in the surroundings. "Whose house is this?"

"Mine."

She turned to look at him with surprise and a question in her eyes. Then she remembered he'd purchased a house recently.

"I bought this place to keep the rows of brick houses out. A local developer wanted to tear down the house and turn the property into a subdivision. I just couldn't let that happen to the old girl," he said, his eyes wandering over the structure. "I've always been in love with this place."

They sat there in front of the house, hushed and still. Bay felt as if she were being introduced to it and was just waiting for an accepting nod of approval. "Can we go inside?"

"There's not much to see, but I do need to check for leaks. You sure you want to?"

"Definitely."

Before he could argue, she was out of the truck and running through the rain toward the door. Mack grabbed the keys and followed her, splashing through standing water before he reached her. After a turn of the key and a quick kick to the bottom of the warped door they were inside.

Chapter 17

"**O**h, my goodness," Bay said as her eyes adjusted to the dim light. "These walls … they're cool and dry and textured. Solid." She slapped a hand against it. "What a wonderful, sturdy home!" She touched everything, sliding a gentle hand down the door facing, acting as if she'd just discovered the house and was calling his attention to it for the first time. "All the greens and grays make you feel like you're wrapped inside a cool mist. I think it even helps you breathe easier in this humidity."

Bay's enthusiasm was contagious, and Mack looked around feeling somewhat proud. Their footsteps echoed in the empty rooms as they crossed the dusty hard wood floor.

"I hope Piper shares your feelings about the place," Mack commented. "Come on, the best feature is upstairs." He led her to a small, wooden staircase just beyond the foyer and began to climb the creaky steps ahead of her.

She hesitated.

Looking back over his shoulder, he said, "I'm taking a risk being here alone in this house with you, but you'll have to promise you won't try anything. I have my virtue to think of."

Bay rolled her eyes and followed after him. "Relax, you're not my type."

"Whew … that's a relief. A guy can't be too careful these days with all the aggressive man-eating females around."

"Well, *you're* safe," she added, with emphasis.

He regarded her with an intensity that made her blush from the neck up. Twisting his lips to cover a grin, he gestured with his hand for her to step in front of him. "If you're through insulting me, step this way."

Half-embarrassed by her outspokenness, she rushed on to explain. "I guess I get kind of …"

"Rude at times?" he said, adjusting the cap on his head.

She halted abruptly, as his brow raised questioningly. "I was going to say that I get careless with my words when I get tired."

"Then you must get tired a lot," he said under his breath.

The stairs led up to a wainscoted hall painted the same calm gray as the ground floor. Down the hall and to the left was the master bedroom, painted the yellow of dried grass. The door stood ajar, and Mack pushed it open wider.

"Wait … let me find a match to light the kerosene lamp. I won't have power for a week or so," he said, patting the surface of an armoire.

As he searched the room for matches, Bay peered through the door of the room opposite the master bedroom. It was dark, with thick gold curtains covering the floor to ceiling windows. She thought how it would be all in shadow in the morning and how much difference light colors and fabrics would make to compensate for the dimness. She decided to keep those thoughts to herself, unless he happened to ask. She was aware of how opinionated she could be at times, especially when it came to decorating. Stepping back across the hall, she saw Mack standing just inside the door, the space now softly lit from the lamp.

The room was rather barren, but the color of the walls warmed it to keep it from being too stark. The brick fireplace was clean, and the scent of ash hung on the air. Bay felt a sudden chill in the room as the wind sighed down the chimney. *Must be a downdraft from the fireplace,* she surmised. A large four-poster rice bed with a simple patchwork covering, an armoire, and a small bedside table were the extent of the furnishings. Still, everything in the room, situated on the back corner of the house, seemed to be positioned to take advantage of a view from the large, mullioned window. Bay was curious to know what was outside to command such attention.

"When the sun rises, I bet the cool colors of the eastern sky permeate this room and make it glow," she commented, looking around at all the tall windows.

"When the candles are lit, their shadows on the walls and ceiling quiver, but it's a lousy place to try to sleep in a few extra hours in the morning. The sun practically comes up in this room ... any suggestions on what to do about it? " He turned his head to hide a threatening grin when he saw her face light up.

Looking around, she quickly appraised the situation. "Since most of the direct light will hit the floor in the morning, you might think of painting these old heart-of-pine floorboards a dark gray to help sop up some of the glare."

Mack ran a hand across his whiskered chin. "What color do you suppose I should paint the walls? Butterfly yellow is just not me."

She walked over to the window and looked outside. "This place has a tropical feel, especially with all that vegetation climbing up the walls and across the balcony. I'd go with a cool white on the beaded-board walls and ceiling. A sisal rug and dark mahogany furniture will add warmth without being too heavy, and a few ..." she abruptly stopped talking and turned to look up at Mack. "Sorry ... I kinda get carried away sometimes."

"I asked, didn't I?"

To the right of the windows, there stood a pair of small French doors. Releasing the rusted bolt, Mack pulled the doors open wide and stepped through to a small covered balcony.

She followed closely behind but stopped in the doorway as she took in the sweeping view. There it was, the mighty Mississippi River. Barely visible off in the deep channel was a long industrial barge shrouded in rain, making her way slowly down the Old Man ... her yellow lights casting streaks of gold across the wind-tossed water.

Turning over two old wicker rocking chairs, Mack wiped out the seats before gesturing for her to sit. "When a house is as much a part of the marshland as this, nature becomes the decorator. Sometimes, these porch chairs literally have to be untangled from the vines before you can sit."

"You come here a lot?" she asked, taking a seat before taking her eyes off the river.

His answer was a nod.

"I can certainly see why."

"I always feel a little guilty for enjoying it so much. I'm no earthly good when I'm here."

Sheets of rain began to move across the water in wide sweeps, turning the twilight pewter.

"Look!" Bay said, in a voice so astonished it caused Mack to turn to her suddenly. "The ground is starting to flood, and the river is rising!"

Bay's fascination with everything around her made Mack aware of how invariably fixed his sight was on the horizon these days. He should have noticed the rising water and the potential for dangerous flooding. Sugar Land was prone to flash floods. The close proximity of the river made them even more susceptible to swift currents and dangerous undertows. "We'd better ride this out … I'd hate to get swept away down river."

"I'll call Mother and tell her … oh, never mind, they're in the movie theater."

Everything was quiet, except for the sound of the wind and the rain. They sat in silence, watching the rushing river push against its banks.

Thinking back to his boyhood river days, Mack asked, "Did you spend a lot of time on the water in … where are you from again?"

"Moss Bay, and, no, my mother told me to stay out of it … 'cause if the water even touched my skin, I'd have to go to the hospital."

Mack pulled his head back sharply and looked at her. "What?"

"She's always been terrified of the water. So here I am, a grown woman who can't swim a lick." Bay pointed across the river, changing the subject, "Why is that boat not moving?"

"That's an old steamboat, and it's more like an island. It floats there year round. I think it's been turned into a restaurant or something. I hear music coming from it on the weekends." He watched her expression as she took in the sights of the river. "Are *you* afraid of the water?"

"No … but, I don't know too much about it. Jace loves to fish, but I've always been a little leery of taking him to a pier. I'm afraid he might fall in, and we'd both drown because I'd jump in after him, and there we'd be. Back home, I'd let him fish in a little ditch in our backyard after a good rain. That seemed to satisfy him."

He looked at her incredulously, narrowing his eyes. "You did … what? You let that boy stand out there and fish in a drainage ditch?" He put both hands against his forehead. "That's not … right! I'm taking him fishing … in a boat … on the water … soon!" Mack shifted in his seat and, from the set of his jaw, it appeared that this comment would evolve into a long, one-sided conversation.

Taking special care to lower his voice, Mack continued, "Growing up, we weren't obsessively monitored like kids are today. In fact, my dad didn't monitor us at all. He just wanted us back before supper. If we weren't working around the place or in school, we were on our own. And, most of the time, we were on the river."

Bay swept her hands through her hair and pulled it on top of her head. "Where was your mother?"

"She wasn't around. My dad raised us."

"Well, I'm not sure I'll ever be able to give my son up to the river. But," she conceded, "I don't want to be an overprotective mother either and make a sissy out of him. I moved here for that very reason. More than anything, I want my son to have a happy childhood and be around men who will teach him things he needs to know, like how to be a man."

Mack relaxed a little and eased back in his chair, satisfied with her response. "The boy just needs to be taught, and so does his mother."

"Taught? Me? Taught what? To swim?"

He nodded, "Among other things."

The translucent hazel eyes narrowed. "Such as?"

He gestured toward the river with his finger, then casually pulled a roll of butter rum Life Savers from the pocket of his jeans. He tipped it toward her, offering her one, then took out a piece and rolled it around on his tongue before he continued, "After a heavy rain, you'll see a swirl of froth where the water has rushed quickly into the main current. That creates a vortex beneath the surface … a whirlpool, and that spells danger. And over there," he pointed to an area in the water just off the bank. "A trailing braid in the water is a sure sign of a snag. Just underneath the surface is a tree limb or some other obstruction ... you don't want to run up on something like that in your boat. It could capsize you, and you could get trapped beneath the debris."

Bay shivered, staring wide-eyed at the swift current of the river with a new respect.

He peered at her thoughtfully, wondering just what to believe about her. "Danger is everywhere, Bay, and not just around water. The key is to understand what's going on around you and make adjustments to *avoid* danger."

Her finger lightly traced the small scar at the corner of her mouth as she thought about his words. "Henry Clay told me you're on a leave of absence for hitting a man. You hit another man *tonight*. It doesn't sound like you take your own advice," she chided. Her voice was so smooth and soft that it nearly sent shivers all over him.

A trace of humor played across his lips. "I have a reputation for ... not being gentle-natured."

Bay rewarded him with a gracious smile. "I would hardly call what you did tonight 'not being gentle-natured.'" She grew serious as she carefully stated, "But, if you're trying to change your ways, I've found that the best way to do that is from a kneeling position."

Frowning slightly, he tried to figure out her frame of mind. "I'm really not a monster, you know. I don't hit women, and I don't eat small children."

"So what you're telling me is that you're completely undisciplined *only* when it comes to grown men. And especially when they don't act the way you think they should act."

Mack stared at her, then flashed a wide grin. "Exactly." He leaned forward, looked out to the river as if contemplating his next words. He turned, his cool green eyes meeting Bay's confident gaze and a slow smile crossing his face. Something about her intrigued him. He found himself studying with more and more intensity the small scar curving upward from her lip. "Where did you get that scar?"

She shrugged, "Walking away from danger or trouble without taking action can be more demoralizing than taking a chance. I decided to interfere in something. That's when I got this scar."

"I'm listening."

Bay's chin came up. The long moment stretched even longer as his eyes bore into hers. "My former employer did certain *favors* for a few high profile guests at the St. Bonitus Hotel. I didn't know about it until one day I happened to walk by a room where a girl was screaming out for help. I pushed the door open and saw a man struggling with the young girl. He was trying to force himself on her. I grabbed him from behind and pulled him off her. That's when he backhanded me. His ring sliced my face, leaving this scar. The young girl got away and called for help. Hotel security got there in time to keep me from further harm. The man said that it was a simple case of cold feet and that the girl had come to his room willingly. My boss agreed and, after a closed-door meeting with the girl, didn't file charges. Soon after that, I got a promotion and the attention of the boss's son, Sterling. I know now that they were trying to keep me quiet." She gave a soft laugh, tracing the scar lightly with her finger. "My scar bothered him, though. He told me one night after he'd been drinking that he just pictured his wife differently. I took it to mean 'without defect.' We were having trouble before that, though. What we each wanted in life was too different. So, in a way, my scar was a blessing. In the world's version of what makes a person attractive, I come up short," she said, with a wave of her hand. The lateness of the hour must have loosened her tongue to share all this with him. "But that's not really unusual. A lot of men seem to value beauty."

"I've never really stopped long enough to know what I value."

"Oh? Well, there's Piper … weren't you two high school sweethearts?"

For some reason, he was having difficulty getting his thoughts together. "We were." He took a sip of his coffee.

"I think she is stunning," Bay offered. All she has to do is walk into a room, and she commands the attention of everyone present. I've never had that. Just once I'd like to have that kind of effect on people."

He shifted his gaze from the river and settled it on Bay before stating, "I find that hard to believe."

"Oh, it's true. But you really can't blame people for staring at her. It's not every day you see gorgeousness like that."

"No, I mean I find it hard to believe that you've never been the object of a man's attention."

"Well, there's always Crawford, but he loves all women so that doesn't count."

Mack kept quiet a moment. He always seemed to be gathering his strength, like storm clouds on the horizon. "Crawford knows nothing about love."

"Oh? And, you do?" she teased.

He turned the cup in his hand and looked at it as if he understood something. "I know that love has no limits to its endurance. It can outlast anything. In fact, it's the one thing that still stands when even the one loved is no more."

She paused, mid-sip, surprised by his response. Passing her eyes over him briefly, she judged the sincerity of his words. "True," she whispered, swallowing hard against the knot of emotion forming in her throat.

Chapter 18

*T*he St. Bonitus Hotel reflected the fortunes of its owner. With grand views of Mobile Bay on one side and a twenty-four-foot high garden pavilion on the other, the hotel offered its guests the secluded feel of a private estate with all the attractions and conveniences of the city. Capturing the feel of a Spanish hacienda, the white-colored structure with its red-tile roof and stucco exterior blended harmoniously with the garden surroundings. Bright fuchsia bougainvillea in bountiful baskets graced the archways with bursts of color. But, within the walls of the seemingly serene and composed structure, a sinister plot was being devised. And, like an elaborate performance, the stage was being set as scenes being developed, ready to be played out.

Sterling Geroux emerged from his private quarters, leading a dark-haired beauty by the elbow across the central courtyard as bells pealed the hour from a nearby tower. Stopping beside the tiled fountain, he turned to the woman. "It's been a great pleasure meeting you, Mrs. Harding. I look forward to seeing you again … soon."

"Please, drop the formality, and call me Piper. After all, we've just discovered we have so much in common ... I already feel a developing bond between us."

Sterling lifted her hand and placed a gentle kiss on her fingers. "I feel the same way."

Jace Rutherford rose early in the morning on Saturday and slipped out of the cottage undetected. He walked across the damp grass to the kitchen of Briarleigh and plopped down on a step stool beside the pantry door and waited without a word.

Mack was seated at the bar. After a long moment, his eyes slowly raised over the top of the newspaper. He lowered his coffee cup as he found the boy staring at him curiously.

Derlie glanced between them, then slid a small plate across the bar for the boy.

"Something on your mind?" Mack asked and waited before taking another pull of the hot brew.

Jace got up and slowly wandered over to the bar, laying his small arms across the counter and resting his chin in such a way that only his green eyes showed over his folded arms. "Fishin'," he answered, in a voice low and muffled.

"Fishing? Well, what a coincidence! That's just what I've been sitting here thinking about myself."

Derlie's smile widened as she quickly busied herself with breakfast, slicing more smoked ham as she listened to the conversation.

"Eat your breakfast, boy." Mack pushed back from the table and rose. "Course, I always fish better with a partner. That jon boat has a way of getting caught too close to the bank at times. I need somebody to help me guide her to the best fishing spots without running aground. You know anybody that could handle a job like that?"

"Me!" Jace blurted out quickly.

Mack drew back as if in amazement. "You?" He reached out a hand to feel Jace's muscle. "Here, let me see if you're able to do the job. Make a fist, now pull your arm up slowly." He whistled low. "Yep ... you've got what it takes. Now, if only we can convince your mother to let me take you along." Scratching his cheek, he shook his head. "That might be hard to do. Especially after she finds out you left the house without permission. You did leave without telling her, didn't you?"

Jace nodded slowly, looking defeated.

"You know, she just might ground you."

"I'll take a spankin'!" Without a backward glance, Jace took off through the kitchen door. As the screen door slapped against the frame, Mack's shoulders shook with a chuckle.

Bay was deeply engrossed in typing entries into the computer and confirming reservations when she realized the sound of heavy footsteps had ceased in front of her door. Looking up, she saw Henry Clay standing there with a troubled look on his face.

"Is everything all right?" she asked anxiously, jumping to her feet. The thought of Jace out on the water with Mack had been at the back of her mind all morning. The only way Mack had been able to convince her to let Jace go was to assure her that having a paramedic in the boat with you was about as safe as you can get.

Henry Clay waved her back down to her seat, "Yes, yes … I just need to make you aware of something. Something … well, let's just call it a recent development."

"Oh?" Bay felt relieved. Whatever it was, it couldn't be more important than the safety of her child.

Before taking a seat across from her, he tossed a magazine down on the desk. "Looks like someone is trying to ruin us."

Bay carefully lifted the magazine and scanned the cover of the traveler's guide before opening it to the feature story. She read out loud, "Briarleigh, The Most Haunted Inn in the South." After skimming the article, she casually gave it back to him.

Immediately, his manner changed from one of worry to one of annoyance, and he dropped the magazine on her desk. "Well? Don't you have anything to say about that?"

"Are you asking me if these ghostly visions and … sounds they're reporting are bad for business? Hardly—the most haunted places remain popular tourist destinations, with ghost towns having the biggest draw." She tapped the magazine with her finger lightly. "It's clear someone wants to do us harm, but they obviously don't realize they're actually doing us a favor. I mean, a beautiful woman in a flowing gown who visits your room while you sleep, then perches on the balcony to watch for a long-lost love. And a former soldier from the Civil War wailing out a lament across the grounds each night … these stories can work in our favor."

Henry Clay placed his head in his hand and shook it. "No, Bay ... this is a challenge. I mean, who wants to bring their family to a haunted inn besides a few freaks? We can deny it, but what's going to happen once they hear those murmurs coming up from the cove?"

"It may seem like a challenge to you, but it's really very simple. The key is to play up the stories and not try to cover them up like we're hiding something. In fact, we need to pick a room where the ghost lady supposedly visits." She ran a hand through her hair as her gaze roamed the ceiling. "We'll call it 'Julia's Room' after Julia Breckenridge and tell a brief history of the part she played in the Civil War. As for the murmuring cove, after recounting the history of the house and grounds, we'll just let their imagination take over. We'll provide brochures of local battle monuments and markers along with books on local history. I was thinking of providing a room for books and coffee and a small fridge stocked with bottled drinks. Maundy can bake up a fresh batch of cookies each evening for the kids, and I think I can talk Ezra into telling a few stories. He's a natural-born storyteller."

Shifting in his seat, Henry Clay eyed her warily. "That's all well and good ... but what are we going to do about the cove scaring the kids?" He took a deep breath, then slowly exhaled. "Your mother seems to think they'll get used to it. She hardly even notices it. It's like people who grow up near a train track ... after a while they don't even hear the whistle."

"We'll set up a bonfire area near the cove for the bravest of souls and make it known that it's off-limits to anyone under the age of twelve. That'll make it a challenge and something for the younger kids to want to come back to once they reach the age." Bay shrugged. "If you put limits on anything, kids will always try to go beyond them; then you'll have created interest. Whoever is responsible for this article did us a huge favor. Remember the old saying, 'There is no such thing as bad publicity'? Besides, that's a great shot of the house."

Henry Clay rubbed his chin then reached into his shirt for a cigar. Searching his pocket for a lighter, he leaned forward, pointing to her with his finger. "You just might have something there. When Mack gets back, I'll have him set up a place near the cove for a bonfire. We'll keep one lit down there."

The pipe smoke curled through the air around Ezra's face as he rocked. "You eatin' that ice cream too fast, boy. Roll it around on your tongue and get the good out of it … same with life. Most folks swallow down their food half-chewed. They can't enjoy nothin' these days." He took his pipe out of his mouth and pointed with it. "And you know why? 'Cause God-denying folks ain't never content with nothin' they have or who they are. Don't be like that, boy. Thank the Good Lord for all you got, even ice cream."

Jace tilted his head. "You mean … be good and go to church?" he asked, squinting up at the old man from his position on the porch floor.

Sitting on the steps nearby, Bay felt a stab of guilt as she listened to their conversation. She'd only darkened the door of a church once since her daddy's funeral.

Ezra became silent and continued to stare out into the yard. Carefully, he placed his pipe beside the rocking chair and spoke. "That's just it. You can't ever be good enough for God. He's perfect. That's why he came down here to this earth, to tell us that He'll be perfect for us 'cause he knows we surely can't do it. All we got to do is trust in him and follow his ways. He takes care of the rest."

Bay sat in quiet amazement. In all her life, she'd never heard the gospel presented so clearly.

The rocking chair creaked as Ezra leaned forward. "Now, boy, go rest so you can catch lightning bugs after supper."

Smiling, Bay got up slowly and took Jace's hand, walking him to the cottage. After settling her son down for a nap, she left him with her mother and went back to the Briarleigh kitchen.

She stepped through the door and noticed Mack wiring a hanging lamp above the sink. Yanking on the refrigerator door and hearing the bottles clank, she reached inside to grab a drink. "Want a Coke?" she asked, popping the cap off and taking a swig.

"Jace."

Holding the bottle to her lips, she asked before taking another sip, "What about him?"

"He's a Blackwell."

Bay choked on the Coke and coughed to catch her breath, making her reply hoarse. "What?"

"You heard me," he stated bluntly, as his fingers worked the wires.

Her chin lifted in a brave little show of defiance. "Well, that's none of your business. It's not like you're the father," she said, gently placing the bottle on the counter.

He kept a carefully-controlled expression as he climbed down the ladder. "Oh, trust me; I'd remember if I was." He tugged his work gloves from his back pocket and put them on, watching Bay's small hands close in tight fists. She was protecting Shannon, and it annoyed him. As he saw it, Jace was the one suffering. No boy should grow up without a father, if it could be helped. He snapped the ladder shut, lifted it, and brushed past her, fully convinced Bay would never admit to his brother's role in Jace's life. He mumbled over his shoulder, "Jace is doing without a father while you keep the man hidden behind your skirt."

The sound of his boots hitting the porch floor drowned out the sharp comment Bay hurled toward his back.

That evening, Bay left her office and pushed through the swinging door into the kitchen. Derlie was busy chopping onions, Maundy was sitting at the bar cracking pecans, and the monotone voice of the Atlanta Braves announcer filled the room.

"Versidy Williams's husband died," Derlie said, wiping her hands down the front of her apron. "Didn't even put it in the paper. I had to find out from the mailman."

"Who is Versidy Williams?"

"Our closest neighbor … I always knew she was odd, but not to tell folks when your husband passes is just plain wrong. Kinda makes you wonder, don't it? Ezra said she wasn't always like that. Said she used to go to his church when she was a young girl. He said her husband was so jealous of her that he kept her locked up in the house. Why, she didn't even buy groceries; he did all the shopping so she wouldn't be seen out."

"How sad … no wonder she didn't tell anybody. She's probably forgotten how to communicate with people." Bay thought for a moment. "Maundy, when you get a chance, make up a batch of your pecan bars, and I'll take them over sometime this week."

Maundy nodded and hopped off the stool. "May I go with you?"

"Of course," Bay assured her, looking over the young girl with amusement and a little confusion. Maundy rarely showed interest in anything besides baking.

Derlie spoke up. "She won't let you in … but, guess it don't hurt to try."

Looking out the screen door, Bay noticed Ezra asleep in the rocking chair, his flyswatter over his chest and his mouth hanging open. A homemade ice cream bucket sat at his feet. Stepping near it, she shooed the flies and pried off the lid, making the thick, sticky cream fall off the blade and plop inside the container.

She smiled down at the old man. "I guess we've all had about enough excitement for one day."

Chapter 19

A confused storm had blown in, beating the loose shutters against Briarleigh for most of the day, but, as night settled, the wind suddenly stopped, and all was quiet. A shroud-like mist began to form, creeping up from the marshes, spreading white vapors over the ground like the searching fingers of some beleaguered ghost.

The squeak of iron hinges reverberated in the silence as Bay passed through the gate that led to the cottage. A snowball bush by the fence twitched unnaturally, causing her to search the enclosed yard. Hurrying her steps, she quickly hopped inside the cottage and closed the door.

After Bay had taken a warm bath and put on her pajamas, she heard a rapid knock on the door. Her eyes widened with surprise as she pulled the door open to find Derlie standing there with her hands on her hips.

"What's the matter? You expecting Mel Gibson?"

"Derlie … I thought you'd left hours ago."

"Since everybody but that old recluse that calls himself a writer is gone, I thought I'd keep you company tonight."

"Well, get in here then." Bay held her relief in check. Before shutting the door behind Derlie, she glanced into the darkness. A murmur like a poor, demented soul repeating mindless sounds drifted to her ears. She stopped and listened closely to the whispers as the low, disconcerted moan became clear. *Grace ... grace ... God's grace ... grace that is greater than all our sin ....*

"Do you hear that?" Bay inquired.

"Do I hear what?" Derlie asked, straining to see into the darkness.

"Grace ... grace ... God's grace ... grace that is greater than all our sin."

"Can't you hear that?"

Derlie turned her head to try to catch the sound. "Nothing but those same old murmurs."

Slowly, Bay's eyes traveled over the grounds as the sweet, cloying scent of magnolias filled her senses. Moisture dripped from moss-covered branches arched high above Briarleigh as moonlight pierced through the clouds, illuminating the house in pale shades of gray. Suddenly, she didn't feel quite so afraid. "I'm glad you're here, Derlie," she said, as she stood at the door. "Mother and Jace won't be back until the end of the week. He's getting immunizations back home before school starts, and Henry Clay volunteered to help move some more of their belongings. I think Mother is considering spending a few extra months here, just until Jace gets settled into school, anyway."

"Where is Mack?"

"I don't know. He's been gone all day."

Just then a flash of lights swept through the mist as a truck pulled into the drive. "That must be him now," Derlie noted, watching with keen interest.

The truck pulled under the magnolia tree in Mack's usual spot and both doors opened at the same time. Piper's high-pitched voice chattering in the stillness and echoing in the damp air. She laughed at some comment, then hurried to take hold of Mack's arm before disappearing inside the house.

"So, when was the last time you were invited to a sleepover?" Bay asked playfully, closing the door. She led the way to the bedroom and waved toward the twin beds.

"Wouldn't *you* like to know … I'll not be tellin' my secrets now."

Bay twisted her lips. Derlie punctuated everything with the word *now* in her singsong voice.

"Why does that fine man want to go and ruin his life with the likes of that woman?" Derlie asked as she removed her rain jacket to reveal her two-piece pajama set in faded cotton floral.

"Did you ask him?" Bay yawned sleepily as she threw back the covers. Climbing in, she pulled the quilt up to her chin.

"No … but I've been wantin' to. I'd like to slap some sense into him sometimes and make him like it. But, there's no way I'm touching that man's face." Derlie walked to the window and threw back the curtains before opening the window to the scent of rain wafting in with the slight breeze. Climbing into bed, she reached over to turn out the lamp.

Bay peered up at the ceiling thoughtfully, listening to Derlie settle into bed. "So, if he were ugly, you'd slap him?"

"I'd flat-out smack him across the face for bein' so stupid!"

Bay half-laughed before stifling another yawn. "Well, you can't blame the man ... Piper is a beauty."

"Beauty is as beauty does ... or didn't your momma tell you."

"Good night," Bay whispered, as she rolled on her side, smiling.

Coming to Briarleigh had simply begun as a job, a way to earn money and give her son a chance to grow up away from all the sadness and loss associated with home. But now, Sugar Land with all of its quirky people was fast becoming a place to call home.

Chapter 20

"Bull alligators sound like what?" Bay asked, staring at the back of Mack's head as he walked down the path in front of her. She picked her way through the marsh grass in her attempt to keep up with him, placing her feet in exactly the same spots where his foot had been.

"Like lions. They bellow this deep, throaty, gurgling sound. The ladies love it." He turned back to look at her, the corners of his lips barely lifting.

He wore blue jeans and a white T-shirt that made his back and shoulders appear much wider and more muscular than she first thought they were; his tanned arms were corded with muscle. The way he handled himself bore the mark of a man well-accustomed to the outdoors; he was definitely in his element.

"So … I take it I'm here to have a lesson on alligator mating rituals? And we need a boat for that?"

He nodded his head and smiled a little. "We do." He watched as her eyes began to fill with fear.

She took in a sharp breath and let it out slowly. Her head began to swim, and she wondered if she might be having another dizziness attack. *Please, God, don't let me faint and fall down in front of this man!*

He noticed her breathing quicken as her apprehension increased. She looked as if a torrent of panic had washed over her. "There's a life jacket in the boat. I want you to wear it ... just in case *I* should have a heart attack and die. That's the only way I'll *not* protect you from drowning, should you fall out of the boat, just so you know."

Over a small rise, the pier came into view. Tied off to the side of the dock was a small jon boat. The dock's boards popped as Mack's heavy boots hit them, which startled a white crane out of the marsh grass. He untied the boat, holding it secure as he helped Bay step down into it, waiting until she was seated before climbing in.

Moments later, Mack steered the boat through the bayou and into the cove near the opening of the river. In the middle of the cove, he cut off the engine and dropped the anchor line.

Bay felt like a little Brownie about to earn her first wildlife explorer badge on the habits of reptiles. The puffy orange life jacket didn't make her feel any more like an adult; her face began to redden at the thought of how ridiculous she must look. Clasping tightly to the sides of the boat, she gradually loosened her white knuckles as the boat's rocking motion slowed.

"In the spring, bull alligators will mate, and female alligators lay their eggs in June and July. It's never a good idea to get too close to her nest. She's a fierce defender of her babies. Once we flew over a nest after take-off, and the mother alligator leapt toward us with her jaws open to attack our helicopter." He pointed a good distance away to a grassy pile of brown hay. "That's a nest."

Holding down the front of the life preserver, she moved her neck to look and asked, "Will they hunt people for food?"

"No, not usually, but they will fight. They're strong, like an armored battleship, but they have a brain the size of a lima bean. That limits their thinking to eat, bite, fight, and mate in an endless cycle. They have an average life span of about seventy years."

Sliding her sunglasses onto her face, she asked, "So, should we restrict guests from swimming in the cove?"

"No swimming at dusk or at night, especially. But we hope to have a pool in place by summer's end. Keep in mind that the chances of your getting attacked by an alligator are about one in twenty-four million. Small children and small animals have the greatest risk if they're near the bank. Feeding alligators is strictly forbidden. You never want them to see a human and think, 'Dinner time.' And, at night—oh, you've got to see this some time— when you shine a light on a gator, you'll see blazing red eyes. They don't blink either."

"Why's that?"

"Because they're hoping you'll come within range of their jaws."

She stretched her neck backward to cover a shudder and watched as puffy white clouds drifted along effortlessly overhead. "What made you decide to become a flight medic? You seem so suited for the water and this environment."

His response was a head shake. "I worked on a barge called the *Voyager* when I was a teen."

Bay's eyes lit up.

"It has a romantic sound to it, but, trust me … nothing could be further from the truth. The truth is, I stayed in a fight most of the time. Our manners were not much better than our friend the alligator's."

"You mean, eat, bite, fight, and mate?"

He glanced away. "Yeah, pretty much."

A light breeze caressed Bay's face, increasing her awareness of her surroundings. It suddenly dawned on her how wildly beautiful and untamed everything appeared to be.

"River life can get pretty monotonous at times … guess that's how we let off steam."

"Sounds like you must've met up with some interesting characters."

"This one old man," he laughed low as he remembered, "kept a bucket on a long rope so he could dip it into the river. He'd lower his bucket into the current, snatch it up, and guzzle it down straight. He claimed the river mud was good for you … called it his tonic."

She laughed, "That's what you call a hard-core river man."

Mack's face took on a slight mellowness as a shadow of a cloud passed over the boat. "But, at night … the scenery would take your breath. The moon and stars just shimmered on the surface of the water. On a clear night, you felt like you were sitting under a faucet of stars as the Milky Way just poured all her brilliance over you." He glanced at her as if embarrassed, shifting his position on the seat. "Wow ... did I just say that? I sound like a pansy."

"You sound like a poet."

"Same thing."

"No, it's not. Crawford is a writer *and* a poet, and he's far from being a pansy."

As Bay contemplated their conversation, she realized how much Mack intrigued her. There was something unpredictable about him, as if any minute he could go slightly wild and veer off his carefully calculated path. He embodied strength and character, but there was uncertainty about him, too.

Mack didn't say anything right away. He seemed a little conflicted about how to respond so he changed the subject. "So, how do you like Louisiana so far?"

"Coming here is a good way to find out if you have the gift of discernment, and I obviously don't."

"Not sure I follow you."

"The murmurs from the cove ... what are they, really?"

Wearing a slight smirk, Mack leaned toward her, as if inviting her to share an intimate secret. "It's the spirits of the cove."

She jerked back as if slapped, then seeing his amusement, reached over and pushed him back, annoyed.

He then took on a serious tone. "Sugar Land has a high tolerance for eccentricity among its citizens. Come on, I'll show you what I think it is."

He pulled up the anchor line then cranked the engine, easing the boat out into the river before giving it full throttle. Unconsciously, she rubbed the scar near her lip with its familiar dead feel and then relaxed some, enjoying the feel of the wind on her face and the sound of the humming motor.

They hadn't gone far when Mack pointed to something over her shoulder. He shouted over the sound of the motor. "That's my place."

Twisting in her seat, Bay was surprised to see a house come into view, though partially hidden behind trees and undergrowth. It sat back on the land which slightly jutted out into the Mississippi River. As they approached, she could make out the second-story balcony where they had waited out the storm.

"I didn't realize your house was so close to Briarleigh!" she said, raising her voice to be heard over the boat's engine.

He nodded, slowing the boat as he eased closer to the bank. The waves bulged under them as Mack killed the engine. They drifted slowly in the calm water of the protected little inlet. Overhead, a flock of geese flew by, and Bay pointed up. Her fascination with all things natural was almost childlike in its freshness, causing Mack to smile.

She adjusted herself on the boat seat, tucking one leg under her. "Do you plan on moving here? Permanently, I mean."

"Not too many positions open for flight medics in the boondocks."

She shrugged. "Maybe you could split the time. Work away during the week, and come home on the weekends." A smile of hope brightened Bay's face as her eyes met Mack's. "But I don't really need to be offering advice on how to do life."

"Why's that?" Mack asked and squinted, fixing his eyes on her.

"Isn't it obvious?"

"If it was ... I wouldn't' have asked."

"Some people think I'm here because I'm running away from something. That's not true. I'm running toward something ... a simple life. I guess sometimes you have a dream that's been with you since childhood. My dream has always been to have my children grow up around trees and water and experience the freedom nature gives. It's important to me to make sure Jace knows how the people who've come before him are connected to him."

"So that's why you brought him here?"

"Yeah."

"Well, that makes perfect sense ... since he's a Blackwell."

She avoided the challenge in his eyes, not willing to be goaded into a confession. Calmly, she reached over the side of the boat and pushed her hand through the water.

Mistaking her avoidance for embarrassment, he explained, "I used to be so black and white in my opinions, but I'm not like that anymore. I still struggle with it sometimes, but most of the time, I live in a kind of gray grace that floats along beside me most days. The people around me get covered in it, too."

Bay was quiet for a moment, then she nodded. "Good way to be."

A barge had passed moments ago, and its wake now reached them, rocking the boat.

"Hold on," Mack warned, reaching over to steady her in the boat. His gaze caught hers, and they froze, with eyes fastened to each other. The moment passed as the sound of a fish jumping near the boat drew their attention away.

Mack cleared his throat, eager to fill the awkward silence. "Between my place and Briarleigh, through those woods," he pointed, "there is an old trail and a tumbledown chapel. Years ago, there was this circuit riding preacher, Reverend Hezekiah Agnew. He'd march his converts down to the river for baptism on what was called the 'road to redemption.' Quite an interesting character ... he rode his horse bareback and carried an albino squirrel on his shoulder. There have been so many tales told about him and his road to redemption that he's become a legend around here. People from all around these parts walk that trail. I've seen and heard a lot since I've been working out here on the property."

"What sort of tales?"

"Not too long after the preacher passed away, some of the townspeople found his diary in the pocket of an old coat. What they found there was shocking. Hezekiah kept a ledger record of all the wrongs done by the people of Sugar Land, right along with the births and deaths. He made mention of thefts and incest, drunkenness and laziness, everything people could possibly do wrong. He would name individuals, too. But once they repented and turned to Christ, he'd mark out their transgressions in that little book, not to remember their sins against them anymore."

Bay objected sharply, "He didn't have the right to do that."

"Oh, but he did. God forgives us in the same way, and he chooses to forget. Aren't we supposed to do the same?"

"Yes ... I guess you're right. It's just harder to forgive yourself sometimes." Anxious to change the subject, she added, "So, you think people are making those sounds?"

"I do."

The gentle hum of a lawnmower became louder as they slid up to the dock and tied off.

Mack offered her his hand, and she stepped from the boat. "Speaking of which ... there is someone you've got to meet."

After unfastening the life jacket and tossing it into the boat, Bay followed as he walked toward the young man pushing the mower. Bay noticed a woman sitting on her knees under a tree in the distance. "Who is that?" she asked, gesturing with a slight nod in the direction of the woman.

"That's Timmy's mother. Timmy's the one pushing the mower. He was born with certain mental disabilities due to his mother's use of alcohol and drugs during pregnancy. Mercy took her in at the home and talked her into staying in

Sugar Land. My dad kinda took up with Timmy. I didn't realize all he did for the boy until he asked me to take over when he moved away. Timmy cuts the grass here and over on my dad's property."

The sound of the mower died, and Timmy began running toward them with a wide grin on his face. "Mr. Mack, Mr. Mack! Hit me on the top of my head … go ahead, hit me."

Mack made a fist and gently tapped his knuckles against the boy's head. "Timmy, I want you to meet my friend, Bay."

Bay smiled and greeted him. "Hi, Timmy!"

"You're nice … not like that other one."

"Thank you." Bay didn't have to wait long to find out about the other one.

"Mr. Jesse married some whore from church, and now he's gone." Timmy's face was drawn into a scowl. He kicked the ground with his tennis shoe, causing a puff of dust to rise in front of them.

Mack's face grimaced. "Now, Timmy, be nice. You know we don't have any of those in church. Mr. Jesse is with my mother again, remember? They love each other, but he still loves you, too."

A smile broke on his face, and his brown eyes gleamed. "He loves me?"

"Of course he does. Now, you're doing a good job here, but you'd better get back to work. The sun will set soon."

Timmy turned and ran toward the mower, yanking on the cord so hard that it started on the first pull.

"He won't stay out here after dark," Mack explained. "His mother comes with him now." He looked back toward the edge of the trees. "She seems drawn to the place somehow. Once, when I was working on the house, I heard the words to an old hymn drift up from that direction. I guess she was singing as she walked down redemption road."

Bay shivered. "I just know I never want to get caught there after the sun has set."

"We all have to face fear of some kind in this life … and, in the end, we all have to fight this battle for ourselves." He glanced at his watch. "And I need to take you back."

Bay suddenly felt compelled to go, probably out of embarrassment as she remembered Mack saying that he needed to return early to have dinner with Piper. Quickly, she crossed the yard to the dock and managed to climb into the boat rather clumsily, nearly capsizing before he got there.

Glancing up, Bay found Mack standing on the pier in front of her. His arms were crossed, and though the cap's bill partially hid his face, she detected disapproval in his stance. As he looked down at her, they stared at each other for several seconds when his green eyes lightened to a seething gray against his scruffy, tanned face. The relaxed look from a moment ago was gone, and, in its place, was an expression that struck her as one of intense seriousness. She felt like a small, reckless child about to be disciplined.

He spoke almost as a stern father to his errant child. "As I recall, Bay, you can't swim. That being the case, you've just risked your life in your hurry to leave. Tell me, what is so important to get back to?"

She shook her head, offering no answer.

He peered closer, puzzled by her actions. "Are you wearing anything that you don't want to get wet?"

She shook her head.

"Good." He extended his hand to her, and she took it with some hesitation. "You're having your first swimming lesson."

He pulled her out of the boat, and she looked up at him, confused. "Here?"

"Here," he replied, removing his cap and pulling off his shirt, tossing them aside. He pointed to the ladder at the end of the dock.

Bay's teeth began to chatter and her legs stiffened as she tried to convince him that this was not the time for a lesson. "We need to get back … Piper is waiting for you. She'll be upset."

"This is more important."

He climbed down the ladder and into the water, then lifted his hands up to help her down.

She took his hand and let him guide her until she touched the oozing mud of the river bottom.

"Do you feel it?" he asked.

"You mean the pull or the mud?"

"The pull."

"Oh, yes, I feel it. If you let go of my hand, I could get lost down that river in no time. It wants to take you along with it, doesn't it?"

"Absolutely … now, don't be afraid, I've got you. When I lift you up, I want you to kick with your feet against the current and move your hands, like this." He made a paddling motion. "Got it?"

"I think so, just don't let go of me ... okay?" Her eyes filled with apprehension and her lips began to tremble.

"Not on your life."

Bay felt his firm hand on her stomach as he gently lifted her. Water threaded through her fingers as she broke the surface, focusing all the strength she could muster into her strokes.

"Cup your hands," he instructed, guiding her through the water. After making several rounds, he said, "Good, now, kick your feet and paddle with your hands; it will help you stay afloat. It's called dog paddling." He removed his hand for a second to allow her to drop slowly into a vertical position, but pulled back sharply as she shot up. Splashing wildly, she desperately grasped the air until she caught a fist full of his hair.

"I've got you, I've got you!" he said through clenched teeth as the breath left his lungs.

"You said you wouldn't let go of me!" Bay sputtered, her free arm thrashing in the water wildly.

"I won't let go this time, I promise." He wiped his hand down his face and shook his head, clearing away the water. "Now, I'm just going to hold you up on your back and let you get a feel for floating. If you kick your legs in this position, the motion will propel you."

Her strength was nearly spent but she agreed to try. "Just don't take your hands away again ... I need to feel your hands on me."

"I won't … just relax. I've got you." He supported her from underneath as she floated on her back, then told her to kick, following along as she moved backward. They went back and forth in the water until Bay's kicking began to slow. "Good. Now that's enough for today."

Gliding her toward the ladder, he stopped and let her feet find the bottom rung. She turned around, the step putting her eye-to-eye with him. The concentrated look he gave her made her heart catch in her throat.

He caught her chin and brushed the hair out of her eyes. "You did well," he said, proudly.

The simple gesture and his simple words made her throat tighten and her voice crack. "Thank you."

The way Mack Blackwell made her feel was dangerous. She'd made mistakes in the past, but she hoped she'd learned from them. The best thing she could do now was stay as far away from the man as she possibly could.

Chapter 21

*T*he rain pounded hard upon Briarleigh as evening tints of gray mist floated up from the marshland. Light shone from the windows, hitting the porch at odd angles. Within the walls, chatter, tinkling glass, and the sound of forks scraping across plates filled the dining room. Bay looked around the table, the very one she had dined at so many times before, and wondered why she felt so uncomfortable this night. Virginia and Jace had been back for a few days, and Henry Clay seemed happier than before. Mack and Piper were seated near Mack's brother, Shannon, who had dropped by unexpectedly. So what was wrong?

Shannon turned to Bay, and his eyes gleamed. "Tell me, how's my 'Bama girl getting along over here in Cajun country?" His grin deepened, then he winked. "These two old goats aren't working you too hard, are they? When I heard you were here, I had to come see for myself."

"No, I'm afraid it's the other way around," Bay replied. "But, everything seems to be coming together for our big day tomorrow."

He frowned as he noticed the distance between his place at the table and Bay's. Shannon said, "I have a complaint to whoever made the seating arrangements." Seizing his plate and glass, he moved them closer to Bay.

Mack glared at his brother a moment then lifted his drink, never taking his eyes off him as he swallowed back his tea.

As Shannon sat down next to Bay, Jace got up from his place at the table and moved to the seat next to Shannon, smiling with impish delight.

Trying hard to keep his temper in check, Mack commented dryly, "If you've all finished playing musical chairs, I'll ask Derlie to bring in coffee and dessert."

Bay glanced over her shoulder at Mack and noticed his scowl, but she quickly turned her attention back to Shannon and smiled warmly, puzzled at Mack's sudden change in mood.

Piper spoke up, and the sound of her voice seemed to Bay's already taut nerves the same as a china plate hitting a ceramic floor. It annoyed her how Piper turned every statement into a half-question. "So, Jace is used to being around different men? Most children are afraid of strangers, wouldn't you agree?"

"Yes, and ... yes," Bay carefully stated and brushed the hair out of her eyes. The fewer words she exchanged with Piper the better.

Shannon spoke up. "There're words for it, Piper. It's called being well-adjusted. But, I'm no stranger. I'm Uncle Shannon, isn't that right Jace?" He reached over and tousled the boy's head.

"Oh ... how original," Piper shot back, with a smug look on her face. The meaning was not lost on anyone present.

Bay felt slapped by the words, and she turned sharply toward Piper. However, it wasn't Piper who caught her attention—it was Mack! His face darkened and his cheek flexed tensely as he glared at his brother. In a flash of revelation, she realized what Mack must be thinking, and her heart jumped to her throat.

Placing her glass down on the table, Bay pushed her chair back and stood up to get everyone's attention, "Please." Her call was barely noticeable to anyone but Mack who turned quickly to the low and soft summons. "I have something to say."

A startled hush fell over the room as Bay's words registered to first one, then the others. She went to the window and looked out on the rainy evening, offering up a silent prayer for wisdom. The rain beat down upon the house with a vengeance, but there was a great calm within the dining room. She knew this was the time to speak.

Mack caught the meaning of Bay's delay and quickly got the attention of Derlie who had been watching the scene with open-mouthed fascination. "Derlie, will you take Jace into the kitchen for dessert? And, put some ice cream on that pie. Everyone knows that you can't eat pie without ice cream."

"I sure will. Come on little fellow. Derlie will fix you right up."

The chair scraped the floor in the silent room as Jace got up from the table. He looked to his mother for approval. At her nod, he followed Derlie into the kitchen.

Bay tried to pull her reeling thoughts together. She didn't just want to blurt out the truth. She had to use wisdom. And everyone she loved depended on it.

"Mother?" Bay looked to Virginia for direction.

"The floor is yours, dear," her mother said, smiling reassuringly.

"What would you like to know about my son?" Bay steadied her trembling hands, holding them together tightly as she walked toward the table.

With tenderness in his eyes, Henry Clay spoke up. "It would seem that the Blackwell men have never been too successful with their women, Bay." He cut his eyes sharply to his nephews with a warning. "So, please, tell us about Jace."

"Of course … what would you like to know first?"

"Is he a Blackwell?" Mack asked pointedly.

"Yes."

The thought suddenly occurred to Mack that Bay might actually be Uncle Henry's daughter. A thousand implications raced together in one tragic conclusion. Bay could be his cousin!

Shannon leaned his head back against the chair and stared up at the ceiling as if he already knew the answer to the questions and was just waiting for it all to play out.

Henry Clay raised a hand, halting any further comment and asked the question. "Who's the father?"

Bay shrugged, "I don't know … I suspect someone from the university."

"What! You don't know?" Mack asked incredulously. He threw his hands up in exasperation.

Smiling knowingly at Bay, Piper was obviously pleased with the turn of events.

Henry Clay leaned his elbows on the table and turned his head to consider her words. "Then, how do you know he's a Blackwell?"

"Because his birth mother is your daughter, Rachel."

The room was quiet, and, in the stunned silence, Mack asked his brother, "So, why do you not seem surprised by any of this?"

Shannon answered, "I was the one to suggest to Rachel that she contact Mercy. Mercy then contacted Virginia. I drove Rachel over to Mobile … she wanted to meet them."

The kitchen door creaked as Jace pushed it open. He paused, as every eye fell on him. "Do I need to leave, Momma?" he asked, making his way to her side, a little frightened at all the attention he was receiving.

"No, son, we were just finishing up." She gently brushed the hair from his eyes and discreetly wiped a tear from her cheek.

There were still so many questions to be answered, but no one dared ask another. It was enough for the moment to take in the wonder of seeing Henry Clay's grandson for the first time, and the astonished look on the old man's face.

Virginia tucked her hand through the bend of Henry Clay's arm and squeezed. "It was always hers to tell, Henry, but now I can finish the whole story," she whispered low in his ear, "when we're alone."

Chapter 22

Measure by measure, the realization had dawned on Mack that he'd never really known the girl, Bay Rutherford. She had been an intrusion into their lives, a welcome one and a much-needed one to be sure. But, what did he really know of her? After leaving Piper at her cottage door for the night, he pulled the hood of his rain jacket over his head and walked toward the side of the house. The same drizzling rain fell on the subject of his thoughts as he rounded the corner of the house, finding Bay on her hands and knees digging in the garden.

Virginia and Jace were on the way to their cottage when they spotted Mack crossing the yard. Virginia waited under the umbrella for him to approach. "Whenever Bay is troubled, she digs," Virginia said, motioning with her head toward the kitchen garden on the side of the house. "After her father died, I sat and watched her dig an entire pond in our backyard … with a trowel! It's best to leave her alone. She's battling a few private demons right now. She'll exhaust herself soon enough, and that'll be that." She turned, and they continued on their way, as if this was nothing out of the ordinary.

Water ran down Bay's cheeks, making it hard for Mack to determine if she was crying or if the rain was washing down her face. He snatched off his rain jacket and walked over to her, draping it around her slick shoulders. She didn't seem to notice and didn't look up, just kept stabbing the ground and turning it over with her trowel. The rain-soaked dirt seemed to melt into mud as it hit the ground. He stood there a moment then decided to sit down against the side of the house and wait her out.

After a while, he sensed she was running out of steam. Her movements began to slow, and her breathing became labored. Dropping the trowel, she looked up at him, her brow creased in pain.

In his profession, Mack was well-accustomed to seeing the face of pain, but nothing prepared him for the feelings that assaulted him as he looked upon Bay. The sorrow he saw in her hazel eyes was almost unbearable. Without thinking, only reacting, he reached out and took her hand, pulling her beside him.

She glanced at him, taking in his features with uncertainty, as if drawing out the truth behind his action. She relaxed beside him, satisfied with the answer in his eyes.

For ten minutes or so, Mack sat in the rain beside Bay. He was aware of the rhythmic pattern of her breathing and smelled her lavender scent with each rise and fall of her chest. She stirred and glanced at him again.

Mack smiled but didn't say anything.

"Sorry ..." she managed to say, trying to find her voice as she got up and handed the jacket back to him. She didn't know what else to say or what else to do.

He didn't move, didn't reach for the jacket, but allowed it to fall across his leg.

She stepped back before turning then walked away toward the cottage.

The next day, Mack sat at the window of the Thibodaux Cafe and watched as Ludie Earl made his way across the street. It was good to see his old friend. He hadn't changed much since high school, only becoming a little thicker around the middle. For a second, Mack felt sucked back in time. It somehow seemed inappropriate to go there. But that's exactly what he wanted to do. He wanted to conduct friendships and love affairs with the zeal of a nineteen year old and to feel wild and free again. Given the chance, he thought to himself, he'd go there in a heartbeat. Only he'd be wiser this time around.

Mack sought out his friend, anxious to get away from Briarleigh for a while. As soon as Shannon and Piper left to return to New Orleans, he found a private moment to call Ludie Earl. Now, as he waited for his friend, Mack reflected on the day's events.

They'd worked all morning getting ready for the noon opening and their first guests. Bay set up a dessert station with iced sugar cookies, lemonade, and toasted pecans to greet guests as they arrived on the porch. A lush hydrangea centerpiece filled with sprigs of lemon leaf graced the table, bringing a warm Southern greeting of welcome.

Mack had started to wince every time he heard the words, "Oh, one more thing." Bay was in her element. Gone was the distraught girl of the night before and, in her place, was a gracious woman, fully alive and in charge of the household. He smiled as he remembered the way she'd pensively nibbled at her fingertip, trying to decide between magnolia blossoms or wisteria for the entrance table.

Mack's thoughts were interrupted by the clanging bell at the restaurant door when Ludie Earl came inside the cafe. The typical crowd in their usual spots nodded a greeting to the police chief. Spying Mack next to the window, Ludie turned toward the waitress and held up two fingers. "The number two special, Tibby, with a Pepsi."

Mack pushed out a chair with his foot. "'Bout time you got here. I thought I was going to have to come looking for you. Tibby said that the barge came in last night and the men were pretty rowdy."

"Nothing I can't handle."

Laughter drew their attention to the counter. "Don't let him sit there and lie to you, Mack. One of them pulled a knife on him."

"Oh, for Pete's sake, Tibby, that guy barely qualifies as a man ... still had fuzz on his cheeks."

"Don't matter none when he's totin' a knife," Tibby retorted, before turning to exchange words with the cook in the kitchen. "Y'all get catfish today—cornmeal-battered and fried to a deep golden brown—hush puppies, and slaw."

Mack watched in amusement as Ludie Earl picked up his menu and waved it in the direction of the waitress. Having lost all patience, he snapped, "You sure could've saved yourself a whole lot of money on these menus. Why didn't you just print up a big sign that says, 'You'll eat whatever the heck I want you to eat'?"

Tibby stuck her tongue out at Ludie Earl and the chief's mouth softened into a lazy smile. He carefully avoided meeting Mack's eyes which made his friend want to take another look at Tibby. She'd always been a pretty, country girl—pretty with a certain pride in her appearance. If she never said a word, you'd never know she was straight from the backwoods simply by looking at her.

Eager to change the subject, Ludie Earl asked about Piper. "I saw Piper in town going into the Lavender Jar yesterday. Is she staying out at Briarleigh?"

A quick nod answered him, and Mack picked up his tea and took a swig.

"You two back together?"

The reply was barely audible. "I'm not sure."

"What happened?"

"If you can believe it … nothing. And not because I didn't have plenty of chances." He ran a hand through his hair. "I don't know what's wrong with me, Lud. Why have I waited so long for her in the first place?"

"Maybe she was just safe because she was married. You never were one to get too close to women."

"Have I wasted ten years of my life waiting for a woman I'm not sure I even like anymore? She left this morning ... and all I felt was relief."

Ludie Earl glanced at him, and his eyes grew thoughtful. "You have to figure things out as you go, Mack," he said, "just like the rest of us."

Tibby approached their table, skillfully balancing a large tray with one hand as she placed their plates in front of them. When she left the table, she called back over her shoulder. "You'll have Coke and not Pepsi."

Mack laughed lightly then turned his attention to the tantalizing food in front of him.

Ludie Earl began munching on a piece of fish and continued with the conversation. "We're living in no man's land these days. We're not young like we once were and not quite settled either. Just don't lose yourself in regret. The way I see it, you never know what's around the bend in the river ... it may be something you've been waiting for your whole life and just didn't know it."

"Did she change ... or did I?"

"Both. Some things are beyond our control. Like what people turn into when they grow up. Listen, Mack," he leaned forward in his chair and spoke low and deliberately. "You banked on feelings from adolescence. Heck, those were mostly hormones ... raw testosterone. At least now you've got some sense mixed in with it. What did you think you were getting with her anyway?"

"Someone who knew me ... someone I knew. I wanted what we had back then, I guess."

"You can't go back, not to stay anyway. Every once in a while, I like to climb a tree or turn circles in the boat just to make donuts. But, if I did that all the time, they'd lock me up in an insane asylum. It's okay to visit your past, just don't stay there."

Mack rubbed his rough cheek in thought. "Maybe all we need is more time to figure things out."

Ludie Earl hooked his hand around his drink. "That's something only you'll know."

Chapter 23

The long summer evenings were under way, and the heat of August had sapped the energy from everyone but the children. Since the opening day of Briarleigh Inn, to the amazement of all, the days that followed ran smoothly. Under Bay's careful management and easy charm, business thrived. She began making it her habit to stroll the grounds just before dark and listen to the light flow of conversations at gathering places here and there. Hearing Ezra's deep and husky voice, she paused by the back porch to listen, noticing a scattering of children and parents surrounding his rocking chair.

"Many's the night I've passed right here on this porch," Ezra slowly tapped the arm of the chair with his long, brown finger for emphasis, "in the company of someone that's been dead two hundred years or more. All I have to do is sit still and wait and then my mind goes wandering back ... back to the war that took place on this very land."

"What do the murmurs say?" asked one man, seemingly more interested in the old man's tales than his distracted children who were busy poking each other with sticks.

"If you discover the message behind the murmurs, the river will sing, and joy will break out on the surface of the water." Ezra leaned back in his chair and pointed to the man. "You just watch and see if it don't. Makes me want to go to church on Sunday just to thank God for takin' the time to whisper them things to me."

Bay smiled and stepped away, rounding the side of the house to the front lawn. Only then did she lift her eyes to find Mack and two others talking near his truck. She had no desire to be seen, so she quickened her pace to the front door.

"Bay!" Mack called to her from across the yard.

She stopped and turned around, waiting for him to continue. He mumbled to his companions before they all began walking toward her. He approached with measured steps, and she eyed him with curiosity.

"Bay, I want you to meet my flight partners, Lauren Lansing and Nicholas Straight."

"Pleased to meet you," Bay said, noticing the familiar ease between the three. Lauren's sleek, fawn-colored hair fell to her shoulders in soft, light layers. She was pretty with a warm and engaging smile while Nicholas seemed sunny and optimistic with a full sense of himself. "I'm Bay Rutherford, and I hope you're here to stay for a while," she said, extending her hand to each of them.

Mack looked at Bay seriously. "Please tell me we have room. I don't like the thought of bunking down with these two anymore than I have to. You've never heard such awful buzz-saw snoring

... it'll wake the dead. And around here, that's not a good thing to do."

Bay dismissed his comment with a flip of her hand. "Oh, I'm sure Nicholas is not as bad as all that."

"Nicholas? I'm talking about Lauren."

Lauren punched Mack in the arm. "Do you have to tell everything you know about me?"

Bay was not willing to wade into that discussion, so she quickly changed the subject. "We have a room available upstairs. I'm sorry to say that it's the only room we have unoccupied right now."

Lauren was quick to respond. "One room is all I need. The guys can cozy it up tonight. I wouldn't want to keep anyone awake with my *buzz-saw snoring*." Walking back to the car, she lifted a small suitcase from the back seat and joined them again. "Lead the way, Miss Bay. The sooner I can take a bath, the better off I'll be."

Going inside, Bay went up the stairs and paused at the landing, waiting for Lauren to follow her. Mack grabbed Lauren's hand and pulled her back to whisper in her ear before letting her pull free, a devilish grin spreading across his face as he laughed.

Lauren rolled her eyes and climbed the stairs. "Men ... do they ever grow up? If I see a ghost, I'll be sure to tell him that you're looking for him," she said, never looking back.

Bay looked back at Mack, amazed that Lauren seemed so unaffected by his smile. Slow and powerful, his grin could disarm her in seconds, and it was the one thing about him that she feared the most.

"This room is my favorite of all," Bay said, as they made their way down the second-floor hallway. "It has a view of the river and the sky that will take your breath. But, you can close the curtains if the morning light bothers you. At night, I sometimes come up here and find the whole room flooded with moonlight."

"Sounds wonderful … maybe I can find a little peace of mind here. The last few months have really taken a toll on all of us," she said, blowing the hair out of her eyes as she followed behind her.

Turning the key in the lock, Bay wondered if Lauren was referring to Mack's absence, but didn't ask. "I'll do all I can to make sure you're comfortable here. If you need anything, just call." She handed Lauren her business card, then pushed the door open.

It was not a cluttered room full of objects, but open and spacious with the soothing colors of moss and sage lending a cool, tranquil feeling to the space. A white-painted iron bed laid out with fresh white linens and a softly colored duvet spread across its foot dominated the room. The room felt calm, shadowy, and sheltered.

A sigh seeped from Lauren as her suitcase hit the floor with a thud.

Crossing to the bed, Bay gently turned down the soft, cool covers. She stepped to the French doors and pulled them open to allow the sound of cicadas into the room. She indicated a grouping of wicker chairs on the balcony. "The last guest spent hours on this veranda. He said he liked to watch heat lighting in the afternoon and imagine that it was a Civil War battle with firing gunboats on the river." She pinched off a few dead leaves from a hanging ivy geranium and tossed them over the railing … unintentionally noticing Mack and Nicholas talking near the steps. "All these leafy trees seem to enclose the house in summer. This is the only room where you have an uninterrupted view of the river any time of year." As Bay turned around, she noted Lauren's careful concentration while staring at her from her place in the doorway. Bay raised her eyebrows, waiting for a question.

Lauren's mind began to flash back. The patient was a woman in her twenties with summer-brown hair. She wore a blood-stained T-shirt that read, "Proud Mom" and had a child's painted hand prints stamped on the front. This young woman was hooked to the EKG monitor, its generating information kept Mack's attention as he administered treatment. In the past, he had never encountered this heart rhythm but knew he could handle it. The woman was unconscious after losing control of her vehicle and slamming into a bridge railing. The crash resulted in a head injury producing loss of blood due to the force of the air bag against the patient's head. The patient had had a brief incident of tachycardia before being transported by med-flight.

Lauren remembered observing the woman strapped to the gurney. She noticed a silver chain around the woman's neck and gently lifted it to pull it free from the scooped neck of her shirt. A tiny elongated silver bar flashed under the light. Under close scrutiny, the pendant indicated the patient's diagnosis with the arrhythmic pattern of Wolff-Parkinson-White Syndrome. Lauren poked Mack, drawing his attention to the bar. Recognition dawned on his features, and he briefly smiled down at the woman. It was as if their patient had accepted the rare condition as part of her life and had made peace with it.

They knew that common symptoms of WPW were palpitations, dizziness, and shortness of breath, with fainting or near-fainting possible under the right circumstances. But still, the condition drew their interest.

Lauren and Mack had been partners for four years, long enough that she perhaps knew him better than most women did. She knew that he came alive in a crisis.

Now, looking at the woman preparing her room for the night, Lauren knew without a doubt that this was the patient. She also knew that Mack, being animated whenever someone was injured or dying in flight, had had his full attention on saving the woman's life and very little else. There was a good chance he hadn't made the connection.

"Is everything okay? You look like you've seen a ghost." Bay smiled warmly, hoping she realized she was teasing.

"Oh, yes … everything is perfect. I'm zoning out … guess I'm just tired and need a bath and a nap."

Bay nodded. "Well, I just stocked the bath with Briarleigh's signature bath products for your enjoyment. I'll send Maundy up with a snack tray while you're relaxing." That said, Bay crossed the room to the door.

"Thank you, Bay. Mack's lucky to have you. You're the perfect hostess."

Chapter 24

The little crowd of guests around the bonfire dwindled down to four, with the sinking sun against their backs, its fading light turning the tops of the river trees a soft, golden orange.

Ezra let out a sigh. "I stabbed a man once in a bar fight, and he died. I got sent to prison. Best thing to ever happen to me," he drawled, as he rubbed his chin reflectively. "'Cause, you see, that's where I met the Lord. I finally stopped my running when those iron bars closed in front of me. Yes, sir … that's where he found me. I picked up a Gideon Bible someone left on the bunk, and I began to read, mostly because I didn't have anything else to do. I discovered that King David, Moses, and Paul had all been murderers. Some of his *best* had been murderers, just like me. I found out that he forgives sinners when they ask him and then cleans them up for his service. Yes, Lord … that's what he did for me all those years ago, and I ain't never been the same."

Crawford Benton shifted uncomfortably in his seat, then stood to leave. Leaning over, he kissed the top of Bay's head and said, "Goodnight."

"Goodnight," she whispered, still thinking of the truth of Ezra's words. She looked across the fire to Mack, his face shadowed and lit from the flickering firelight, then to Ezra's weathered face, cracked and deep from years of living. His eyes shone in the amber light, as if compelling her to confess. Then he spoke again, only softly this time.

"Lay it out there. Lay it *all* out there … your hard life, your sins, your failures. Now, once you've spread it out you wait. Wait on the rain of grace to fall, and it will. As surely as God lives, it will. And after it has soaked into all those dried-up places, something amazing happens … new life. Old things pass away and all things become new."

Bay sat still and quiet for a moment. Everything around her hushed, but the hiss of the fire. "Five years ago, I lost my baby," she blurted out. "After my father passed away, I was seeking comfort. That's when I met Crawford. He was a guest at St. Bonitus where I worked. At the time, all I saw was a kind and intriguing man. It felt good to be in his arms. It had been so very long since I'd been held like that and really listened to. Then I made a poor choice. When I found out I was pregnant, I wasn't prepared for his response. He was tender and supportive, but he made it clear that marriage was not part of his plan. He shed a few tears and explained to me how selfish he was. Then he told me that writing was his first love and that he doubted he'd be much of a husband, much less a father."

Ezra nodded his head once, took out a pipe, and tamped the bowl with his thumb, pressing down the tobacco. With the strike of a match, Ezra's face glowed while he puffed the pipe to life. Bay could feel Mack's eyes on her, but she didn't look at him, glad he was covered in darkness.

"Financially," she continued, "he said that we would be secure. And so, the good outweighed the bad most days until the day I miscarried my baby. The pain I felt after I came home from the hospital was like no other. It rocked me to the core of my being. I can only describe it as a desperate kind of loneliness, a horrific emptiness. That single event brought me to my knees. Everyone else returned to life just as before. My mother, Crawford, but not me. I would never be the same." She turned her eyes to Ezra and smiled. "And, like you, that's when I grabbed hold of God's rescuing lifeline. He saved me from drowning in my own sorrow and shame and gave me another chance at motherhood. Jace is that chance."

Mack sat gazing at the fire, his thoughts running rampant. He sat and stared in silence, offering no words.

Ezra lifted his eyes to watch Bay stand, brush off her jeans, and walk off into the darkness toward her cottage. He called after her, "That boy of yours sure has a good momma. I call that a double blessing."

A narrow silvery beam of moonlight pierced the crack between the closed curtains as Bay lay sleepless, curled against the pillow. Her thoughts rolled over one another like waves during a turbulent storm at sea, causing her to finally toss the covers back and seek some relief. She tiptoed out of the room, careful not to wake her mother who slept peacefully in the twin bed beside hers.

Quietly, she made her way to the back door of Briarleigh. Easing the door open, she stepped inside. Navigating her way through the obstacles in the dark room was no trouble … she knew the kitchen by heart. Reaching the cabinet, she gently pulled it open and had her hand on the bottle she was seeking when a movement from across the room made her turn.

Mack's bedroom door was open and Bay's creeping motion roused his curiosity. He swung his long legs over the side of the bed and sat up. He strained in the darkness, trying to make out the form through the doorway of his bedroom. "Are you sick?" he questioned, his voice clear in the hushed silence.

Bay could only stare into the darkness. Her voice seemed to catch in her throat as she stood there like a child caught with her hand in the cookie jar.

He reached for his jeans at the end of the bed and yanked them on, then grabbed a T-shirt from the back of the chair and pulled it over his head. He flipped the switch, squinting in the light of the wall lanterns as he walked toward her. Gently, he removed the small bottle from her hand. Turning it, he read the label. Their eyes met as he lifted a brow. "Benadryl?"

She nodded.

"Are you having an allergic reaction?"

Her mouth curved, and she replied, "Yes … I seem to be allergic to public confession. All I have to do is talk about my past, and I break out all over."

His tone became quite casual. "Well, that explains it then."

"Mind giving it back? It helps me sleep," she said, presenting her flat palm.

He didn't answer her question, though he heard it. Instead, he asked, "Why can't you sleep?"

"Too much on my mind, I guess."

As Mack looked at Bay, it amazed him that in one short evening she had made herself vulnerable. Truth was, he'd not been able to sleep either but stayed awake trying to make sense of Bay Rutherford. He'd foolishly thought he knew women. Now this one was teaching him a thing or two. She would not easily fit into a neat little compartment. Bay was a woman, less than perfect, but a woman fully alive. There had been women in his life like Piper whose features were so fine that they could be called beautiful. Not so with Bay. She was pretty, but far more intriguing scarred than those that seemed to be flawless. She had strength of character and grace ... admitting her failings, sins, and weaknesses openly and facing the consequences with courage. Most of all, she loved her son ... and he valued that about her much more than fleeting beauty.

"Here," he said, popping the lid with his thumb. He shook out a tablet and gave it to her. Mack tried to imagine his life without her after these few months and his mind rebelled, shutting off the thought. He turned and stared straight ahead into the backyard through the kitchen window. His voice grew husky as if the words came hard. "I'm leaving in the morning, going back to Baton Rouge with my crew. There's a hearing, and some people from corporate are coming in."

Bay shrugged casually. "I guess it's time to get your boot back in the stirrup and face the showdown. Are you dreading it?" The thought shocked her like a bucket of ice water poured over her head, but she remained outwardly calm and collected.

"Yes and no."

In his eyes, she saw a strange emotion. Was it regret? He pressed his lips together until a white line formed, as if holding back what he truly wanted to say.

The silence that followed was no longer comfortable. Bay glanced away, searching for the proper words. "Well, I'll e-mail reports to you weekly ... keep you posted on how things are going around here."

In the soft light from the wall lanterns, she suddenly looked very small and fragile. Mack cleared his throat. "That'll be good. I'll try to come up on the weekends when I can. If anything comes up ... just handle it the way you think best, like you always do. Go to Henry Clay with anything you're not sure of and then e-mail me if you don't mind ... keep me in the loop." Rubbing his jaw thoughtfully, he added, "Remember to keep an eye on the sky. The weather around here will trick you. Just be careful ... especially if you or Jace are near the water."

"Okay ... *now* you're sounding like my mom," Bay said, smiling to take the edge off of her words. "So, are you going to miss it here?"

Running a hand through his hair, he let out a shallow breath. "Being on the river the first and last thing every day is my idea of the good life. Sure, I'll miss it."

He looked so adorably rumpled with his wrinkled white T-shirt, tousled hair, and close-cut beard. She almost stopped breathing. Having found her voice, she said, "I guess you're just a river man at heart."

"Guess so." A slow smile crept across his face. "I kinda get this calm feeling when I see that river roll by. No other place but the banks of the Mississippi keeps me quite as sane." He looked at her, as if asking whether she understood. "But, it's back to the real world. I'm certainly no earthly good when I'm here."

Bay tried to swallow the words before saying them, but found she couldn't. "I disagree … strongly." She went to the refrigerator and took out a pitcher of lemonade, pouring a glass. Placing the pill on her tongue, she swallowed down the tablet.

Mack watched her intently, marveling that she could be at one time so transparent with her sins and faults then another moment as graceful as a nymph whose movements were a study in rhythm and grace. He began to realize that it would be easy to become bound by more than the river. There were other ties that seemed to begin to entwine around him, making their way to his heart as fast and steady as any vines that grew on the land.

"Couldn't you at least pretend you're going to miss us?" Bay teased, as she pulled out a bar stool and slid onto it, holding her glass. "I doubt very seriously you'll ever come across another fainting medical case like mine."

A corner of his mouth quirked upward. He watched her closely as he answered, "Of that, I have no doubt."

The certainty in his voice caused her to lift her eyebrows. His clear green eyes studied her, making her suddenly uncomfortable under their scrutiny.

"How long have you had WPW?"

Bay dropped both feet to the floor and stood to face him. "How did you know that? Did my mother …?"

He cut her off mid-sentence. "No, I transported you to the hospital after you hit the railing of a bridge near Baton Rouge. All this time, I didn't recognize you, but Lauren did immediately."

She gave a tiny nod that was stiff and difficult. "So … I guess that's going to change things. I mean, who wants an employee with a heart condition … one who may be a liability."

He held up his hand to stop her from saying anything more. "Your condition is not something that can't be managed. It seems to me that you've done a pretty good job of it so far."

"Yeah, well, I've noticed employers tend to skip over my assets and focus more on my liabilities. I would have told you if you'd have asked about my health, you know. My previous employer used my condition as a kind of hold to keep me bound to them. They reminded me often how fortunate I was to work for them. After all, not many people would be willing to continue to employ damaged goods."

"Damaged goods! What? Bay, there is nothing damaged about you. You just happen to have an extra circuit in your heart, that's all."

"The night of the accident, I was in Baton Rouge making a delivery for Rachelle Geroux, Sterling's mother. I never know where I'll be when I have a spell."

"How long have you had the condition?"

"I was born with it. When I was around nine, my doctor gave me a stress test to see how my heart handled activity. The delta waves disappeared with an increased heart rate, so I'm considered low risk for sudden cardiac death."

"Have you considered catheter ablation?"

Bay shook her head. "As long as I can handle the symptoms okay, I won't have the procedure. I'm getting used to the palpitations. But, the dizziness and fainting really scares me sometimes, especially if I'm driving. I've learned to ease off the road when I begin to feel it. Holding my breath, standing on my head, or sticking my head in the refrigerator can convert my heart back to a normal rhythm, but you sure do get a lot of strange looks when you do things like that."

He laughed, reaching over to trace his finger around her neck until it slid underneath the silver oblong tag with the engraved EKG. "Now, this is definitely a first. I remember smiling when I first saw it. Lauren pointed it out to me," he said, his warm breath in her ear. "I'm sure going to miss a case like yours."

Chapter 25

*F*or the first time in her life, Bay Rutherford kissed a man first. Lifting up on her toes, she pressed her lips softly into Mack's cheek. He smiled broadly, his teeth white in the shadowed stubble of his face.

"What was that?" he questioned, touching his cheek as he tried to hold back an escaping grin.

"A goodbye kiss, of course," she said quietly, as if it was the most common thing in the world. "Haven't you ever been kissed goodbye?"

"Can't say that I have, not like that, anyway," he hesitated a moment, rubbing his scruffy face as if in thought. "But I'm certain I can do a better job of it than that."

She scanned his face, trying to determine his intention. What she saw there was not easy to read, but whatever it was … it was genuine. "Well, that's mighty big talk for someone who's never even heard of a goodbye kiss."

He didn't speak, and she thought that maybe he wasn't sure how to respond. Then, just as she turned to the door, he reached for her hand and pulled her back into his arms. Lowering his head, he moved his lips slowly across hers, gently at first, then he drew her closer as he deepened the kiss. She trembled in response, savoring the feel of his rough jaw against her skin. Then, just as suddenly, he pulled away. "Blackwell men are more about action than talk ... usually."

Without meeting his eyes, she whispered a quick good-bye, then hurriedly left. She headed back to the cottage, rubbing her eyes with the back of her folded hands trying to put McRossen Blackwell far from her mind.

It was almost six o'clock the following morning when Bay made it back to the kitchen of Briarleigh. As she stepped through the door, she was surprised to see Mack seated at the bar cradling a cup of coffee in his hands. He was quiet and introspective, staring into the dark brew completely lost in thought.

Derlie smiled up at Bay. "You want the usual ... coffee and a pastry?"

All thought seeming to vanish from her mind, Bay paused then responded, "Yes, please, and can you bring it to my office? I've got to make a quick call. I've hired some workers who should be here shortly."

"Oh ... and I'll make sure you have a lovely hydrangea for your desk. The deep purple ones are just gorgeous this morning, all glistening with dew. I know they're your favorite flower, and it doesn't even matter that they have no fragrance ... you are fragrant enough for the both of you."

At times, Derlie's Irish prose got a little embarrassing ... particularly *this* morning when all Bay wanted to do was disappear to her office and forget about the man seated at the bar.

Wiping her hands down her apron, Derlie turned to Bay and said, "Before I forget, Maundy wanted me to ask if you'd mind taking her to church next Sunday." She shrugged. "I didn't ask why. And Mr. Benton wants to know if you'd mind delivering his breakfast this morning. He said he knows it's your day off, but it makes him uncomfortable having Maundy in his cottage ... her being so young and all. He said he'd really prefer that you deliver it from now on."

Mack swallowed back his coffee and set his empty cup on the bar with a bang, startling both women. "I'll take it to him."

Neither of them said a word but watched as he lifted the tray from the counter and kicked the screen door open with his foot, letting it slam behind him. He left without another word, leaving them to stare after him. Once his feet hit the grass, he jerked the flower out of the small vase and threw it to the ground.

Pulling her attention away from Mack, Bay said, "Um ... I'll be in my office should you need me."

A light tapping sound drew Bay's attention away from the computer screen. She pushed back from the desk and got up to investigate. At the window, she lifted the sheer drapes away and watched as Ezra tapped the bottom of a large clay pot with a rubber mallet. Letting the curtain drop, she wandered outside to see what the old man was up to.

"I've got a mind to fix this old fountain. The bottom's cracked, but I got the stuff to seal it off for good," Ezra informed Bay as he wiped his forehead with the back of his arm. "Found me some wild ferns down by the bayou. Thought maybe I'd plant them around it ... right here out front ... what you think?"

Bay sat down on the porch steps near him, tucking her skirt beneath her. "I think that's a great idea. I love the soothing sound of a fountain. I can even open my office window and enjoy it. Need some help?"

"Could always use help. Here, hold this shovel while I get the wheelbarrow. We'll go on down there now before it gets too hot."

Mack was walking away from Crawford Benson's cottage when Henry Clay was coming out of his. His uncle raised an eyebrow in question.

"I delivered breakfast to our guest ... just trying to help out," Mack said, a little sheepish.

"Well, now ... wasn't that sweet of you?" Henry Clay crossed his arms over his chest and looked at him knowingly.

Henry Clay was anything but stupid. Thankfully, Virginia and Jace diverted the old man's attention away from Mack by crossing the yard at just that moment.

Mack's gaze moved over Virginia's shoulder. "I'll be along in a minute. I want to check with Ezra and Bay before I go."

"I'll go with you," Henry Clay chimed in. "We need to discuss a few things before you head out today anyway." He turned toward Virginia. "Keep the coffee hot for me; I'll only be a minute."

They'd almost made it to the bank of the bayou when they heard a large splash in the water. Mack's eyes scanned the area, and he declared, "That was too loud to be a fish."

The men quickly approached Bay and Ezra who were now bent over, tugging on a stubborn fern. Bay moved closer to the water, improving her position so she could dig around the tightly held plant.

"Get back from the water!" Mack commanded sharply. "And toss that shovel to me!"

Bay stood before Mack with a clear challenge in her stance. "Here, come and take it." Bay was not used to the potential dangers lurking within the water.

Not comfortable enough to turn his back on Bay, Mack spoke to his uncle without turning around. "I detect a note of hostility."

"Maybe she doesn't like being told what to do so forcefully," Henry Clay said under his breath.

"Did I sound forceful?" Not taking his eyes off Bay, he slowly walked up to her and took the shovel from her hand.

Henry Clay nodded. "Now come on … let's find what made that noise."

Mack backed away slowly. "Whatever it is, it's not half as frightening as that little swamp fairy staring me down right now." A shadow of a smile played across his lips. He was beginning to find way too much pleasure in this woman.

After surveying the area and being satisfied it was safe, Mack returned the shovel to Bay's waiting hands, thankful he didn't have to use it to dissuade a gator.

Ezra sat down on the ground abruptly and looked up at Mack with a kind of smirk on his face. Bay and Ezra had developed an odd friendship in the brief time they'd known each other. They seemed to speak the same language, sometimes making it hard for others to keep up. Once, Mack came upon them engaged in a deep discussion about the scissor grinder cicada — how it sounded in the trees and how that little creature needed to feel warm to sing and fly around happily. Another time, he'd walked up on them asleep in their Adirondack chairs with their faces turned to the moon. He would never admit it, but he had some serious envy going on. They seemed to go as far as any humans he'd ever known toward simply tuning in to the created universe. They enjoyed it as if it were made for that specific reason, just to give them pleasure.

"What are you two scheming now?" Mack asked, ignoring the look Bay was giving him. "You both look guilty as sin. Are you burying stolen money in that hole?"

Ezra picked up his trowel to begin digging around the plant, answering in his slow drawl. "We robbed the First National Bank of Tallulah. Now we're digging up our money so we can buy a schooner and set sail for the Islands. Wanna throw in with us?"

"I'll pass. Just the same, it'll be a good idea not to let Bay drive the getaway car." Mack's eyes raked Bay, taking in the sight of her grass-and-dirt-stained skirt before grinning. She still looked mad, and it was all he could do not to continue with his teasing.

"What are you saying, Mack?" She could not keep the exasperation out of her voice.

"I'm just saying that good driving sense was never a fault of yours, that's all."

An easy, playful breeze stirred the marsh grasses as the familiar scent of lavender and wild primroses blew up from Bay's temper-heated body. She smiled sweetly, then asked, "Can someone please tell me where I can find a voodoo priestess? I'm in bad need of one of those dolls they're famous for. Oh, and some pins ... *plenty* of *sharp* pins." Pulling beggar-lice off the hem of her skirt, she avoided his amused stare.

Henry Clay coughed, covering his laugh with his fist. "We heard something, thought it might be an alligator. Just keep an eye out. Now come on, Mack, breakfast is calling."

Hearing the rattle of a loose tailgate and the grind of gears, Mack turned his attention to the cove. "What do you suppose those two are doing?" Recognizing the truck, he motioned for Henry Clay to go on as he started walking toward the men.

"I'm going with you ... those are the sort of men you've got to walk upwind from even if there's no wind blowing," Henry Clay followed close on Mack's heels. "No tellin' what they're up to."

Bay spoke up. "I hired them to clean up the fallen branches near the cove and cut down a few dead trees that are blocking the view."

Mack stopped dead in his tracks and looked over his shoulder at her. "You *what*?" he asked incredulously. His lips grew thin, so thin they looked bloodless. He stared at her as if all the reasoning ability had suddenly drained out of her head.

Bay sneered; she could certainly do without his fatherly correction. "I hired them to help around here. We can't do it all, especially now that you're leaving. I'm taking the money out of the general fund you gave me. You told me to use my best judgment, didn't you?"

Frustrated, he ran a hand through his hair, making every effort to remain calm. "Bay, you've just hired two of the area's most notorious thieves and con artists! That's Shoob and Terrell Jackson. They kidnapped their last employer and forced her by knife point to withdraw money from an ATM! If their convictions weren't overturned on a technicality, they'd be in prison today!"

Bay was stunned. "I just thought …"

"Stay out of sight. I'll take care of this." Mack calmed slightly, trying to regain his control over the situation. Never in his life had he had so much trouble with one woman!

Shoob was unloading a chainsaw from his truck as Mack approached.

"That won't be necessary," Mack stated plainly. "We've made other plans."

Propping the chainsaw on the tailgate of the truck, Shoob eyed Mack hawkishly. "We was hired to do a job."

Mack nodded and pulled out his billfold. "Yes, I know, but we've had a change of plans. Here," he said, handing him two twenty-dollar bills. "Sorry for your trouble."

Shoob cut his eyes sharply at Mack, then Henry Clay. He had only gone a few feet when he paused and half-turned with a question. "Suppose the lady asks us to come back and help her again?"

Mack gave a tight smile and a brief warning. "She won't." The briefest of smiles curved his lips. "Next time I see you around here … I won't be as generous *or* as friendly."

"Just tryin' to help the lady out, that's all."

Without another word, Mack watched as Shoob passed his brother a twenty, cranked the truck, and pulled away, leaving a trail of dust behind.

Ezra sat back on his elbows and rested a minute, watching Mack as he headed toward the house. "Yeah … love don't make no sense at all. Sure can make a mess of a man's life. Cause him to worry himself to death."

"Who are you talking about?" Bay plopped down next to him, brushing away a few dead fern leaves from her clothes.

"Mack. My guess is he's fallen for someone who ain't his type at all … someone who has blindsided him when he was lookin' the other way. Now he's leavin', but his heart is stayin' … that'd be my guess."

"I keep forgetting. I'm in the presence of the one who *knows*," she muttered low, as if to herself. "But you're wrong about that one. He doesn't have much use for women at all."

"We'll see," he said, as a deep throaty laugh escaped him. "We'll see."

Chapter 26

Mack drew a deep breath and held it as he walked across the foyer to the dining room. Derlie stepped to the side, clearing a path for him. "What is Bay doing down at the bayou?"

"Whatever swamp fairies do on their day off," he answered flippantly, still annoyed with her. Then he saw concern on Derlie's face. "Ezra is with her … she's fine."

"Is that woman still here … your guest I mean?"

"If you mean Piper, no … she's gone back to New Orleans."

"Gone? Thank the good Lord. That woman can't get a good night's sleep unless she's made life miserable for somebody around here."

He counseled slowly, "You need to keep a closer check on your mouth, Derlie … it has a way of outrunning your mind most of the time."

She dismissed his comment with a wave of her hand, determined to say her piece. With Mack leaving, there was no guarantee he would return with the same mind as when he left. Piper had been spouting off to anyone who would listen long enough that she'd return to Briarleigh as Mrs. Mack Blackwell. She made no secret of the fact that she would pursue Mack, even if it meant keeping the road hot between New Orleans and Baton Rouge or camping out on his doorstep at every opportunity.

"*You're* the one who needs to keep a close check, and on more than just your mouth, if you know what I mean. And whatever you do, don't let anything *you* have outrun *your* mind either!" Satisfied that her meaning was not lost on him, Derlie slapped the swinging door open with both hands for emphasis and disappeared into the kitchen.

It took Mack less than a minute to decide to return to Briarleigh as soon as possible. Something just didn't seem right.

The long, warm days of summer shortened as the end of August grew near. The early morning was warming up quickly and a threat of storms loomed on the horizon. Small gusts of wind filtered through the screen door as Bay sat across from Henry Clay at the bar. In the days since Mack's departure, Bay's fondness for the old man had grown. In many ways, he reminded her of her own father. He was direct and sometimes harsh in his comments, but underneath it all, she saw kindness and love for all he valued.

She sought him out over matters concerning the inn or for his advice in dealing with Jace. The latter seemed to please him more than anything. On more than one occasion, she'd noticed his stature rise to full height when she'd approached him with a question pertaining to her son.

That particular morning, Bay sat quietly and listened in rapt attention as Henry Clay spoke of Mack and Shannon and their boyhood days. She listened with eagerness as he told about witnessing their mother's rejection of the boys firsthand and how each one handled that rejection differently. Mack declared he didn't need his mother while Shannon seemed to take it all in stride. With a shrug, Shannon would say, "The woman has issues."

Mack struggled with understanding his father's continued love and devotion to his wife. Even after she'd abandoned them, Jesse never stopped loving her.

Meeting Rudd England had been Mack's saving grace according to Henry Clay. At their first meeting, Mack declared to Rudd that he wasn't interested in having a family ... all he wanted to do was work.

Taken with Mack's frankness, Rudd pressed him to join up with his team of flight medics and go through all the necessary training and requirements. Rudd persuaded him, and Mack found a man he could respect. He was well-set in his loyalty to Rudd and his profession.

Sipping her coffee, Bay asked over her cup, "So, do you think Mack hates women ... because of his mother, I mean?"

"Hate? No, he loves the company of women ... now whether or not he'll ever trust one remains to be seen."

Though Bay made every effort to keep her mind on the business at hand; restlessness set in, and her attention was never very far from Mack.

Piper had come back to Briarleigh, insisting that she occupy Mack's room at his request. He was to join her there for the weekend.

Just after the morning crew began to arrive, Bay paused to listen as the familiar clicking steps of her mother came down the hall toward her office.

"Knock, knock ... may I come in?"

"Of course, have a seat." Closing her appointment book, Bay smiled up at her mother. "This place agrees with you, Mother. You look beautiful this morning."

"When I'm here, I feel nothing but a sense of safety and a kind of nurturing love ... it's home. But, at the same time, with all these strange happenings," she scanned her daughter's face before continuing, "Henry Clay is afraid someone is trying to hurt our business. We'd just feel better if you kept a careful eye on your surroundings."

Virginia Breckenridge Rutherford had never forbidden anyone over the age of twenty-one to do anything. She would find it too disrespectful and distasteful to do otherwise. And for that simple reason, Bay always heeded her advice.

"Come on, Mother. Let's go for a walk. I need some air."

A gentle wind ran through the trees, stirring the moss on the live oaks. Bay glanced at her mother, and, momentarily, it seemed that the essence of the place and her mother were one entity. Then without warning, the murmuring began, low and whispering. Virginia seemed somehow immune to the unquiet murmurings of the cove. They never disturbed her peace of mind.

Virginia slid her arm around her daughter's waist as they walked toward the cove. "I'm aware that it can get sort of ingrown here. Everybody is connected by birth, marriage, or circumstance. It's hard to find your place, but you will." She squeezed her daughter gently.

Bay gave a small, reluctant shrug. "I haven't helped matters. I do need to make an effort to get out more. Maundy wants me to take her to church on Sunday ... I think I will."

"Church is always a good idea, dear. I suggest the small community church on Old Verbena Road if you're interested. They need some fresh blood. The big church in town ... well, I can't see you fitting in there. You'd feel caught in the machine. The minute you walk in the door, they slap a nametag on you and shuffle you off to the age-appropriate room. You're enough like me that you'll not care for that one bit."

"Isn't that where the Blackwells go?"

"Yes, well ... that's just because they don't know any better," she answered, then winked. "One more thing, dear ... Henry Clay and I would like to take Jace to Disney World before school starts. This is something we want to do while we're still young enough to get around. We may get married while we're there, so don't be surprised if we do."

She cast her mother a quick glance, too stunned to respond. Virginia rushed on with her speech, unaware of the stress her words were having on her daughter.

"If we do ... we plan on moving into Mack's old room. Henry told me that Mack has hired a contractor to finish up over at his place. He's also having a rope bridge built to cross the cove and connect the properties. We're thinking he's planning to stay at his place from now on ... when he travels up."

Swallowing hard, Bay stared into the distance, trying to wrap her mind around this surprising turn of events. "Do you love him, Mother?"

Virginia hesitated, then explained in her customary dramatic way. "Just look at that." She pointed to the bayou water as it flowed from the cove out into the main channel of the majestic river. "The bayou water is deep and green and slow-moving. But look what happens when it meets the rush of the golden river. They come together, blending with each other and getting all stirred up into one harmonious mix. Blending requires several miles of side-by-side flowing together, but eventually they become one. So to answer your question ... yes, I've always loved Henry Clay Blackwell, just as much as I loved your father. Henry and I *blended* a very long time ago."

Bay raised an eyebrow, but let the question pass, not sure if she was prepared for the answer. "So, when would you like to leave for Disney World?"

"We want to leave today, if it's all right with you. Henry has asked Ezra to move into the smokehouse cabin while we're gone, and he's agreed. He knows you can handle the inn, but we'd ... *I'd* feel better with a man around the place just the same. He'll be here later on tonight."

The decisions of Henry Clay were usually accurate down to the nth degree. Bay had no doubt everything had been thought out and planned way in advance with every minute detail attended to.

"Are you sure you want Jace to tag along on your honeymoon?"

"Oh, for heaven's sake, Bay, the purpose of our trip is to spend time with Jace. Henry Clay wants to make up for lost time with his grandson. We'll have plenty of time for ... all of that later."

Bay clasped her mother's hand tightly. "I want you to know ... I approve. Henry Clay is a fine man, and he's extremely blessed to have you."

With her family well on their way to Disney World, Bay decided noon was a good time to pay a visit to their neighbor, Versidy Williams.

"Maundy ... fix a basket for our neighbor Mrs. Williams, and let's go pay our respects."

They got in the car, and Bay turned the key in the ignition ... nothing. After several tries, she finally gave up. "I'll call a mechanic."

After being told it could take an hour or so for the mechanic to arrive, Bay and Maundy decided they could walk to Mrs. Williams's house and get back before he got there. They entered the kitchen to tell Derlie of their plans.

Derlie glanced around from her work and announced, "We've got large cat-head biscuits and molasses, fresh salad dressings for a nice leafy salad, squash, meatloaf, and a piping hot chocolate sheet cake cooling on the counter. So, whatever you're up to ... it'd better wait until after supper." She looked at them suspiciously, raising her brow.

Maundy looked shamefaced and wouldn't look the woman in the eye.

"Looks like we've got plenty to eat … do you think we could squeeze out another plate for our neighbor, Mrs. Williams?"

"Why, of course! Why didn't you tell me that's what you're up to? Hang on and let me pack it up real nice. That poor woman needs all the help she can get."

Bay winked at Maundy behind Derlie's back, and the girl grabbed her mouth to catch her giggle.

"Here, now go on before it gets dark." Derlie smoothed her apron in a quick fashion before turning back to the stove. "I'll tend to the guests and get a tray to Mr. Benton. Now run on."

"Oh … one more thing, I've called a mechanic to look at my car. It won't start. We should get back before he gets here, but if we aren't …"

"Here," Derlie said, crossing the kitchen to the pantry. She lifted her purse from the hook inside the door. "Take my car."

As soon as Bay climbed into the seat, she groaned. "A stick shift."

Maundy glanced at her apprehensively.

"It's all right … I can drive it. It's just been a while."

After cranking the car, she eased off the clutch and accelerated a little too fast, causing the car to jerk forward and stall. "Hold on … it may take some getting used to, but I'll get the hang of it."

Maundy's terror-stricken eyes fastened on Bay as they lurched down the road. Finally, after many failed attempts, Bay found the rhythm of the vehicle. Maundy relaxed her white-knuckled fingers, releasing her hold on the seat and eased back with a sigh of relief.

The Williams's home was at the edge of Sugar Land, a good distance before rows of streetlamp-lit houses and tree-lined sidewalks created a path toward town.

As they pulled into the drive, a dog barked a warning to anyone inside that strangers were near. Just then, the door opened and out stepped a woman in, of all things, a royal blue box dress reminiscent of the Kennedy era. Her hairstyle looked as if she'd apparently chosen it for life in the early sixties. It was flipped out at the ends just above the shoulders and wrapped with a scarf tied around her head and knotted just behind her ear. The woman glared at them from the doorway with a hand fastened tightly on her hip.

"Come on, we can do this," Bay said, as much to herself as to Maundy.

Bay scanned the yard looking for the dog that broadcasted their arrival and felt relieved after spotting it inside a fence.

"Good afternoon, Mrs. Williams," Bay said politely.

"It's evening," Mrs. Williams corrected aloofly, not yet ready to receive them. "And it's a little late to be out selling, don't you think?"

"We're not selling anything; we're your neighbors, from Briarleigh. I'm Bay Rutherford, Virginia *Breckenridge* Rutherford's daughter, and this is Maundy. We heard about your recent loss and just wanted to pay our respects. We brought a plate from our cook, and Maundy made some pecan bars for you. Ezra Perkins said to be sure and tell you hello."

Mrs. Williams stepped away quickly, vanishing inside the dark house, not giving them an opportunity to say anything else. Bay turned to Maundy and shrugged. Just as they were about to leave, Mrs. Williams came back to the door.

"Won't you please come in?" she said politely.

Chapter 27

*D*usk had deepened over the land, and the sky to the west was painted softly in muted shades of melon and pink as Bay and Maundy made their way back to Briarleigh. Noticing Maundy's sudden change in demeanor, Bay's mind filled with questions.

"Did you enjoy the visit with Mrs. Williams?" Bay's eyes looked over the girl briefly, before turning back to the road.

Worry drew Maundy's brows together. "She's lonely, near to the bone I'd say."

"Yeah … I think so, too."

"Maundy, if you don't mind my asking," she approached the subject hesitantly. "Why was it so important for you to visit Mrs. Williams?"

"Cause I've been lonely … and Jesus wants me to love people the way I want to be loved. He also wants me to remember his sacrifice … the covenant sealed with his blood, and make sure people know about it, too. That's what *Maundy* means. Ezra told me … and those murmurs told me, too."

For the first time, Bay saw the raw pain in the young girl, and her heart ached. "Well, Ezra would certainly know about that." She glanced at Maundy and questioned, "Do the murmurs frighten you?"

"Not after Ezra explained them to me. He knew what they said to me."

"Oh? What did *he* say they said?"

"Lay aside the garments that are stained with sin,
And be washed in the blood of the Lamb;
There's a fountain flowing for the soul unclean,
Oh, be washed in the blood of the Lamb.
Are you washed in the blood
In the soul-cleansing blood of the Lamb
Are your garments spotless, are they white as snow
Are you washed in the blood of the Lamb?"

The moment Maundy began the song, Bay recognized it. "Yes ... I know that song. That's an old hymn. And that's what you heard from the murmurs?"

"I couldn't quite make it out, so I asked Ezra, and he listened and told me what he thought the murmurs were saying."

Bay shook her head slowly, knowing she had someone watching her reaction. "If you still want to go to church on Sunday, I'd like to go to a little community church on Old Verbena Road. My mother recommends it ... how does that sound?"

"Yes, ma'am," Maundy agreed. "I've never been to a ..." she let the sentence drop.

"To a what?"

"To a place where God lives … a church."

"You can't put God in a specific place, Maundy. He's everywhere. But if his people are there, even just two or three, he'll be there, too. That's what his Word says."

"I want to be a healer and soothe people's hurts," Maundy announced and trained her eyes on Bay intently, as if taking her full measure. "My grandfather was a traiteur, and I'm going to ask God if I can be one, too. Grandfather asked me to take his gift 'cause he's getting old. At the time, I didn't know if I wanted it. Now I know I do. I called him and told him I wanted it, and he prayed with me over the phone."

"Is that why you want to go to church … to ask God for something?" Bay didn't know what a traiteur was, but she assumed it had something to do with treating sickness.

Maundy nodded.

Taking into account the young woman's ill-fated upbringing, Bay wasn't surprised by the unconventional request. She only hoped she wasn't referring to some type of black magic. She'd heard of snake handlers and such, but never of traiteurs.

"Maundy, you don't have to go to a church to speak with God. You can talk to him right where you sit. Church is good for connecting with other believers and hearing God's words, serving, and worshipping, but you always have access to God. Jesus took care of that for you on the cross."

But before Bay could comment further, Maundy pointed and called out, "The mechanic is here … and so is Mr. Blackwell."

With her heartbeat quickening, Bay scanned the grounds, but there was no sign of Mack. Disappointed, she parked the car and got out, making her way to the mechanic who backed away from the raised hood and straightened, waiting for her with a ready smile.

The mechanic lazily wiped his hand on his shirt before extending it. "Ma'am … I'm Justain Lemelle. Is this your car?"

Bay took his hand and shook it firmly. "Yes … I'm Bay Rutherford. Thank you for coming out so quickly."

Justain was a kind-faced, rumpled young man who had the ability to make slouchy look sexy. His hands seemed permanently stained with grease. From the conversation Bay had had with Justain's boss, the boy worked on nearly everything in Sugar Land bearing a motor. His warm and open smile put you at ease almost immediately.

"Oh, this is Maundy," Bay explained, turning to bring the girl into the conversation.

Maundy smiled tightly and glanced away.

"Sure is nice to meet you ladies … wish I had better news for you, though. Look here." He walked back to the car and leaned over the motor and pointed out the severed battery cable wires for their inspection. "Cut them suckers so low it took me forever to find out they'd been cut. If you just looked at them, you'd never know anything was wrong. But I tugged on one, and it came lose at the cut." He scratched his head under his cap, as if expecting an explanation to pop into his head as the result of the effort.

Bay examined the wires. "Who would do such a thing?"

Justain shrugged, "Don't rightly know, ma'am … but I'll fix you up in the morning, early as I can."

Baffled by the evidence that someone tampered with her car, Bay could only nod.

"Ma'am, I sure hate that this has happened to you. Some mighty strange things have been goin' on around Sugar Land lately … seen more strangers in town than I ever seen before."

"Really … well, do you know what they're doing here?"

"It's kinda silly if you ask me … but this one fella was goin' around sayin' he'd been staying out here at the inn until he saw a ghost. Said she was blockin' his way up the stairs, and she was beautiful and looked kinda milky and wavy. He said he could look straight through her to the stairs. Then the weird part, he said a voice spoke inside his head and told him to leave the house. He said he'd learned never to come between an apparition, and the house she was haunting."

"What did this man look like?"

"Fancy sort … like the kind of guy that has his hair and fingernails done up at the beauty parlor." He spread his hands in a helpless gesture. "But, hey, that's just me talking. I sure ain't judging the man."

"Well, thank you for coming out, Mr. Lemelle. What do I owe you?"

"You can pay me tomorrow, ma'am, once I fix it. And I'm just plain ole Justain." His smile turned to a grimace as he rubbed his shoulder before picking up his tool box.

Maundy eased over to him quietly, almost without notice.

Bay half-turned to look at the girl curiously before going into the house. Still pondering Maundy's odd behavior, she stepped through the kitchen door in time to hear Mack's clear voice coming from the bedroom.

"When I said you could stay in my room, I didn't mean I'd be staying with you. I'm staying over at my house now. Sorry for the misunderstanding … but that's how it is."

Bay's jaw dropped to the floor. Then she heard Piper respond.

"What is going on here, Mack? Is there someone else? You never used to turn me down."

"People change, Piper. I'm not who I was."

"Are you telling me you're *gay* … or some *religious fanatic*?" Piper questioned, caustically. "Does that little scar-faced girl have anything to do with this? Or is this how you're punishing me for marrying someone besides you?"

Dismayed, Bay stepped back to the door hoping to get away undetected, but before she could make her escape, she heard Mack's remark. "It's clear from the tantrum you're throwing that you're not used to being turned down. Maybe it'll do you some good, Piper. Call it character-building. Now get dressed. I'll drive you over to the house so you can see that I'm not harboring a harem over there."

Sensing that Mack was about to leave the room, Bay quickly went out the door and fled to the safety of her office. Passing by the window, she noticed Justain's work truck through the sheer drapes.

Easing the curtain back, she observed Maundy and Justain engaged in some bizarre ritual. Maundy was tying something that looked like a knotted string around the mechanic's shoulder.

"Have you no shame?" Mack accused, grinning from the doorway.

Bay jumped back, dropping the curtain. "You scared me to death!" she scolded, holding her hand hard against the pounding in her chest.

"Who are you spying on?" he asked, stepping over to the window and pulling back the curtain.

"Please tell me what they're doing is not voodoo?"

Mack responded in a more serious tone. "No, it looks like Maundy is a traiteur."

"And what, might I ask, is *that*?"

"A faith healer, basically," he shrugged casually, as if it were just that simple.

"And *you* of all people are okay with that?

"Doctor's visits are rare in some of our rural communities, so I have to negotiate the gaps between biomedicine and faith healing all the time in my profession. *Traiteur* means "treater." They treat things like snakebites, warts, sunstroke, aches and pains, nerves, earaches … that sort of thing."

"And you believe they can cure people?"

"Faith in God's power to heal is at the heart of the practice. I believe *God* can heal. Whether or not *I* believe in the practice is really not important — *they* believe. Most use a lot of herbal remedies, the laying on of hands … strings. But all use prayer. You're never supposed to thank a traiteur or the treatment won't work. You can give them a gift, but never money. The traiteur is interested in the nature of the suffering, not the nature of the disease. Does that make sense?"

Bay nodded, then peered out the window again. "Maundy told me she wanted to be a traiteur … said her grandfather passed the gift to her. I guess she thought she'd try it out on Justain."

"The gift is usually passed down from an older traiteur to a younger person, often in the same family. The practice is dying out in some areas, growing stronger in others, and it's been around for a long time."

The click of Piper's sharp heels could be heard coming from the foyer. "There you are." She came up to Mack and rubbed a familiar hand down his arm. "See, it didn't take all that long to get my clothes back on."

Mack met her gaze without any warmth and replied dryly, "You do have a way with words, Piper."

Bay went to the desk and snapped the laptop closed, grabbed her purse, and moved past them. "If you don't mind, just lock my office door on your way out."

With a last smug look, Piper turned to Bay and said, "I sent Derlie to the woods to pick berries … when she comes back, tell her never mind about the pie. Mack and I are going to his place." She tossed her head arrogantly, smiling up at Mack. "I'd rather have you than pie any day."

Of all the audacity, sending Derlie away to do her bidding! Bay fumed. "As it's been explained to you before, we don't have servants here. The next time you want or need anything, you ask me. After today, none of the employees of Briarleigh will act as your personal attendant, and they'll come to me with whatever you request. Do I make myself perfectly clear?"

Piper squinted and thinned her lips. "Are you so simple that you've forgotten who owns this place?" She tossed her head and adjusted her shoulders. "Mack, tell her she has no authority here."

Showing not the slightest inclination to obey Piper, Mack grinned. "Ah, but you're wrong. Bay has been given full authority here. In fact, she decides who stays and who goes. So if I were you, I'd try harder to be more ... agreeable."

Responding with honeyed words, Bay gave a gentle reply. "Relax ... I could never ask you to leave and disrupt such a blissful union."

Bay was the greatest stumbling block Mack had ever known to his peace of mind. With a casual line or two, she could level him. She met his scowl head on. Neither one yielded until finally Piper spoke up.

"We should go, Mack. I want to see your place before it gets too dark."

Finding no other excuse, Mack led Piper to the front door. Before reaching for the knob, he turned and asked, "If you're having car trouble, I'd be glad to look at it for you."

"Thanks, but don't trouble yourself. It's nothing Justain can't fix." There was no way she was going to give them the satisfaction of knowing someone had tampered with her car.

As they left the house, she moved again to the window and peered through the sheer curtains. Mack motioned for Piper to get in the car. Left alone with Justain, he turned to him with a question in his eyes. As the mechanic began his story, Bay was startled to find the ice-green eyes fixed on her, penetrating the sheer curtain. The intense way he looked at her made her shiver. It seemed his scowl deepened as Justain talked on. She knew what was being relayed to him, but never would she have imagined his distress over it. Finally, he shook Justain's hand, got into the driver's seat of the Lexus, and drove off.

Chapter 28

A river breeze moved across the moonless, blindfold-dark night, lightly stirring the trees. There was a sleepy stillness around the inn. A few dim lights shone from cottage windows and rooms, and beneath the sighing wind, all appeared to be well.

Bay crossed the yard toward the back door of Briarleigh, her slippers slapping loosely at her heels. Disturbed by the events of the day, she'd unsuccessfully fought her premonitions. Sleep eluded her as apprehension mounted. Going inside to her office, she wondered, *Why would someone want to disable my car?*

When headlights flashed across the office wall, Bay turned to see the silver Lexus turning up the lane leading to Briarleigh. She realized that Mack and Piper soon would be coming in the door. Getting up from the desk, she shut off the computer and turned off the lamp.

Making her way across the foyer to the darkened library, she slid onto the cool leather of the couch, tucking a soft pillow under her head. At once, she was reminded by the lingering fragrance on the pillow that Mack used this room as his office.

That same pleasant but elusive scent comforted her now as it had the night she'd slept in his bed. She had no intention of sleeping alone in her cottage. At least there were other people in this house.

Daring no movement, she waited, listening as the front door opened and closed. The sound of Piper's sharp heels clicked across the wooden floor, disappearing into the kitchen. Then she heard Mack's bedroom door shut.

Where is Mack? she wondered. Then it occurred to her. *He must have gone back to his house.*

Satisfied with the answer, she hugged the pillow tightly against her body and drifted off to sleep.

When Bay woke, she opened her heavy lids without moving. The room was still and quiet; a mild panic grew as she failed to recognize her surroundings. Raising her head off the pillow, she saw Mack at his desk reading something on the computer screen. Patting herself lightly, she realized a cover had been draped over her, nearly covering her. Turning her attention again to Mack, she wondered if he'd even noticed she was in the room, engrossed in his work as he seemed. She might have been part of the couch for as much attention as he paid her. She watched him quietly, thinking of her options and debating whether or not to try to slip out of the room unnoticed.

"Sleep well?" he asked suddenly and found her eyes fixed on him. He rose from the desk and lifted the chair with one hand, setting it down in front of Bay.

She sat up, clutching the cover close to her chest as her light brown hair fell in disarray around her shoulders. Her eyes traveled up and found Mack's stern expression fastened on her. There was a tense, almost angry look to his jaw line. She watched his cheek flex, as if clenching his teeth somehow restrained him.

"I believe, Bay," he began with a disapproving frown, "that you either have a bent toward self-destruction … or you're somehow testing my response time. Which is it?"

Each moment that passed was longer than the moment before as Bay weighed her words. Finally she said, "I apologize for intruding into your office space … but I wasn't comfortable sleeping alone in my cottage."

For a moment, he looked at her with some surprise. "You think I'm upset because you slept in my office? You don't mesh well with me, do you? I spent half the night searching for you. When we got back last night, I went straight to your cottage to check on you. No one answered the door, so I used my key and went in. After *not* finding you inside, I turned this place upside down until I finally found you here. Luckily, this was the eighth place I looked or else I'd have disturbed every guest here. Did it never occur to you that whoever did that to your car could just as easily be in this house? That you may have been safer in your cottage?"

She had not thought of this … or that he would be so concerned for her safety. She felt warmth begin to grow inside her. Looking to the spot beside him, she noticed a gun sitting on the corner of the desk. "Do you expect trouble?" She sat up straighter, waiting for an answer.

He glanced back, seeing the gun on his desk. "It's just a precaution. I'm not at ease with what's happening around here. It doesn't make sense ... why someone would tamper with your car. I always try to adapt to the circumstances. I have a gun and a license for it. This one," he gestured to the desk, "is for you." He took note of her reaction. "Have you ever fired a weapon?"

"Yes ... my father taught me how to shoot a rifle, but I've never used a pistol."

"I'll teach you ... it'll be a good idea to start right away." He didn't want to scare her, but something was up. Someone had deliberately disabled her car.

"My car is not all that new ... do you think those wires could've just snapped?"

Mack shook his head, "Clean cuts, all of them."

"Oh ... well, I don't really know too much about cars. This is only the third vehicle I've ever owned. "

"Really?" Amusement softened the sarcastic edge of his voice.

Not knowing why, she began explaining her limited experience with cars. "Of course, you saw what happened to my first car. I smashed it up pretty good on the bridge railing. The car I had before this one was basically rust, had to be started with a screwdriver, and leaked exhaust so badly that you had to drive around with the windows down, even in winter. The door was held shut by a clothes hanger which, fortunately, also acted as an antenna for the radio. You could see the ground under the brake pedal, and the passenger seat was a five-gallon bucket."

There was something about Bay Rutherford that totally amused and intrigued him. He found himself almost mesmerized as he watched her movements and listened to her soft voice. He had the distinct feeling that she could've been talking about gutting a fish and he would have found it equally fascinating. But there was something else, too. She seemed both confident and coolly put together, vulnerable and in need of protecting. And, for some odd reason, he found the combination mighty appealing.

"What, pray tell, happened to your car?"

"Nothing … I bought it that way. I guess you could say that I was financially embarrassed at the time, to quote Charlie Brown."

He commented, before getting up. "Guess that's why you didn't seem to mind the decorative strip of duct tape on the seat of my truck."

"Nah, just adds character."

"Come on, we'd better clear out of here before people start stirring."

Soon guests would be arriving in the common room, reading the Sunday paper as they waited for breakfast. Mack knew Bay would prefer not to be caught coming out of his office first thing in the morning with mussed hair. Following her through the library door, he suddenly halted to keep from plowing into her back.

Bay froze as Crawford brushed passed in a hurry, buttoning his shirt. Catching Bay in his peripheral vision, he stopped and turned to see her standing in the doorway.

"Well … isn't this a cozy sight?" Piper commented, stepping into view. She slowly raked Bay with her eyes, taking in the disheveled hair and crumpled clothes. "Poor timing. It looks like we got in the way of your little escape."

"Escape, Piper?" Mack moved in front of Bay. "So what do you call what you were doing?" He directed his gaze to Crawford. "Inspiring the writer?"

Piper rushed on to explain. "Crawford came to me this morning wanting to know if we'd found Bay. He was so concerned; he was half-dressed when he knocked on my door. He said that you were out looking for her last night, and he was worried. But see," she turned to Crawford, "you had nothing to fear. She's been with Mack all night."

Since Crawford's arrival at Briarleigh, he had not ventured often from his cottage, though from time to time he'd sought out Bay when the mood for female companionship struck him. This was not unusual behavior for the man. Obviously, he'd just met someone willing to take him up on his offer last night.

The idea of going to Crawford's cottage had nibbled at Bay's thoughts occasionally, especially when she felt lonely. However, her overriding fears were that she would go as far with him as she'd gone before, a fear that usually put to death her meandering thoughts.

"I can see that you're both happy that Bay is safe and sound," Mack stated, sarcastically. "Although I think I've seen better smiles on a plate full of steaming clams."

Mack stepped aside to allow the now-anxious Bay to pass and make her way to her cottage. She glanced briefly at Crawford, noticing his unusual expression, then hurried out, ready to put some distance between them.

"I thought you'd be relieved to know that Bay is safe. Especially since someone on this property," he emphasized, "sabotaged her car!"

Crawford spoke up. "Ah ... well, as long as I've known Bay, she has always managed to land on her feet. I never worry about her too much. She's strong enough to handle most things. I have all the confidence in the world in her."

Mack's jaw clenched tightly before he chose to reply. This guy didn't appear to be the slightest bit interested in Bay's welfare, and the apathy angered him. He forced a smile, but the air of danger about him spoke louder than the grin on his face. "Confidence? Or is it lack of concern? Sometimes it's hard to tell the difference between the two." The longer Mack stood there, the angrier he got. "Don't let me hold you up. You seem to be in a hurry to leave."

Piper stared at Mack, terrified that her lack of discretion may have cost her the only thing she wanted. Oh, she'd wanted Crawford for a night. He had the ability to enjoy the moment and not make too much out of it. She thought she needed that, and now it may have cost her everything.

Chapter 29

*T*he morning air hung motionless over the kitchen garden as sweat trickled a slow path down Mack's forehead. As the sweltering heat rose from the ground, he wiped his brow with the back of his arm, understanding for the first time the therapeutic value of manual labor. "Let's take a break," he suggested.

Bay straightened, slapping her hands together to remove the dirt. "Good idea." She snatched up a handful of weeds and tossed them into the small brush fire burning near the outer edge of the garden.

Mack crumpled a paper and pitched it into the fire. With no regrets and a certain amount of satisfaction, he watched the richly-embossed stationery writhe briefly, then vanish into smoke, just as he'd watched the trail of dust disappear behind the silver Lexus only an hour earlier.

Finding a seat on the back porch, Mack dropped his weight into the chair and let out a deep breath. There was peace and an almost domestic tranquility between them, the likes of which he'd never experienced.

Bay commented, "Thanks for helping me with the garden. With everything going on lately, I'd just about decided to give it up and let the wildlife have it."

"Well … it'll cost you. I've told you before — I don't work for free."

Derlie raised a surprised brow as she came out onto the porch, overhearing the comment. Taking a cold glass of orange juice from Derlie's hand, Bay couldn't help but smile as she noticed the gleam in the woman's eye.

"Thank you, Derlie," she said sweetly, knowing the woman was nosy and curious. "So, Mack, what do you have in mind?"

"A trade off."

Derlie widened her eyes behind Mack's head as she looked at Bay. Dynamite would not have removed her from the spot.

Bay raised a single eyebrow and hesitated, mid-sip, while waiting for him to continue.

Twisting his lips to keep his grin in check, Mack knew by the way Bay's eyes kept moving above his head that Derlie was hanging on every word. "I need help with the kitchen over at my place. It still has an old roll-top refrigerator and this knotty-pine dark paneling. It's my least favorite room in the house. I'm not sure what to do with it."

The slap of the screen door sounded as Derlie went back inside, apparently disappointed with his answer. Bay covered her grin by blotting her mouth with her fist. "I'll be happy to help."

Crawford Benton walked up carrying an over-the-shoulder bag and two suitcases. As he approached, he set the suitcases on the ground and would not meet Bay's eyes but only examined the back of his fingers. "Well, Bay Larke ... I really must be going ... but ..."

"Okay, looks like you have everything." Mack hurried him along by getting up and grabbing his suitcases. There was no way he was going to sit another minute and look at the arrogant, self-centered man. Crawford and Piper had denied any involvement with each other, but Mack was no fool. It further annoyed him that Bay seemed to be sad at Crawford's leaving. For her to even give the man the time of day was way more than he deserved, to Mack's way of thinking.

"You'll be missed, Crawford. Please know that you're welcome here anytime." Bay got up, walked down to him, and gave him a light hug.

Crawford whispered low, "And you should know, sweet Bay, that I'm always available to you, wherever I may be."

Mack thought he just might get sick. It took all the self-control he could muster not to tell the guy exactly what he thought of him. "Here, let me take that shoulder bag for you," he offered, grateful for the chance to hurry the man up and send him on his way.

Releasing the bag, Crawford handed it to Mack. "I'll only be a minute. I'd like a word in *private* with Bay."

"I'd like an *action* in private with you," he mumbled under his breath. Hearing a latch loosen, he noticed the trunk of Crawford's car pop up. "Mighty considerate of you," Mack said, fuming silently. It dawned on him that it hadn't bothered him half as much to think of the guy with Piper as it bothered him now, watching him in the open daylight with Bay. Tossing the luggage roughly into the trunk of the man's car, he turned to see Crawford tucking a piece of Bay's hair behind her ear. Abruptly slamming the trunk shut, Mack threw up a hand as both Crawford and Bay turned to look at him. "All set."

Crawford looked reluctant to leave. Suddenly he grabbed Bay's hand and planted a lingering kiss in her palm. He turned in a dramatic fashion and strode toward his car. Passing Mack, he instructed, "Take care of our girl."

"Which one?" he replied, never stopping to wait on an answer.

As Crawford drove off, Mack commented to Bay. "You might want to wash that hand."

Bay let the remark pass. She understood Mack's reasons and doubts about what may have happened between Piper and Crawford, and she really couldn't offer any reassurance. Where women were concerned, Crawford definitely had a weakness.

"I'm headed for the shower," Bay said, reluctantly. "I'd better get cleaned up before I go to church. We're going to the church on the Old Verbena Road."

"You sound excited."

"I'm dreading it, actually." Her voice took on a note of apprehension. "I'd just as soon avoid the place, but I promised Maundy."

Mack folded his arms in front of him and struggled to contain a confused smile at her blunt statement. "Why do you want to avoid church?"

Bay waved her hand in the air, dismissing his question. "It's not that. I just want more, that's all."

"More what?" he asked, trying hard to make sense of her words.

"Intimacy."

Mack cleared his throat. "I'm sure Crawford would have supplied plenty of that for you if you'd asked."

Bay gave a petulant toss of her head. "What happened between … us was not what I'd consider 'intimacy.' But, it taught me what I *don't* want in a relationship."

"What's that?"

"Shallowness," Bay said. She noticed his uneasy, almost imperceptible glance before he looked away, making her want to continue. "This world is no friend to intimacy and would seem to prefer we keep our love for God to a set, ritualized hour on Sunday morning and our love for another to an act of sex. I, for one, don't intend to settle by reducing love to lust or faith to ritual.. That's what I want—the freedom to love and be fully loved, at all times. And no matter how many times I'm told to behave myself and play along with the game, I won't. I'm not talking about a simple 'Jesus loves me' kind of awareness either. I'm talking about experiencing a love for him and whomever else in the depths of my soul!"

Mack backed around to lean against a post, observing her curiously as he weighed her words.

"Seems to me that you're asking a lot. I get the sense that you've been hurt by church somewhere along the way."

Bay's mild expression shifted to one of sadness. "Try breaking the rules of the game and see how far you get. I showed up at church with a baby, out of wedlock."

His green eyes narrowed in confusion. "But you adopted your son."

"Yeah, well … if my baby *had* lived, I would've been in that same circumstance. I refuse to play the part of an innocent or allow my child's death to be an advantage to me. I'm my child's mother just the same, whether my baby lives on earth or in heaven. To me, it's all the same. I was at church seeking love and acceptance from God's people. Not acceptance of my sin, but forgiveness for it. And I know that no matter what I've done, God forgives me. He forgave me the moment I asked, but clearly those people haven't. Oh, if I'd played along with their games and told them my son had been adopted and kept the knowledge of my other child to myself, everything would've been fine. I was not the only sinner in church that day. They played their parts well and didn't rock the boat by being honest about it. Turning from their sins never entered their silly minds. Just keep up the pretense, keep up appearances. I can't do that … I won't do that … and in the church, of all places, I shouldn't *have* to do that!" Feeling suddenly embarrassed by her unchecked passion, Bay turned away. "I'd better get dressed for church."

Mack was at a loss for words as he watched Bay's retreating form head down the path. After hearing all of that, he began to feel the shallowness of his own spiritual life. He had a vague, unfocused approach to all things spiritual. Over the years, he'd grown used to his sins, imagining that maybe they weren't so bad. He allowed them to sort of free-float over his life so he didn't have to name them. An image of his mother came into his mind and, just like so many times before, he forced it out and barred the door. Try as he might, he couldn't shake the nagging feeling that God seemed to have used another method of zeroing in on a truth, a truth that lay dormant at the bottom of a heart that refused to forgive.

The truck wound around a narrow curve on the back road, then it left the pavement and took the dirt path that led to the old church building. Halting behind a sheltering clump of cedars, Mack hesitated, staring at the white plank church for several long moments before deciding to step out of the truck.

A stout, rather muscular man held the door for Mack as he stomped up the wooden steps to enter the church. He'd never been inside before, but expected the inside to reflect the outside—dreary and boring.

"Come in ... come in, and welcome." The man flashed a ready smile as he extended his hand.

The guy was not what Mack had expected to find passing out bulletins at the church door. He'd seen longshoremen back down from the look of men like him. Genuinely surprised, Mack was even a little mystified by the encounter. "Thank you," Mack said, taking the man's hand in a firm grip.

Glancing inside the church, he caught a glimpse of Bay through the glass square of the interior door. She was crossing the aisle to her seat, dressed in a pale cream, airy dress that flowed just above her knees. Feminine and delicate, she looked soft all over. He could hardly introduce himself to the door greeter for staring at her. Pulling his attention back to the man who still gripped his hand, he stated his name. "Blackwell, Mack Blackwell."

The look on the stout man's face turned to surprise. "Jesse Blackwell's son?"

Mack nodded. "You know my father?"

The lines around his mouth deepened. "Very well ... he's been my mentor for a few years now."

Mack cocked an eye. "Mentor?"

A low laugh bubbled to the surface. "Yeah ... well, I've worn him out over the years ... but I sure do miss having him around. We still talk, online mostly, but it's just not the same. I hope he and your mother are doing well."

Mack peered into the man's eyes, his own narrowed suspiciously. "I didn't catch your name?"

"Oh ... sorry, I'm Sage Davidson. You know, they just don't make men like your dad anymore. Jesse Blackwell is reckless with desire to get his family back. We'd all do well to be like that."

Before Mack could ask anything else, Ezra walked toward him from the sanctuary. "Should I call the deacons to hold up the walls in case the roof gives way?" Slapping a hand on Mack's shoulder, the old man grinned.

Mack laughed lightly. "Might not be a bad idea, considering."

Ezra met Mack's gaze with a calm and deliberate stare. "So, did you hear I was speaking today ... is that why you're here?"

Shifting his eyes over Ezra's shoulder, he concentrated on the small, trim figure of Bay as she whispered to Maundy. "No ... actually, I didn't even know you preached." He looked again to the man. "But it doesn't surprise me. Why didn't you tell me?"

"'Cause there's nothing to tell. Our pastor was called away last night, and I'm just filling in. You'll have to come back when he's here. Try not to allow my feeble attempts at preaching to keep you from coming back." He grinned and waved his hand in the direction of the sanctuary. "Go right in and have a seat."

Mack slid onto a hard wooden pew in the back of the church. Occasionally, someone would turn to him, smile and nod, but mostly everyone seemed occupied with prayer or reading from their Bibles. More than a few times, Mack's eyes fell on Bay. He watched with keen interest as she bowed and clasped her small hands in prayer. The image was soothing to him, and he looked away only when someone blocked his view of her.

As he sat there in the quiet, something popped into his mind. The scene was a small one from many years ago, but he could see it clearly in his mind. It was a summer day, and he remembered being plunged down under the water and coming up smiling, wiping the wetness away from his beaming face. Reliving that moment, he paused, wondering what had happened to the one who, at one time, had had such an excellent start. Life, it seemed, had grown more complicated since that day he'd been doused with baptismal water.

The service began with a hymn, and everyone stood to their feet, followed by another, then another until Mack began to grow nervous and impatient. Looking around, he saw a mixture of races and the thought crossed his mind, *Is this one of those churches where service lasts all day?*

Just when he was about to grow uneasy, Ezra stepped to the pulpit. Without any introduction or fanfare, he began speaking.

"Everything ... absolutely everything takes place on sacred and holy ground. Your job, your relationships, even your entertainment ... they all take place on holy ground. You can't separate things into secular and sacred ... there is no such thing. All of life is sacred. We want to set aside a special time for God, usually on Sunday morning. And that frees us up to have the rest of the time for ourselves. We think that God will wait quietly in the wings until we return to him the next Sunday and honor him with our so-called devotion. What I intend to do this morning is haul you by the ear and unceremoniously thrust you to the foot of the throne of God. There you'll see how utterly immense and staggering it is to behold a holy and perfect God. To find ourselves loved by such a God is far too large a thought to fit into our simple minds. But, *we* must fit into him and receive his love in the person of Jesus. Now, how do we do that? First, we must shake off the small-minded notion that God can be contained. He is good and intends our salvation, and his mercy is our own to receive. The combination of graces is as unique as we are. No one is beyond his grace, but you must receive his son. And when the son sets you free, you'll be free indeed! Why do you think sinners like prostitutes ran toward Jesus, and not away from Him? Because the worse a person feels about himself, the more likely he'll see Jesus as a rescuer. Remember now, we're all products of God's grace, but don't you ever forget how much it cost. Grace is free, but it certainly is not cheap. The giver Himself paid the cost. And, that's just plain shocking if you ask me."

Glancing around, Mack noticed something. Most people were leaning forward, hanging on to every word. Hope had been ignited. Turning his attention back to Ezra, he listened attentively, caught in the sweep of the message.

As the message came to a conclusion, Mack glanced at his watch, surprised to realize he'd been there for hours and had all but forgotten the time. He felt as if the hard soil of his heart had just been run over with the sharp blade of a plow.

As they were dismissed, Bay stepped out from the pew and looked up, stopping suddenly as she saw Mack standing at the back of the church with his eyes locked on her. She smiled, somehow overjoyed to learn that they'd shared the same message. But before she could reach him, a woman approached him with a warm smile and an extended hand, pulling his attention away. Bay slipped past him with Maundy behind her, and they left the church.

Chapter 30

"Mother?" Mack's voice was low and smooth as he tried to disguise the raw emotion threatening to choke off his words. He leaned over his mother, searching her eyes for any hint of recognition.

Leala Blackwell lay on the hospital bed with wide and sad eyes as she studied her son's face for a long moment. The corners of her soft mouth quivered as she fought against the same feelings of grief she always felt in his presence. Light strands of gray mingled with her raven-dark hair. She was quiet, dark, and secluded, just like a moonless night.

Leala's heart was full of secrets, too many for one person to contain. She remembered back to the time when she'd watched her son from the rearview mirror as he ran after her car, crying and begging her not to leave. It had been summer, and once she'd gone far enough away from the house she'd stopped on the gravel road, too blinded by tears to continue. Stumbling out of the car, she'd fallen, the gravel biting into her knees while she sobbed until she was spent.

Mack turned to his father. "How long has she been like this?"

Pain twisted Jesse's face as he led Mack out into the hall. He held his fisted hand close to his lips as he spoke, shaking his head. "There's no reason for it. Her heart is strong, and she hasn't had a stroke … arteries are all good. The doctor is dumbfounded. She's unresponsive … it's like she's just given up on life. Medically, it's unexplainable."

Mack had never seen his father so distraught and, to his recollection, these were the first tears he'd ever seen the strong man shed in all his life. The grief he saw on his father's face was overwhelming.

"Mr. Blackwell?" A nurse questioned, rolling an empty wheelchair near the men.

Jesse ran a frustrated hand through his thick brown hair and sighed deeply, "Yes?"

"We're taking your wife down for a few more tests … shouldn't take more than an hour or so."

Stepping back into the room, Mack watched as his father gently placed a kiss on top of Leala's head.

"We'll have her back in no time," the nurse said cheerfully. "There's a fresh pot of coffee in the nurse's station; help yourself."

Mack nervously rubbed his hands together. "Great. Thank you." He turned to his father, watching him as he watched the nurse wheel away his wife. "Still take it black?" he asked his father.

Answering with a nod, Jesse walked to the window and stared out. "I've called your brother. He should be here soon."

"Good."

Mack was glad to hear Shannon was on the way. He needed help trying to sort through the strange behavior of his father. Usually, when Jesse answered a question, he'd give long sequences of illustrative stories rather than direct answers. And, whenever a family member was discussed, he'd pull out his billfold, flip through until he found an identifying photograph, point to it, and pass it around as if that somehow made the person present. He'd told Mack years ago that that kept him from speaking ill of the person. He always put a face with a name. But this time, his father's hands were unusually still, hanging close to his body from slumped, dejected shoulders.

"I'll get that coffee now, Dad."

On his way back to the room with two steaming cups in his hands, Mack caught a movement from the corner of his eye as Shannon rushed down the hall toward his brother.

"What's going on here?" Shannon shrugged off his wet rain jacket and shook it out with a snap. "Dad said Mother's sick ... what's wrong with her?"

"Her vitals are slipping. There's no reason for it. Here," he handed his brother the coffee cups, "Go on in, I'll get another cup."

"Is she in there?" Shannon's eyes grew wide.

"No, she's having some tests done."

Relief flooded Shannon's face as he let out a stream of air. He'd dreaded the encounter all the way from New Orleans to Monroe. "Okay ..." Gathering his composure, he stepped inside the room.

Mack couldn't blame his brother for his feelings ... he shared the very same ones. But now, their father needed them, and they would have to put away all bitterness toward their mother and man-up, for their father's sake.

Pushing the heavy hospital-room door open, Mack walked up to Shannon, who was seated with his back to him, and clasped his brother's shoulder. Both sons now faced their father who was still standing, holding his coffee cup as he stared out the window. He seemed lost in thought until he began speaking.

"I love your mother," Jesse stated emphatically, as if what he was about to disclose might somehow betray the woman he loved. "Before we met, she was a religious sister, a nun from Holy Cross near New Orleans. Your mother's beauty has always been her curse. She made a habit of visiting the chapel each evening before bed. That was her routine. One night … someone evil entered the church and waited for her. An unwanted pregnancy resulted and threw your mother's religious system out of whack." Jesse turned at the sound of a sharp intake of breath. Waving his hand as if canceling out Mack's thoughts, he was quick to respond. "No … that baby wasn't you, son. You're *all* Blackwell, that's for dang sure." Having settled the issue, he continued, "Your mother was sent to Bon Secour to have the child, but the baby died after only three days of life. Tristan was his name."

The brothers didn't dare say a word … afraid their father would snap out of his trance and go back into hiding the long-unanswered questions about their mother.

"It was bad enough to have been raped, but to have conceived from the overpowering of a religious man, no less, and then have the child die was no less than unimaginable. She left the order and stayed on at Bon Secour. She couldn't bear the thought of leaving her baby's grave.

"The old cemetery past the pecan grove is where Tristan is buried ... and where I first met your mother. I was using a backhoe to dig a grave as a favor for a friend. When I first saw her, she was like a scared rabbit, jumping up from that little grave and scampering away as fast as her legs could carry her. Being smitten from the very first time I ever laid eyes on her, I was more than a little curious and began asking around about her." He laughed softly. "You could say I stalked her."

Shannon narrowed his eyes. "So ... how did you finally win her over?"

"Blackwell charm ... what else?" Jesse flashed his signature smile, easing the tension in the room. "I found out she attended Saint Mary's Chapel in town and made sure I was a common sight around there ... Lord forgive me. That was no easy task, let me tell you. The woman prayed for hours at a time on a wooden kneeler that would make my knees hurt just watching her. I sat in the back of the church and stared at the back of her head. In those days, I had more hope than wisdom and plenty of time. I think your mother really wanted to be rescued because, eventually, I wore her down, and she let me find her."

Mack was so tuned-in to his father's words that his teeth were clenched. Rubbing his tight jaw, he asked, "So why did she leave us?"

"Most likely I waited too long to tell you boys." A flash of lightning lit the darkened window behind Jesse as rivulets of rain streamed silently down the glass. "Her thinking was skewed ... she wasn't crazy, but maybe ... imbalanced. Father Richard, our parish priest, was your mother's confessor. He told me with tears in his eyes that Leala felt responsible for the death of her baby. She felt that somehow she was being punished by God for past sins. The thought of losing her children because of her past was too much for her."

Mack pulled his head back sharply. "What could a nun have done that was unforgiveable?"

"She was molested as a child by a great uncle, and she always felt she'd done something to cause it. I think that was the reason she fled to the church ... she sought penance."

The room fell silent. Then the squeak of a wheelchair could be heard coming down the hall. The sound became louder as it approached the door.

Shannon's face grew pale; he seemed unsure of his reaction at the sight of his mother. He moved quietly into the shadows behind Mack.

Mack drew on his years of experience in the medical field and slipped into the role of paramedic. "Well, now, that wasn't so bad, was it?"

Something like hope flashed in Leala's eyes for a split second before she took control of it. His mother gave a small, tight smile, and they fell into a comfortable silence as she was transported back to her bed. Mack assisted the nurse in getting his mother out of the wheelchair and into bed, tenderly wrapping her slight arms in his strong hands.

Everything had changed in the brief time his mother had been gone from the room. He now saw his mother as fragile and in need of special care. He had the strange feeling — or maybe it was just hope — that something was about to change. That maybe a tiny thread was being offered to connect them, to pull them all together as a family. No matter how weak the line … still, it was a thread of hope.

It was Mack's touch that ignited a spark within Leala as he reached over and held his mother's hand. Shannon stepped near, squeezing her foot under the covers and smiling at her. Of all the people who'd tried to help her, it was the touch of her sons that she needed most. It was a comforting and healing experience.

"Dad … I've got to go back to Baton Rouge and settle some things. But, I'd like it very much if you'd bring Mother to Briarleigh."

Leala was like a little girl out in the cold, shivering. Her thin shoulders slumped forward as her eyes stayed fixed on Mack. The scars she bore were so abnormal that it was as if she always expected some sudden tragedy.

Mack touched his mother's back lightly, feeling her stiffen under his hand. Controlling the slow move of emotion constricting his throat, he swallowed hard and gently asked, "Mother? Do you feel up to a trip to Briarleigh?"

Her eyes left Mack's face and searched out Shannon's, as if waiting for a response from him.

Feeling the need to contribute to the conversation, Shannon added, "I think you should. I may come, too. Besides, there's a pretty little girl down there I've been meaning to visit." Shannon cut his eyes to his brother's annoyed face.

Jesse spoke up. "It's settled then ... we'll all go to Briarleigh. But first, Leala, you'll have to eat." He picked up a cup of broth from the bedside table and began stirring it with a spoon. The boys moved away and allowed their father to feed their mother, realizing that their mother's eyes never strayed far from them.

Chapter 31

*A*nother hot and sultry evening fell. The fading sunlight brought on the throaty croaks of frogs and the whir of cicadas from the trees and swamps as Bay rested on the swing of the front porch.

For Bay, it seemed that she could hardly believe another day was coming to a close. Evening was, by far, her favorite time of day, when the world seemed to let out a deep, satisfied sigh.

Her moods lately were like the changing weather patterns; sometimes she would saunter through a day without a single complaint from a guest. Other times, like this particular night, she would be assaulted by angry words and hurled curses disturbing the peace of the place.

Mr. Drearden slammed the front door closed behind him as he strode angrily toward Bay. "On all those fancy brochures and pictures on your website, you forgot to mention the broiling sun and the pre-historic mosquitoes you have flying around all over the place. I mean, a man would have to be an idiot to be foolish enough to travel from *anywhere* and end up here! The conditions are intolerable, simply intolerable!"

A hint of a mischievous smile played at the corners of Bay's lips. Here it was … her challenge. She hadn't really been tested since coming to the tranquil inn, but, disgruntled guests were her specialty, and she planned on facing this one head-on.

The red-faced man standing with arms crossed tightly over his chest hadn't elaborated on his purpose for coming to Briarleigh, but Bay suspected it had something to do with escaping a stressful situation. As she looked at the man and his bulging, throbbing neck veins, she had no doubt that he'd brought the stress with him. She paused, trying to decide the best way to handle this particular individual. She looked down at his clenched fists and filled with compassion. In all probability, the pity she felt for the distraught man influenced her decision to call for Maundy and ask for her *unusual* assistance.

Despite the demands of protocol, Bay took it upon herself to try to help the man. She never really had a good grasp of the French language, but she knew enough to know that Maundy simply prayed for those who sought healing from her. After all, what could it hurt? It was obvious Mr. Drearden could use a few prayers.

"Mr. Drearden." Bay purposely lowered her voice to a breathy whisper … blinking several times in an attempt to soften her words. She got up from her seat and gently lifted her hand under his elbow and led him to a cooler part of the porch where mottled shade from the lofty trees filtered the harsh heat.

With all of her training in modern hospitality, it seemed unthinkable that she was willing to try such an unconventional method on one of their guests. But, nevertheless, she *was* willing, and if she'd discovered one thing since coming to Sugar Land, it was that people expected a certain amount of eccentricity from its citizens.

Escorting Mr. Drearden to a comfortable wicker rocker, she discreetly slid her cell phone out of her pocket and sent a text to Maundy.

"Have a seat, Mr. Drearden. You must be exhausted." She strongly suspected him to be a career military man. The stress radiating off him could deep fry a turkey!

"I'm hot, and I'm hungry," he complained, "and this unrelenting heat has left me drained. The trip down here was miserable. How do you people handle it? You all must be coldblooded like the snakes and alligators! I need something to calm me down or knock me out ... fast. Drug me, please!"

Bay listened attentively, nodding as if documenting each and every complaint while secretly typing a message to Derlie. Mr. Drearden seemed far more aged than the forty or so years he claimed on the registry. Carefully probing, Bay very soothingly added, "And you've come here hoping for a little peace and quiet ... a little rest."

A stiff nod was her only answer. "Not so sure it was a wise decision. If I live through this, it'll be a freakin' miracle! Don't you have anything to offer? I mean, just give me something to take to relax me!"

Lifting her chin a notch, Bay stated. "Mr. Drearden, if you will permit me, I'd like very much to try to help you. Usually, I would never resort to these measures, but you seem ... desperate."

"You got that right. What do you have in mind?"

"I'd like to have one of our staff say a few prayers over you. Of course, if you're uncomfortable with the idea, I'll understand completely. She's called a traiteur, and although I don't follow the practice, maybe she can help you. Who knows? Only, first, you must ask her for this treatment.

All the white disappeared from Mr. Drearden's eyes as they narrowed in suspicion. He couldn't believe what he was hearing! He rolled his eyes upward as if pleading for divine intervention. The fact that he'd suffered through so many hellish torments caused him to curse and reply sharply, "You might as well ... that's the only thing missing from my Louisiana adventure. Now I can cross primitive ritual off the list!"

"Intercessory prayer knows no boundaries and even extends to one's enemies, Mr. Drearden." She glanced over her shoulder. "Here is Maundy, now. Remember ... you must ask her for help."

Maundy quietly wandered over to where Bay was standing and waited for instruction.

"Mr. Drearden, this is Maundy, and she's here to help you if you would like for her to." Bay stepped back, feeling it necessary to leave them alone. "I'll go check on your snack."

It was a long moment before he asked a question of Maundy. "I'm suffering from a lot of tension ... can you help with that?" he asked, seeing his answer in the almost indistinct turning of her lips at the corners.

"Please tell me your full name."

"Drearden, Weston Blake," he stated, in military fashion. I answer to Blake."

Maundy pressed her small cool hands on his forehead three times while her lips mouthed a silent prayer in French. She asked him to stand as her hands passed down his sides without touching him.

He felt as if he'd been shucked of the tension in his body ... like it just peeled away and left him feeling light and buoyant. As soon as it was over, he burst out laughing ... surprised that he actually felt good. Astonished, he said, "You did it! I actually feel better!"

Violently, Maundy shook her head. "I can do nothing. I pray and ask the good Lord to heal you through my prayers. He heals, not me. Now, you've got to help yourself. You've got to pray and ask God to help you, so it won't come back on you."

Blake's whole countenance changed, his face seemed to relax, losing much of the tight, pinched appearance. "What caused my stress ... and what can I do about it?"

Maundy shrugged. "The cause and the cure, that's God's business, ask Him."

Reaching into his back pocket, Blake pulled out his billfold. He lifted two twenties from the leather fold, handing it to Maundy.

She waved it away. "What I do, I do in the name of the Lord."

"I don't feel right not paying you something ... besides ... I wasn't very nice to you or anybody else around here for that matter."

"To a traiteur, everybody's the same person to you. Jesus tells us to love our neighbor—you're my neighbor." With that said, she turned and walked back into the house, passing Bay as she was coming out.

Bay noticed the difference in Mr. Drearden immediately and couldn't help but smile. "Well, Mr. Drearden, you certainly look more relaxed." She placed a tray down on the small table near the chair. "I brought a supper plate for you. You just barely missed our supper hour when you arrived, but you're in luck tonight. I had a sudden urge to cook." Smiling, she lifted the lid on the plate and uncovered steamy pot roast with carrots, onions, and potatoes. Dark, hard-crusted bread with real butter slathered on the thick slices and a dish of blackberry cobbler sat to the side. "Around here, all tea is sweet ... but not *too* sweet."

"I could stand a little sweetening ... thank you, I'm ... I'm ..."

"You're welcome." Twisting her lips to keep the smirk in check, Bay wiped her hands down her apron and turned to leave.

Earlier she'd fought the temptation to reprimand Mr. Drearden, wanting to tell him to open his eyes and look around! The place almost pulsed with beauty and life. Thankfully, she'd kept her thoughts to herself. Before stepping into the house, she said over her shoulder. "The walking trail goes down by the river ... it's nice this time of day. It begins over there." She motioned to a pea-gravel path near the edge of the woods. "We'll have cookies in the common room around eight o'clock if you're interested."

Chapter 32

The ancient trees of Sugar Land lined the low road, making the sidewalks bulge and crack with their expanding roots. Jesse and Leala drove through the old town under the mottled light from the canopy of branches overhead. Both were quiet with their own thoughts as they passed the road that led to Bon Secour and the little cemetery where her baby lay. This was going to be a challenge. But, Jesse felt ready for it. Now, with God's help, maybe he could finally bring his family back together.

Mack Blackwell just wasn't the kind of man known for paying a lot of attention to clothes. Around Briarleigh, he never wore anything but a ragged pair of faded jeans and mostly-white T-shirts. So, to see him dressed in khaki pants and a light green button-down with rolled-up sleeves made Bay clamp her mouth shut to keep from gawking. His eyes were so arresting that she had to make an effort to pull away from the kitchen window and keep her attention focused on the pot she was washing.

The back porch swing creaked out a protest as Mack put his weight down on it. Ezra eased into his favorite chair just under the kitchen window. They'd just finished settling Jesse and Leala into their cottage and were going back to the main house when Ezra stopped, looked up at Mack, and said, "Jesse is a man to be greatly admired. He has inexhaustible love."

Ezra held out his arm, slowly turning it as he took note of a colorful butterfly that had landed there. "When a butterfly lands on you, it's said to be giving you a blessing."

A little laugh skipped through the open window and Mack smiled, recognizing it to be Bay's.

"I hear you've been keeping company with Mrs. Versidy Williams." Mack leaned back, stretching his arms over the back of the swing, pushing it into slow motion with his foot.

A slight smile flashed on Ezra's leathery face, and he nodded. "We go way back." His eyes took on a distant look as he recalled the old days. "Her momma used to give me a ride to school in her purple car." He wheezed out a laugh that turned into a dry cough as he leaned forward, trying to catch his breath. "That old car squeaked and rattled somethin' fierce … like it was held together by clothes hangers and bazooka bubble gum.

"On our way to school one day, we were just sittin' at a red light, pretty as you please, when *bam!* Mr. Lewis, the mailman, plowed right into the back of us. I was in the backseat when, all of a sudden, this hairy black thing flew at me. I hollered, slapped it, kicked it to the floorboard, and just stomped the fire out of it. About that time, a police officer came up to the driver's side window. Versidy's momma just reached behind the seat and grabbed that hairy black thing I'd stomped to death on the floorboard and put it back on her head! Straw, dirt, and a half-eaten sucker stuck out of it every which way. We laughed so hard that Versidy wet her pants. Her momma never got mad at us either. Lawd, I can't even remember her name. She had a face that could back down a junkyard dog, but she was a kind soul."

It was all too much for Mack's control, and he burst into laughter. "Ezra ... you should be ashamed, talking about that poor woman."

"I just tell it like it is ... no skill in that." Ezra offered his wisdom freely. "Always find the good in everything. It's there, even if you have to wade through a lot of ugly to get to it. What happens after the beauty fades anyway? You're left with just an ordinary person. The question is ... will you like what's left? You sure better know, yes, sir, you sure better know."

Mack leisurely raised an eyebrow, certain the old man had a message for him, and announced, "I think I'll stretch my legs before it gets too dark."

Mack walked away from the house toward the cove. Nearing a cluster of trees, he waited in silence for a long moment as he leaned against the rough bark of an old river tree, lost in his thoughts. Breaking pieces from a twig, he tossed them into the water, then he turned his head, catching the slightest murmur. It came to him more clearly in a low, whispered voice through the damp air.

Grace ... it is love that is given when it is not deserved.

It is forgiveness given when it is not earned.

*It's like water to a soul burning up with condemn-
ing guilt.*
Ah, Grace ... it's how the Father loves us.

Then all was silent, except the usual night
sounds known to surround Briarleigh from her
swamps and lowlands. He mused to himself at how
ordinary it had become to hear the murmurs of the
cove and receive them as though they were
something as common as music coming out of a
nearby church.

Since coming back to Sugar Land, the details of
Mack's early life had become like ashes, easily
blown away. With his mother's nearby presence,
though, all those memories came flooding back.
Maybe Shannon was right to stay away for a week
or so. He'd called, promising to come by after
they'd all settled in.

In the cottage, Mack had helped his mother into
bed. She'd yawned behind a slender hand and
smiled at him before wearily sinking into the
covers. That was the first smile he ever remembered
seeing on her face ... and it was for him! Already
her health seemed to gradually be restored.

The sun continued to sink, dropping to the
swaying line of the sugarcane fields. "What a
turnabout," he mumbled to himself. He was still
annoyed at being persuaded by Piper to see her
again. It was over between them, if, in fact, it had
ever really begun. Seeing her again only prolonged
the inevitable ... but Piper had insisted, saying that
he owed her at least that much. "Lord, help me," he
said, before pushing off the tree and heading back
toward the house.

In the deep dusk, the soft yellow glow from the windows of Briarleigh looked inviting. As he stepped onto the front porch, a movement caught his eye from the shadows. Turning, he saw a man seated there with a pleasant smile on his face.

"Nice evening," Mack said, as he nodded toward the man.

"Yes, I never want it to end," replied the man. "I'm Blake Drearden, and I highly recommend this place."

"Well, Mr. Drearden," Mack stated, as he crossed the porch to shake the man's hand, "I'm glad to hear that. I'm Mack Blackwell; my uncle and I own this place."

"Whatever you're paying Miss Rutherford … it isn't nearly enough. If you're not careful, somebody's going to steal her away from you." Blake pulled a long, slim cigar from his shirt pocket and leisurely eyed the man. "Seems to me, Mr. Blackwell," he spoke as he struck a match and puffed on the cigar, "that a woman like that could make a place like this stay with a man for a long time." He leaned back in the chair and grinned.

Mack faced the man squarely and tossed his head, "Glad you approve. But, Miss Rutherford is not one of our amenities." He turned toward the door before he commented further. It annoyed him to have Bay spoken of so casually. He made a mental note to keep an eye on the guy.

Hearing sounds coming from the kitchen, he crossed the dining room and pushed through the swinging door. Jace sat on a high stool with a measuring cup full of oatmeal in one hand and a bottle of vanilla in the other. With rapt attention, he watched his mother tear off a large sheet of wax paper and smooth it over the counter. He seemed to take special delight in watching her prepare whatever she was making.

Turning his attention to the stove, Mack saw a heavy pot of bubbling chocolate boiling rapidly. Bay signaled Jace, and he added the vanilla, his eyes lighting up as he watched the mixture flare up in a sudden reaction. Then, with her nod, he poured in the oats as she shook off a dollop of peanut butter from a large spoon. Bay stirred quickly before dropping dollops of the mixture onto the wax paper, allowing it to harden into cookies.

They were so engrossed in the process of cookie-making they didn't hear Mack slip into the kitchen. He settled back against the wall, arms folded over his chest and a smile playing around the corners of his mouth as he watched the domestic scene.

Had she expected me for supper? He glanced around, noticing his favorite meal of pot roast and hard-crusted bread warming on the stove. If she had, she'd said nothing to Jace, or he'd have been waiting on him near the road as always. The boy liked to hitch a ride on the tailgate of the truck.

Mack cleared his throat.

Both heads turned sharply.

"Did I surprise you?" Mack asked. He was barely able to keep his grin in check.

Bay froze. It was like looking at someone who saw *her*, really saw *her*. And that caused a shudder to run clean through her. It sometimes surprised her just how handsome he was. "I saw you come in earlier, but I didn't know where you'd gone. I was hoping you'd be able to at least have some supper before going back to your place." She knew she was rambling, but she couldn't stop it.

"Piper is meeting me here ... she and I have some issues to settle."

"Oh, of course ... well, if she's hungry, we have plenty."

Jace slid off the stool and walked up to Mack, squinting as he looked up into his face. "You 'member to get my fishin' pole?"

Mack grimaced. "I knew I was forgetting something. Tell you what, if it's all right with your mother, we'll go to town tomorrow and pick one out." He rubbed the little boy's head, then looked up at Bay, waiting for a response.

Bay nodded. Her son had found a friend in Mack. For most of the summer when he'd found the time, Mack had taught the boy outdoors skills — where and how to fish, what to avoid in the woods, and how to snare a rabbit. She'd worried what Mack's absence would do to her son, but each time he came back to Briarleigh, they just picked up where they'd left off as if time was of no concern at all.

Jace went to the pantry door and took his mother's purse off the doorknob. Placing the purse on the floor, he sat down and started digging around for loose change, making little piles on the floor.

"Mind telling me what you're doing?" Mack asked, as he observed the boy.

"Can't ask a man to buy my fishin' pole. All this kinda money in Momma's purse is mine, ain't that right, Momma?" he held up a shiny nickel.

"*Isn't* that right, and, yes ... it's all your hard-earned money."

"She just keeps it safe for me 'cause I don't have a bank of my own, and my pockets are small with holes." Jace explained. "And boys hate purses!"

"You're right about that. Now, let's see here." Rubbing his chin, Mack looked down at the assortment of coins all splayed out on the floor. "Take that pile and a few of those nickels, and that ought to do it."

Jace cocked his head, looking up at Mack. "You need anything? I got leftover money."

"No, no, I'm good." Mack glanced over at Bay, seeing the proud look on her face. He smiled. "You've got a fine young man here, Miss Bay."

"Yes, I do. Now, son, you just sit there and count out those coins. I'm going to take these cookies to the gathering room and then go check on Mr. Drearden."

Muttering unintelligible words, Mack turned and went back the way he'd come in. There was something about Blake Drearden that just didn't seem right to him. Without a word, he went out to join the man on the porch.

Blake knocked the ash off his cigar. "You really should pay more attention to your manager. Any man with half an eye can tell you she's one in a million."

"You're right about that," Mack agreed as he heard the front screen door pop and noticed Bay as she approached them.

Blake passed his blue, admiring eyes over Bay, unmindful of Mack's stern face as he raked in the full length of her form. "Yes, sir, Mr. Blackwell, seems to me you've done a pretty good job of hiring so far." He winked into the light hazel eyes as Bay looked at him with some confusion. "One of these days, I'm going to work up the nerve to ask you out, Miss Bay. And when I do, I'll do my level best to make sure you have a memorable time." He turned to consider Mack without a hint of expression.

Bay glanced at Mack, seeing a muscle flex tensely in his cheek as if he held his tongue—or his temper—in check. Then he replied curtly, "I suppose we could make it a double date tonight, if you're up for it. Piper is on her way, and we were just about to go out for coffee. Bay would probably feel more comfortable being around familiar people until she gets used to you."

Irritated now, Bay spoke up, "Did it ever occur to either of you that I might actually have something to say about the matter?"

Both men turned to Bay with some surprise.

Seeing the irritation on Bay's face, Blake quickly tried to calm her. "I would enjoy the privilege of showing you off in town. That is, if you wouldn't mind being seen with an old man."

Bay responded with a smile. "Your age has nothing to do with it. I think I would enjoy that very much, but I have a son to consider and no sitter. So, I'll just have to bow out this time."

"Then let's just stay here … I can run to town for supplies for s'mores, and we can toast marshmallows. I'm sure your son would love it! " Blake said enthusiastically. "We appreciate the invitation, Mack, but we'll hang around here tonight."

"Perfect, then we'll stay here with you." Mack added.

Piper climbed out of her car and reached for Mack's hand. "The drive was awful! If I didn't know how important it was for me to be here with you while your mother is here, I'd have sent for you instead, and we'd be having drinks on my balcony, listening to some light jazz."

"You'll have to settle for a bonfire and s'mores. We're joining a guest and his date tonight."

Piper perked up. "Oh? Wonderful … another woman. Do I know her?"

"Yes, as a matter of fact, you do. It's Bay."

"What! How did *that* happen?"

"Why does that surprise you?"

Piper folded her arms. "I just find it hard to believe anyone finds her attractive, scarred as she is."

Mack shrugged. "What's a little mark here and there … it just proves she's daring."

Piper moaned, rolled her eyes, and disagreed. "Or clumsy and stupid. You need to do a better job evaluating people and their worth. Take a few lessons from me."

He spoke slowly, as if to let his words fall with effect. "Oh, I think a lesson will be taught, but to which of us remains to be seen." Mack returned the challenge he saw in her eyes, and a slow smile crept across his lips. As his stare grew more bold and unwavering, her smile slowly faded.

Almost immediately, Mack regretted his decision to suggest the double date. He knew Blake wasn't the kind of guy to get out of hand. He seemed easy enough, but still ... he was a man and would need watching.

Blake took off his jacket and draped it around Bay's shoulders, carefully adjusting it for comfort. "How about some coffee after those delicious s'mores?"

"Oh, of course ... how do you take it?" Bay made a move to get up.

Blake waved her back down. "Hey, relax ... you're off the clock. I'm getting it for you. Cream and sugar?"

Bay smiled and nodded. "Just cream." She glanced across the fire to find Mack's eyes on her.

As soon as Blake was out of earshot, Piper casually commented, "You and Blake seem to be getting along nicely."

"Yes, he's a really nice man." Lost in thought, she reached down and picked up a stone, turning it over as she rubbed her thumb against it."

Mack looked around. "Where's Jace?"

Bay pointed to the live oak tree and its low-hanging branch. "He's sitting in the tree waiting to see the meteor shower that's supposed to happen tonight."

Mack pulled his finger along his jawline in thought. "That's a perfect tree for a tree house … that'll be our next project."

With all the sincerity she could muster, Piper turned to Bay and lectured, "You'd better latch on to Blake. Raising a boy is not easy for a single mother. And, let's face it, not too many men will be interested in taking on someone else's kid. He's older and more mature … and …"

"That's enough, Piper," Mack said finally, as he struggled to get a handle on his emotions. He shifted in his seat, uncomfortable with the conversation. "Bay is doing just fine bringing up that boy. Besides, he's surrounded by people who love him and look out for him."

Bay studied Mack before commenting. "So many things are beyond our control and sometimes that scares me to death. That's why I moved here in the first place, to get away from some pretty corrupt things happening around me. I thought that in a smaller place I could give my son a home and people who could help me shape him into a good and godly man. But, even here …" she let her words trail off. She shrugged, "I guess there is just no getting around simply trusting God wherever you are."

Bay had a pleasant voice, one that gave Mack ease. That she would talk so openly about her faith and her dreams for her son took him by surprise. "Yeah, unfortunately, even here we have troubles. But now … this is still a great place to bring up a boy. I remember being awakened and carried outside on my father's shoulders to watch a meteor shower when I was about Jace's age. You might not realize it, but he's making memories, even now."

The full moon emerged from behind the clouds and the distant sound of a whippoorwill penetrated the night air. All was peaceful around the bonfire as each became lost in thought.

Chapter 33

Mack stepped into an alley off Royal Avenue in New Orleans, the buffeting wind whipping and tugging at his rain jacket as he looked for a restaurant named The Muse. Rounding the corner, he blinked against the rain and looked up to see the black-and-white-striped awning over the door that the caller had described. Pulling open the heavy wooden door, he stepped inside, glancing around. It was an old warehouse-type restaurant with high ceilings, raw brick, and stained glass windows. Low-hung ceiling fans spun lazily, lending an old-world feel to the space within.

"Mr. Blackwell? We were doubtful that you would make it tonight, sir. The weather has turned wicked. Here, let me take your jacket. I'm Pride Redding, and Ms. Charity is waiting for you."

Before Mack had a chance to ask anything more of the man, his attention was directed to an elegant-looking woman, about sixty, descending a few small steps as she approached them. Her skin tone complemented her cream-colored suit, and she carried herself with grace and poise. She was a pleasure to look upon, seeming quiet and reserved, yet quick and observant. He wondered briefly if anything ever escaped her notice. Still, something told him to keep his guard up around the woman.

Charity extended her hand. "Mr. Blackwell, thank you so much for meeting with me on short notice and under these horrid weather conditions." She made introductions before she turned and led the way to a private table on a small landing. Ferns and a blue and green mosaic-tiled fountain partially hid the area from the casual eye.

"Thank you, Pride," she said in a businesslike voice, dismissing the man.

"He seems devoted to you," Mack stated casually, as he pulled out her chair.

"Yes, indeed. He's been with me many years now." She smoothed her pencil skirt as she sat down. "Why are you not married?"

He took a seat across from her. "I'm holding out for the perfect woman."

The tinkling sound of her laughter floated around him. "Well, that should certainly seal your fate as a bachelor."

The woman missed nothing. It was obvious she'd already glanced at his hand and noticed the absence of a ring. Just then, a very distinguished man passed by their table, bestowing a sheepish smile on Ms. Charity and, in haste, hurried away.

"You seem to have dazzled the man," Mack observed, the flickering light moving shadows over his handsome face.

Directing her attention to something less provoking than Mack's intense green eyes, she adjusted the napkin in her lap. "Yes, well I guess I still do have a few admirers in this city."

"I respect frankness, Ms. Charity, even when it's rather harsh. Will you do me the honor of speaking to me directly? I'm certain I can handle it."

Charity's back straightened and her tone softened as she replied. "Whatever standards for complete sincerity I might have had have been so completely lost over the years that I'm afraid I may never get them back." Masking a small smile, she conceded, "It goes along with my profession. You see, I'm a madam." She picked up her tea cup and took a light sip.

Mack smiled without a trace of surprise. "Is your business slowing or the economy hurting to the point that you need to seek out clients? Is that why you asked me here?"

"No, Mr. Blackwell," she half-laughed. "My profession is what you might call recession-proof. No matter the economy, certain men always seem to find time for … recreation." Charity managed a slight smile. "Oh, I took the liberty of ordering for you. I hope you don't mind."

"Not at all." Mack leaned back in his seat as the server placed a sizzling steak with a steaming, salt-encrusted, butter-loaded baked potato in front of him. He smiled appreciatively. "How did you know?"

"It's my business to know men and their preferences."

Privately, Mack agreed that she probably was right about that. "Aren't you having anything?"

"Just tea for me," she replied. "Go ahead and enjoy your dinner while I explain to you why I asked you here."

Nodding, Mack cut into the steak and took a bite. As he chewed, he listened with full attention to her words.

"I own a home for unwed mothers in Sugar Land called Bon Secour. My sister runs it."

Swallowing, Mack asked, "Mercy is your sister?"

"Yes. If you know Mercy, you know we're nothing alike. Our parents lived on the devout side of spiritual things and, to some, they may have seemed rather backward, but they were sincere." She took another sip before calmly continuing. "I've sent several girls to Mercy over the years. I guess my upbringing has given me a few morals after all. I was even a guest there once myself ... about eighteen years ago."

His voice was low, but the question was blunt. "What happened to your child?"

"She's living at Bon Secour and now working for you at Briarleigh. Maundy is my daughter, and that's why I've called you here."

Mack opened his mouth to question, but she waved her hand, explaining further.

"It has come to my attention that a plot is underway to possibly injure Bay Rutherford in some way. I cannot allow that to happen."

"What!" Mack's voice rang sharply in the room as he tossed his fork on the table. "Where did you hear that?"

Charity discreetly cleared her throat. "I service clients in some of the more exclusive hotels in three states. One of my employees brought it to my attention after … servicing a client at the St. Bonitus Hotel in Mobile. The man she was with was drunk and talked openly about his plans. I trust this employee, completely. In fact, she told me that Bay had helped her escape a rather difficult situation once and that she didn't want anything to happen to her. I'd had another employee tell a similar story a month or so ago, but I didn't make the connection with Briarleigh. That story came from a man at a gaming resort in Mississippi. I've found that in certain gambling towns the truth sometimes has a hard time getting out. So, apparently after several failed attempts to shut down Briarleigh Inn with rumors and such, they thought to discourage your manager by causing trouble for her. The whole point, I surmise, is to run Bay back to St. Bonitus and to a man named Sterling Geroux who claims to be her fiancé. Only this time, the stakes are higher."

Mack's jaw tightened, and he was calm, quiet even, but his eyes took on a look of hardened steel. "When is this all supposed to take place?"

"Tomorrow."

Narrowing his eyes, Mack asked, "Why do you care what happens to Bay Rutherford? Who is she to you?"

Charity spoke without hesitation. "She is the woman who has given my daughter what I couldn't, a chance for a good life. I'm indebted to her. And, after meeting you, I believe that you take this threat every bit as seriously as I do." She reached across the table and rested a hand on his arm. "I'm not a cold-hearted person, Mr. Blackwell. In fact, I'm certain that my family, as backward as they seem, evokes the blessed Trinity on my behalf each day. Maybe that's why I have a small measure of decency. I'm not unaware. I know that when you die to sin you don't still live in it. I still choose to live in it." Her eyes took on a mellow softness. "My father once told me that the difference between a sheep and a pig is that the pig loves the mire and a sheep is uncomfortable until he gets it off. I'm still wondering which I am. If I'm a sheep, I seem to have grown comfortable with the weight of the mire," Charity said, stating the obvious. "After the way I've lived, I'm sure God would just as soon do without me."

Mack fixed his gaze straight into Charity's eyes, pausing to form his thoughts. "You're wrong to believe that God is incapable of loving a less-than-perfect human being ... God loves us, and we're *all* imperfect. Sometimes things happen because we've made bad decisions, but even then, especially then, we are given grace to get it right. As long as you have breath, you have a chance to make it right."

"Thank you for that ... it gives me a measure of hope."

Mack rubbed his fingers across his forehead. "I'm still not sure what all this is about. Since opening the inn we've faced sarcasm, then lies which led to criticism and now finally conspiracy."

"Before long, you can look for the inevitable—discouragement—and that's what these people are after. They want to discourage you so you'll give up and close your inn."

Mack stood. "They may try to knock us down, but they're a long way from knocking us out. We'll be ready for them." He walked to the door. With his hand on the knob, he turned around and met her eyes, mouthing the words, "Thank you."

Chapter 34

*T*ime passed slowly in Mack's absence, and, more than once, Bay had to force thoughts of the man from her mind. He had gone to New Orleans on business and hadn't said when he would return. She'd seen very little of Mack's parents in the past few days. Jesse and Leala had come to the dining room for breakfast only once, and Piper had joined them. As Bay poured their coffee, she'd overheard Piper telling Mack's parents that she'd decided to stay on for a few more days to make sure they were well-taken care of. Bristling at the insult, Bay eased out of the room, but not before the dark-haired beauty sent her a triumphant look.

It was late afternoon when Bay glanced up from replenishing supplies for the cottages and saw Piper signaling to her from across the yard.

"Oh—Bay?" Piper waved and smiled. "We need a huge favor."

Bay pulled the supply cart to the side of the path and waited for Piper to reach her. "What can I do for you?"

"We need ..." then she stopped mid-sentence, dismissing her with a quick shake of her head. "Oh, never mind ... I'll do it."

"What?"

"We need the family portrait. Leala wants it, and it's at Mack's house." Piper's dark eyes chilled significantly. "But you're such a ... tender soul. It's best if you don't try to cross the rope bridge, or you might faint or something."

Bay rolled her eyes upward, praying for self-control. The fact that she'd already suffered through a week of Piper's non-stop complaining didn't do anything to help her nerves. But, experience had been a harsh teacher in the past, and it convinced her that keeping a cool head was the only way to overcome someone like Piper. "I'll be glad to go get it, but I don't have a key to his house."

"Oh, that's not a problem. It's hidden under the flowerpot on the front steps. The portrait is in the living room, hanging above the mantle. Of course, if you're *afraid* to cross the bridge, I can go. You just told me earlier that if I ever needed anything to ask you."

Bay shook her head, refusing to share her apprehension with Piper's cold heart. She gathered her wits about her and chose a course of action. "Okay, I'll head over there after I finish my rounds." She pushed the cart toward an empty guest cabin, gathering an armful of supplies before stepping inside.

"Oh, one more thing ... where is all of your family?" Piper asked sweetly.

Her honeyed words sounded nice, but Bay didn't trust the person who spoke them. "They're in town. Why? Do you need something? I can call Ezra."

"No, no ... that won't be necessary. I can manage."

The western sky was ominous as the sun disappeared behind a bank of darkening clouds. In the threatening southern twilight, Bay made her way down the path toward the clearing where the rope bridge spanned the waters of the cove.

The back of Bay's neck prickled in fear as she sensed being watched. Looking around, she thought she saw a movement between the trees. She froze. Holding her breath, she took in her surroundings. Shadows and vague conjured-up images deep in the woods played havoc with her imagination.

Anxious to get across the rope bridge, she stepped gingerly on the first board, thankful for the sturdy support under her feet, then on to the next until she was midway across the bridge.

A coarse scream ripped from her throat as boards gave way beneath her, plummeting twenty feet below. She slipped, holding tightly to a loose plank. A cold dread choked off her scream as the sound of a splash reached her ears.

Hanging, suspended in mid-air with her stinging arms stretched tight, she heard the murmurs of the cove pulling her loose from the bridge. She took a deep breath, sighed and noted the dark, gathering clouds. She had to fight an overriding panic as fear gripped her, but she was determined not to allow the situation to cause her to lose self-control. She had to remain calm; her very life depended on it. At that moment, she heard a sickening pop. Then she fell in a freefall down to the murky water below.

Plunging beneath the water, she kicked with all her strength until she shot to the surface, gasping for breath. Bobbing in the water, she could feel the slight tug of the current but managed to flip over and float on her back, kicking just enough to keep above the water.

A light wind swept over the surface of the water, creating ripples. Bay shivered, then opened her eyes and looked up. A distant thumping sound, like that of an out-of-balance washing machine on the spin cycle, caught her attention. She searched the sky until her sight fixed on a helicopter coming toward her. As she gazed at it, she wanted nothing more than to lift herself from the river and fly upward, but she could only let the river carry her along and pray to God that she'd hit land soon. The helicopter grew louder as it approached then flew over, vanishing from sight as its *thump* faded away.

Maybe it was Mack, she thought, turning her thoughts to anything but her predicament. Thanks to him, she was alive thus far. He'd taught her the basics of the "float on your back" skill. If she survived this ordeal, she'd make sure he knew just how thankful she was!

Staring up into the fading light, she could see nothing but dark and brooding clouds and the arc of trees hanging over the water. It seemed she was doomed to watch the gathering storm as lightning flashed across the ever-darkening sky. A brittle quiet descended — the proverbial calm before the storm.

The only sound she could hear was the distant rumble of thunder and water lapping against her ears. The river seemed to be inside her head.

Feeling a bump against her leg, Bay kicked frantically until her foot hit an object. A piece of driftwood bobbed to the surface of the water, and she breathed out a sigh of relief. As she exhaled, her backside hit the muddy river bottom.

Dragging herself out of the river, she stood dripping and muddy, but alive! The smell of gasoline and oil clung to her clothing. She saw a rainbow effect of fuel clinging to the ground as if a boat had recently been there. Passing a hand over her arm, she noticed a dark spot and quickly removed her shirt, checking her body for cuts and scrapes.

A trickle of blood seeped out from a gash under her arm. Deciding not to put the filthy, fuel-soaked clothing back on, she pulled at her clinging undershirt, hoping it would keep her covered well enough until she found her way back home.

A sudden flash of lightning streaked across the sky, and she looked around seeking cover as large raindrops pounded the ground all around her. Scanning the area, she saw what looked to be a little goat path through the brush. She followed it, not knowing where it would lead.

Pushing through a thicket of undergrowth and small trees, she came to a clearing in the woods. A small stone chapel, half-hidden behind a cape of velvet green moss, came into view. Around the perimeter, the forest trees did not intrude but formed a circle as if sheltering the sacred ground from the evil reach of the world. Even nature seemed to set the place apart as holy, where one could sense only safety.

Bay reached the door and pushed on it. The humidity-swollen wood popped open, swinging back sharply on its hinges with a loud bang. Dust motes twirled and danced in the muted light from the arched windows. Except for a few wooden pews and scattered books, the place was barren and musty, with heavy, stale, motionless air.

Stepping closer to the rough wooden timbers forming a cross on the back wall, Bay recalled something she couldn't place. *He leaves it to us whether to notice him or not.*

As a hard rain started to pound on the roof and beat against the windows with a slashing fury, the old rafters creaked and groaned under the strong wind. As she gazed up at the cross, an overwhelming awareness began to take shape, an awareness of God's intensely great love for her. She dropped to her knees, knowing he was there. She sensed it, the way a sick child senses his mother nearby.

Lost in the wonder of God's presence, Bay didn't hear the door open.

"Bay!" Her name echoed through the empty chapel. Startled, Bay turned in alarm to see the intruder, nearly collapsing in relief as she recognized the tall form of Mack in the shadowed doorway. Grabbing the wooden pew behind her, she pressed a hand over her rapidly beating heart.

He quickly crossed the room, his deep voice filling the small chapel. "You're hurt!" He eased Bay into the seat and raised her arm to inspect the swollen red gash. "This needs to be cleaned and treated soon." He pulled back, seeing fear and exhaustion on her face. "Do you think you have the energy to walk?" he asked softly.

Tears sprung to her eyes for the first time since the start of the whole ordeal. Her throat tightened, preventing her from answering, so she nodded.

"Okay ... let's take this slow." He wrapped an arm around her waist and helped her up, walking gradually to the door. The night was coming on fast. Even with the heavy rain, they knew they had to make it to the house.

Pausing at the door, Bay peered outside and lifted her chin, determined to be brave no matter what they faced outside the protected walls. She now knew that God was with her, inside or outside or wherever she found herself. And that brought her comfort and courage.

Slicing through the wet brush and undergrowth, Mack was still certain that the way through the woods would be quicker than taking the path out to the main road. It seemed to take forever to go a short distance, but as they stepped into the clearing, their sighs of relief lasted only a second before Mack suddenly pulled Bay back into the woods, keeping to the trees' dark shelter. He grabbed her shoulders, pinning her back against a tree. Bracing his hands on each side of the trunk, he encased her between his arms as he lowered his head to whisper in her ear, "Shhh."

The warmth of his breath on her face caused her to shiver as they waited in the dense brush, their eyes scanning the area near the chapel. A twig snapped in the silence. Someone was close by. Sounds of movement came from the woods as three people crept cautiously toward the chapel. Mack and Bay heard the chapel door creak open and, moments later, the three were standing outside, talking over the sound of the rain.

"She must've drowned ... there ain't no sign of her nowhere!" A man's raised voice sounded through the night.

A second man chimed in. "It don't look good for us ... he wanted her alive. And look here, I found this bloodied shirt that washed up on shore near the boat."

All was quiet, then a third voice said, "How was we supposed to know she'd go and get herself killed? Bet she hit her head in the fall and drowned. That ain't our fault. Piper was the one to come up with the idea to make her fall from the bridge with those loose boards. That weren't none of us."

Bay gasped, and Mack quickly covered her mouth with his hand.

The three men looked around, suddenly spooked by their surroundings. "This place gives me the heebie-jeebies—let's get out of here."

"Who's gonna tell Piper?"

"I'll text her later. And if she knows what's good for her, she'd better get us our money, or we'll be paying a visit to the St. Bonitus Hotel!"

Bay was shaking as hard as she was praying. Mack tightened his arms around her, trying to comfort her trembling body. After hearing a boat motor start up and whine away, they moved from their hidden spot, both their minds reeling with the implications of what they'd just heard.

Chapter 35

A calamity, like any major upheaval, has a way of putting one's entire life into perspective in a few short moments. Piper had been someone Mack thought he knew, but until now, he'd never really seen her clearly.

As if in a daze, Bay stared at the door to Mack's house as he fumbled with the keys. With a deep breath, she followed him inside the darkened house, feeling so exhausted that she wondered if she might sprawl headlong across the floor behind him.

Mack didn't turn on the lights but reached back to put a hand on Bay's upper arm, guiding her through the house. With his face close to hers, he whispered, "We need to keep the house dark just in case someone comes prowling around." He led her to the couch. "Wait here while I go upstairs to find something for you to sleep in. There's a bathroom without a window down the hall; it'll be safe to turn on the light in there so you can shower."

Disappearing up the stairs, he returned shortly with an oversized button-down shirt. He held it up for her inspection. It looked as if it would reach her knees.

"After you shower, knock on the door, and I'll come in and treat your injury. Just keep a towel wrapped around you. I should be able to get to the wound that way."

Any relief Bay may have felt at the thought of a hot shower suddenly evaporated at the hurt and disappointment she saw fill Mack's eyes. Softly, she said, "Mack … I'm sorry for the way things …"

He dismissed her comment, shaking his head. "It's gonna be okay. Get in the shower while I heat up some soup."

She looked at him for a long moment before glancing down.

"What is it?" Mack asked quietly.

"Nothing," she said, avoiding his eyes.

"Bay, what are you afraid of? That I'll leave you here alone? I won't, you know. In fact, I think we both need to camp out in the living room tonight in case those guys come back. I recognized two of them by their voices. They're the guys I ran off from Briarleigh … the ones you hired to clean up the property."

Bay swallowed as her mouth suddenly went dry.

"I'll make a few phone calls … we'll see what needs to be done. I keep a rifle here for snakes, mostly, but, under the circumstances, I think it might be a good idea to keep it handy. I wish I had my pistol."

She put her hand on her forehead and rubbed, feeling a headache brewing. "It would be a lot easier just to believe that it was all an accident and that there was a logical explanation for what happened."

"Yeah, but that wouldn't be the truth, would it?"

With a shake of her head, she slipped into the bathroom. For nearly an hour, she allowed the steamy hot tub to soothe her aches.

A tapping on the bathroom door drew Mack's attention away from the stove. He grabbed the supplies he'd gathered and headed for the bathroom.

"Okay, just sit down and let me have a look at that cut." As Mack began treating Bay's injury, carefully tending the wound under her arm, he explained in a low, reassuring voice, "This is witch hazel ... it's a great healing agent, especially for sensitive areas." Her rosy-colored skin was warm and soft to the touch, and she smelled fresh, like soap and water. She reminded him of the climbing roses that grew over his house. He'd been romanced by those roses so much that he'd bought the house, in part, because of them. And now, it seemed, they were not the only things that held a spell over him ... or had not-to-be-reckoned-with thorns on occasion.

His face was less than an inch from hers, so close that she could see the beads of sweat gathering on his forehead. "How often should I treat it?"

"Dab a little on the cut several times a day to speed the healing." His eyes met hers. "But as long as I'm here, I'll treat it." He watched her reaction to his words, seeing a new expression in her eyes ... trust. He shifted uncomfortably, waiting for his pounding heart to slow. Struggling with his impulses was getting hard on him. What he felt stir in his heart could not be reasoned away. He tried to discount it by calling it mere infatuation, but that was only partly true. He'd never before wanted to be in a woman's presence so much. The fact was that he'd resorted to find any excuse at all to be around the girl.

The cell phone in Mack's jeans pocket beeped. Relieved at the distraction, he stepped out to read the text.

A moment later, Bay walked into the living room, squinting in the darkness until she could make out Mack's form near the couch.

He looked around, putting a finger to his lips to silence her, and motioned for her to sit down on the couch. Cocking his head slightly, it wasn't long before they heard the sound of a key in the lock.

Bay's eyes grew wide. When she looked up at Mack, her skin was a little pale, but she sat still, waiting for whatever was going to happen next. As she chewed on her lip, waiting for the inevitable, a loud, deathly moan came from the kitchen as the old percolator let out a final gasp.

The rattle of keys stopped, followed by a scrambling sound. Mack stepped to the window and pulled a corner of the shade to peer out. "Well … that got rid of her. Too bad, I really wanted to see the look on her face when she found us here. But remind me never to throw away that old coffee pot."

Bay felt as brittle as spun glass. "Piper?"

"Yeah, she texted me asking if I still kept a key to the house under the flower pot. She said she'd left a set of keys over here and needed to get them." He shook his head. "She's just wondering if you're here."

Bay looked at him as if waiting for an explanation. Then her eyes moved to the unadorned mantle where the portrait was supposed to be. "Piper asked me to come over here and get your family portrait for your mother."

"This is getting interesting." He smirked a little. "We have no family portrait." Mack ran a frustrated hand through his hair. "She needs to worry about what might have happened to you. You could have drowned, hit your head, been bitten by a snake ... any number of things."

"Where does Piper think *you* are?"

"She thinks I'm still in Baton Rouge and I'm coming in tomorrow. The guys flew me in on their way to pick up a part in Monroe." He could tell there was something else she wanted to talk about—something he wasn't sure he could answer.

Light hazel eyes glowed warmly in the candlelight as Bay searched Mack's face. "Why does your girlfriend want to harm me?"

He was silent for a moment then drew a deep breath and sat down next to her on the couch. "I don't know," he said quietly, "but I was warned."

She tried to read his eyes, but they were hidden by the flickering shadows cast by the candlelight. "Warned? Who warned you?"

"Maundy's mother, Charity."

A puff of air left her lips. "But ... Maundy's mother is a ..."

"I know," he interjected. "But when she got word of a threat to you, she acted quickly. Seems Derlie isn't the only woman who has your back. She told me that she knows how you've helped her daughter. I just found out that Charity is Mercy's sister, and I'm sure Mercy keeps her posted on Maundy."

Bay sucked in her breath and, for a long moment, wasn't sure she understood what he was talking about. Bay slowly exhaled. "That's ... hard to believe."

"Charity has girls at the St. Bonitus Hotel, and one of them happens to be the girl you helped save the night you got that scar."

As Bay listened, she lightly traced the scar on her face with her finger.

"She was with Sterling when he was drinking, and his tongue was loose. Seems he wants you back pretty badly. You must've made quite an impression on him."

Bay shook her head, dismissing the idea. "Rachelle, Sterling's mother, wants me back ... not Sterling. But, he'll move heaven and earth to please his mother. Those two have the strangest relationship I've ever seen."

Mack gave a dry laugh. "There seems to be an epidemic of strange relationships these days."

Before she could stop herself, she blurted out, "So what's going on with you and Piper?"

"There is no *me and Piper*. Not anymore."

Bay bit her lip, wishing she hadn't brought it up. "I'm sorry, Mack. Something tells me that Sterling has gotten Piper involved in trying to drive me away from Briarleigh."

"He's probably paying her."

"The woman hates me enough to volunteer her services."

Mack lifted her hand from the back of the couch and squeezed it. "It's not your fault, you know. I've had my doubts about Piper since the first day she came back to me." He leaned forward and kissed her on the forehead. "So put it out of your mind." He rubbed his slightly whiskered face. "On second thought, maybe all this *is* your fault. If you were lousy at what you do, none of this would be happening."

She laughed weakly and shook her head. "I'm not delusional … this is all about money, bottom line. St. Bonitus has had five consecutive successful years and, with number six, they get lots of recognition plus worldwide attention. That's all they're after. They think I'm the reason."

Mack raised an eyebrow. "Aren't you? Tell me, how long did you work at St. Bonitus?"

Her eyes met his, and she blushed. "A little over five years."

Running his hand through his hair, Mack stated, "Enough said. I've contacted my attorney and Ludie Earl to see where we need to go from here. Conspiracy to do harm is hard to prove, but that's exactly what I plan to do. In the meantime, I want them all to stew in their own juices tonight. I've called Henry Clay and told him what's going on, but he's not saying anything to your mother until tomorrow. You and I know that if Virginia gets wind that someone's trying to hurt her baby, she'll take out half the state of Louisiana then ask questions after the smoke clears."

"I guess Mother's premonition about the danger of water came true for me tonight."

Mack looked at her, his eyes darker than usual. Softly he said, "Yes, but you survived it."

"Thanks to you and my swimming lesson."

"Are you okay with staying here tonight?"

She looked down at her lap, seeing her hands clasped tightly together. "As long as you're here, I'm fine ... just don't go anywhere."

"I wasn't planning on it." Mack hesitated before offering his hand to her. "Come on, we can eat by candlelight tonight. I've heated up some soup. I wanted to make a few sandwiches, but the peanut butter is so sticky you could mortar bricks with it."

"Do you have honey?"

"Yeah, some. Do you want honey?"

"Adding honey to peanut butter makes it smooth and creamy — plus it tastes good, too."

Mack lit a small candle in the center of the kitchen table and moved to the stove where he began dishing up two bowls of soup. After Bay made the sandwiches, she slid into a chair and waited for Mack to join her. Under different circumstances, Bay thought she'd enjoy this simple dinner with someone as interesting and attractive as Mack.

Slowly, the night lightened as the clouds rolled away and the round moon rose to perch above the treetops like an enormous pearl. The peaceful, homey setting drove some of the ache from Bay's mind as she relaxed and settled in, watching Mack dip out their soup.

"So Maundy's mother is Mercy's sister. Wow, that's hard to believe," Bay commented, as Mack placed a steamy bowl of soup in front of her.

"Not only that, but she owns Bon Secour. She has convictions against harming the unborn, but not so much with regard to other sins of the flesh."

"That surprises me."

"Why? People do it all the time. Some people would never dare drink alcohol or cheat on their spouse, but they'd cheat in business, gamble, or gossip … and on and on."

"Thankfully, God initiates grace, or we'd all be lost. Grace gives us the chance to get it right," Bay stated the obvious, a little surprised by her own words.

"I'm sure the word *grace* is the favorite word for many of the former residents of Bon Secour. I've met quite a few who've been chewed up by life. Most of them have chosen to make their home here in Sugar Land. And, now, most live a different kind of life under grace than what their old life was under sin. We're kind of like the island of misfit toys … my mother is one of those misfits."

Bay stared for a moment in mute surprise as Mack casually picked up his spoon and began to eat. She kept her face averted as she toyed with her food, allowing the statement to pass without verbal comment.

Looking up, Mack noticed a deep blush coloring Bay's cheeks. "I'm sorry; I shouldn't have said that. *I* still have a lot to learn … especially about forgiveness, but I'm getting there. Before meeting my father, my mother had a tragic life. I'm just coming to grips with it. More than anything I want her healed and whole. And oddly enough, I think she needs to be here, at Briarleigh."

"Why is that?"

"For her well-being. I have no doubt she'll be in good hands under your care." With elbows on the table, he scraped his fingers through his hair. "My life is full of complications right now, but I'm hoping to get a few things worked out ... soon."

"You know I'll help you in any way that I can. I'll take good care of your mother."

"Of that, I have no doubt."

After receiving the news of Bay's danger, Mack knew helplessness for the first time. This feeling was one that no training or personal experience could prepare him for. On the trip up from Baton Rouge, he tried to imagine life without Bay, without her smile and graceful presence, without her soft laughter and unpredictable behavior. Then it came to him, suddenly. He loved Bay beyond all reason, more than his own life. He was surprised by how easily he'd accepted the fact. It was a natural feeling, and he welcomed it. He suddenly realized that one can't judge the beauty of another until he has watched that person, what she enjoys and how she lives and loves and treats others. That's when one knows how beautiful someone is ... when she has life and joy spilling out all over the place.

Yawning behind her small hand, Bay sank a little lower in the chair.

Gulping down his iced tea, he placed the empty glass on the table. "Come on. Let's get you to bed on the couch."

One green eye opened, showing pained forbearance. "Are you always so squirmy in bed?"

Bay glanced at Mack and thought he looked a little put out. "Am I bothering you?"

He grunted and closed his eyes.

"It's just hot … I can't sleep when it's hot," Bay explained as she flipped the pillow over once more and tried to get comfortable. "And this couch is itchy. What's it made of? Wool?" She lay on her back and stared at the blades of the circling ceiling fan.

There were very few things that could bring Mack Blackwell to heel, but seeing a woman in distress, no matter how minor the trouble, was one of them. He rolled to his feet. "Come on … we're going upstairs." Snatching the rifle, he led the way up the stairs.

A soft, cooling breeze swept through the room, stirring the curtains to life. Mack propped the French door open with his boots and grabbed a chair from the balcony. "Go on, climb into bed." He watched her as she carefully peeled back the covers. Hopping up on the side of the large tester bed, she turned and slipped her feet under the sheets. There was an elegance about Bay that he'd somehow overlooked. She did all things with a certain amount of grace and refinement, from scraping gunk off the floors to getting into bed.

Pulling the covers under her chin, she sighed a breath of contentment as she snuggled into the downy bed. "Mack?"

"Hmm?"

"Are you comfortable?"

Mack shifted in his chair. "I'm fine, go to sleep."

A moment passed. "Mack?"

"What is it now?"

"This bed is really big ... I wouldn't mind if you'd like to share it with me." A short silence ensued before she added, "As long as you stay on top of the covers."

Inwardly, Mack groaned. *What is this woman trying to do ... kill me?* "I'm fine where I am."

"Mack?"

"Yes ..."

"Thank you."

"You're welcome." He felt himself relax a bit from his earlier tension, and he smirked. "Bay Rutherford is going to be the death of me yet," he mumbled under his breath. Two seconds ago she had him quaking like an aspen and now ... well, he didn't know what he felt. He'd had women after him, and he knew when he was being played, but this girl had thrown him. She didn't seem the least bit interested in him, and all he seemed able to do was think about her. If he followed his original inclination, he would leave for Baton Rouge in the morning, after making sure she was safe and sound. But he knew that he wouldn't do that because he'd be leaving the better part of himself behind.

Chapter 36

*B*ay rubbed the sleep from her eyes, the aroma of hot biscuits and savory coffee wafting toward her as she slowly sat up, stretching.

"Sleep well?" Mack asked from the doorway. He tossed the dish towel over his shoulder casually, smiling warmly as he looked at her tangled, matted hair. After taking a sip of his coffee, he said, "Your mother and Henry Clay just pulled up. It might be a good idea to get dressed. I'll occupy them while you're in the shower."

Snatching off the quilt, Bay scrambled from the bed and headed for the bathroom.

"I put your clean clothes behind the door." Mack gave a low laugh before lifting the cup, drinking deeply of its content. He smiled as he walked down the stairs to the front door to let in a very troubled mother. Pulling the door open, he reached out and reassuringly clasped the slender hand that stretched toward him.

"Where is she?" Virginia asked, her eyes scanning the interior of the house.

"She's in the shower. Come on to the kitchen and have some coffee. She'll be out in a minute."

Henry Clay came through the door with Jace in tow. "Remember what we discussed, Virginia ... about little listening ears?"

As if Henry Clay's words finally appeased her, she quieted down and followed Mack into the kitchen. "Do we know anything yet?" Virginia whispered, under her breath.

"Ludie Earl wants to meet with us at Briarleigh around noon. He's been working all night piecing things together. He said he's bringing some people with him, so I guess we'll see."

"Good ... at least something is being done about it and quickly."

Bay's nails dug into the bare skin of her tightly folded arms as she and Mack sat alone in Briarleigh's study. Ludie Earl had asked them to wait for him there; he wanted a chance to explain a few things before allowing the others to join them.

Mack rubbed the cool leather of the arm of the couch beneath his hand as Ludie Earl came into the room and leaned against the corner of the desk. "I wanted to talk to you two privately before everybody gets here. Seems there's been a lot going on behind the scenes which none of us were aware of." Rubbing his hands together slowly, Ludie Earl continued. "I'll get right to the point. The FBI is investigating the St. Bonitus Hotel. Seems there's been some drug activity going on there, and they're closing in on the major players of the operation. Even as we speak, the owners, the Gerouxs, are being questioned by the authorities."

Bay swallowed hard, her light hazel eyes briefly touched Mack before coming to settle again on the chief. "I had no idea about the drug activity. I knew about the prostitution ... or I suspected it, at least."

"Yes, well ... you've been thoroughly checked out by two informants with the agency. Both have cleared you of any involvement. It appears you were unsuspectingly transporting drugs for the Gerouxs when you had the accident in Baton Rouge. One of the agents called for help and confiscated the packages of drugs before the authorities got there. The other, after making sure you were alive, stayed with you until Mack and his team landed. They waited until you were transported out then secretly set fire to your car so the Gerouxs would think the drugs had been destroyed. "

Bay gasped in horror, and Mack turned quickly to her, reassuring her with a gentle smile. "You were unconscious when we arrived. No one was around, but someone had placed a blanket under your head."

Ludie Earl looked sheepish. "One of the informants insisted on coming here today. He wants to explain his part in all of this to you ... personally."

Bay's eyes widened. "Who are they?"

"Blake Drearden is one of them ... the other will be here in a minute."

She shook her head, as if to clear her thoughts. "I don't understand ... what does any of this have to do with me? Why would Piper want to harm me?" Confused, Bay met Mack's gaze, sensing his growing frustration.

Mack turned his stern face to Ludie Earl. "They needed Bay as a cover for their operation. With her running things smoothly, winning all kinds of awards for them, they had no fear of discovery. Who would dare suspect a four-star hotel of running a drug operation?"

A mild degree of surprise crossed Ludie Earl's face. "Not bad, Mack … not bad at all, but you've missed one piece of the puzzle … Piper."

Bay chimed in. "I can tell you one thing … it somehow involves Mack."

"You'd be right." Ludie Earl tapped his fingers on the desk. "Piper insists that she was only trying to scare Bay back to St. Bonitus. She told me that she had contacted the Gerouxs asking about any problems they may have had with Bay or her job performance. She was posing as someone from Briarleigh checking references. The Gerouxs quickly stated that they wanted Bay back and would gladly pay a hefty sum for her. That led to a meeting between Sterling and Piper, where one twisted mind met another. Guess Piper wanted the best of both worlds," he looked at Mack before continuing. "She *wanted* you, but she quickly found out she *needed* her husband to fund her lifestyle. And, with what the Gerouxs were paying her, she could afford to go slumming with you." Ludie Earl gave a good-hearted laugh before turning serious once again. "I had Piper right where I wanted her, then all of a sudden, it was like a light flipped on in her head, and she demanded to see her attorney. Her attorney happens to be her ex-husband. He didn't waste time getting here, either. The last I saw of them, they were all hugged up and consoling each other." He winked at Bay. "Course, neither one of them knew you were alive. You were still missing as far as they were concerned."

"It might be a good idea, Bay," Mack said, trying to keep the strain out of his voice, "if you stay close to the house for the next few weeks." He glanced up at Ludie Earl. "All this talk of taking Bay makes me uncomfortable ... I don't like it. How long until all this goes down, and some people are arrested?"

Ludie Earl shrugged. "I know it's been going on for several years. From what I've been told, this is the final showdown."

A light rap sounded on the door, and Ludie Earl called out. "Come in."

The door opened and in stepped Crawford Benton.

An audible intake of breath came from Bay, and she stood up slowly, facing Crawford.

Ludie Earl scratched his head then pushed off the desk. The slow, pondering deliberation of the chief seemed to draw out the scene. "This is the other informant, Crawford Benton. He works for the FBI."

Crawford's eyes fixed on Bay. "I wanted to tell you a million times, but I was afraid of what they might do to you. I was the one who disabled your car. I had to keep you close ... things were getting crazy around here for a while." Taking her hands in his, he said, "Go for a walk with me, Bay. Since I left, I haven't been able to stop thinking about you. There's so much I need to tell you."

Blushing under the intensity of his gaze, she opened her mouth to respond, wanting to say both *yes* and *no* at the same time. She was painfully aware of the other men in the room, especially one certain man. "Okay ... if we're finished here?"

Ludie Earl nodded. "We are ... for now. Just remember to keep what you've heard quiet until it all plays out. It's extremely vital that the identities of both Blake and Crawford remain hidden ... for their own safety."

"Oh, of course ... well, we'll just be outside if you should need us."

As they walked out of the room, Mack sat back down, suddenly feeling as if the wind had been knocked out of him.

Watching his friend, Ludie Earl saw a muscle jerk on Mack's face. "So, did any of this surprise you?"

"Crawford Benton surprised me," Mack stated and slapped his palms against his thighs. "I thought he was a much bigger fool than he apparently is."

The days swept past and autumn was upon Briarleigh. Justice seemed certain for all involved in the drug-trafficking operation. And, even though Piper's ex-husband worked every angle for her defense, punishment and restitution seemed inevitable as justice was served.

Just after breakfast, a mild, southwesterly breeze sprang up to set the curtains above the kitchen sink aflutter. A movement through the kitchen window caught Bay's eye as she poured her morning coffee into her cup. She glanced up in time to see Mack, dressed in his hooded med-flight jacket, trudging down a back trail toward the woods, swinging an ax in his hand. She continued watching until the forest swallowed him whole into the dense brush.

Sipping her coffee, she casually questioned Ezra as she stared out the window. "Do you happen to know why Mack has gone into the woods with an ax?"

Ezra shrugged as he leaned over the bar, folding his hands together. "Saw him checking out the woodpile early this morning ... he was wrapping the outside water spigots, too. If I didn't know better, I'd say he was preparing for a paralyzing snow storm by midweek."

Bay turned from the window. "Do you have harsh winters here?"

Ezra cackled, "Mercy, no ... cold nights and chilly days, like today, but rarely snow and ice. Here it is October, and we've yet to see a hard freeze. Oh, we'll have a few, but nothing to write home about."

Curious now, she slid onto a bar stool across from Ezra. "So, what's he up to? Why did he suddenly come back? I mean, he's been gone for a while ... why show up now?"

Tugging on his ear, he replied, "Looks to me like he's planning to stay away for a while again. I heard he got his job back."

Bay's shoulders slumped, and she let out a heavy sigh. Looking around the kitchen with its polished pine floors, rough brick fireplace, and the slanted doorjamb to Mack's old room, she began to feel heaviness in her heart. The weight of losing Mack again was almost too much to bear.

Leaning forward with his elbows on the table and his hands clasped as if in prayer, Ezra spoke to Bay, pure and deep. "Why do you insist on going it alone? What are you not letting go of?"

"I'm not alone; I have my son, and that's enough."

Ezra sat back, staring long and hard at her until she began to squirm beneath his gaze. He motioned with his head toward the back door. "Those murmurs, they're like dreams. They mean different things to different people. What do they say to you?"

Bay was quiet for a minute. Drawing a deep breath, she replied in a soft voice, "I hear words about grace, God's grace."

"If you hear words about grace, then most certainly that's what you need to hear. Grace allows us to get it right. So, do that, get it right. Forgive who needs to be forgiven and get on with living ... even if *you're* the one who needs your forgiveness."

The bridge had been repaired and strengthened. Mack inspected each board, walking slowly over the structure, testing, examining every inch of rope railing. Looking down, he saw Bay sitting on the dock below, dangling her feet off the side, skimming the water with her toes. Beyond the dock, the Mississippi River flowed swiftly on its course. But here in the cove, a finger of land kept the currents at bay and the water calm, like a still pool.

"I'd keep my feet on dry land if I were you," Mack called down to her. Ducks fluttered along the surface of the water at the sound of his voice. "Your toes could be mighty tempting to a snapping turtle."

Bay glanced up, smiling over her shoulder at him without a reply.

As Mack walked from the bridge, he made his way down the footpath toward her, startling a graceful white egret from its nest. The bird flashed over the reeds, landing in a more tranquil spot at the base of a cypress tree.

Coolness hovered over the water as a small, solitary cricket called out from a nearby blade of marsh grass. "That's a lonesome sound to me, sort of like a quiet lamentation to a dying summer," she whispered as Mack sat down beside her.

"Down here, I find I'm always listening for the murmurs."

A breeze rose up and ruffled her hair. "I'm gradually trying to become aware of these great messages Ezra says are occurring all around me. They don't frighten me as much anymore. When I first got here, I had trouble sleeping. I couldn't shake the feeling of being watched. I felt … haunted, or maybe the word is *pursued*." A mild wind blew across her skin so caressingly gentle that it tickled her arms. She rubbed them, smiling up at Mack.

"Cold?"

Bay shook her head. When he spoke, she could smell butter rum Life Savers on his breath. "No, just satisfied with life right now." She let out a contented sigh. "Jace loves school … especially his teacher. She has blue eyes, you know. I think he has his first crush."

Since meeting Bay, Mack felt like he was being nudged awake. But, the one thing about awakening is that one has to face whatever is found upon regaining consciousness. "So I guess you and Crawford are working it out? It's what you want, isn't it?"

Everything in Bay wanted to scream out, *No! I want you!* Instead, she simply shrugged. "I guess I had my chance with Crawford, but I decided against it. That ship sailed a long time ago." She gazed down into the water, seeing his reflection and detecting a slight sense of relief from him as his shoulders relaxed.

Mack was quiet for a long moment, then his voice took on a reflective tone. "My dad was told that our ancestors crossed this river when there were no bridges. It was like a venture from the civilized world into the unknown. The crossing made an impression on the first Blackwell. He was so captivated by the Mississippi River that he never wanted to move away from her. He never grew tired of her ... it was a love affair that exhilarated him all of his life, back before bridges were built over the river." He leaned back on his elbows and closed his eyes, listening to the wind stir the leaves in the trees.

Bay pulled one leg up and crossed it beneath her. "You're like that river, always flowing on with a look of urgency about you, as if you're either coming from danger or heading to it. Sometimes, when I look at you, I haven't the slightest idea where you'll end up, but just like the river, I know you'll end where you're supposed to be."

He sat up to lock eyes with her. "And you're like the bayou, fresh and alive, fragrant and nurturing to everything around you. It lets you sit beside it quietly when you don't feel like doing or talking, just being. I love that about you. In fact, I love you," he said, unable to stop the words. "It just took me a while to realize it. And just like that river out there, I need your life with mine."

Bay's heart began to pound … this was what she'd most wanted to hear from the man she loved. "I'd like that very much, Mack." Almost shyly, she leaned into him and slipped her hand over his.

Taking her offered hand, he moved his thumb gently over it. "If you'll allow me, I'd like to be a father to Jace." He shook his head, looking awkward. "I know this is probably a lousy proposal. I'm not good at this sort of thing. Heck, I don't even have a ring!"

Twisting her lips as if she were trying hard not to smile, she whispered quietly into his ear, "Yes."

He pulled back, looking into her smiling face. "Yes?"

"Yes!"

Leaning forward, he pulled her to him, and, as he lowered his face, she met his lips and responded to his kiss the way she'd always wanted to. Drawing her fingers down the line of his rough jaw, she pulled away, turning her face into his shirt, comforted by the masculine feel and scent of him. Peace surrounded them.

Mack sighed contentedly. "We'll live here ... I'll come home."

Bay looked up and saw Mack watching her. "What makes you think for one minute that I want you hanging around here all the time? Keep your job, and come home when you can."

"You just try to keep me away," Mack said, with a roguish gleam in his eye. "Rudd will work with me ... of that I'm certain."

The river was quiet as was the cove. It gave nothing to the wind and asked nothing in return. An odd light bathed the surroundings. Then, the wind came faintly through the trees and so barely there that they could not be sure they'd heard it. It was repeating the words it knows: *Grace ... it is love that is given when it is not deserved; it is forgiveness given when it is not earned ... Grace, it's how the Father loves us.*

In the years to follow, Mack and Bay would return to the cove, but they would never return the same. Their love was a merging and a blending like the river, and they gave all they had to the other. In return, they found joy. Weathering every storm together in love and a strong faith in God, happiness and contentment surrounded them.

And the murmurs continued, just as before, reminding those who heard that each life starts with grace, continues with grace, and, finally — the comforting thing — ends with grace. And isn't that, after all, the message of the murmurs?

Made in the USA
Lexington, KY
15 July 2017